D0822551

VOID WYRM

MAGITECH CHRONICLES BOOK 2

CHRIS FOX

CHRIS FOX WRITES LLC.

To every kid with their nose buried in a book.
Keep reading, and someday, start writing.

Want to know when **Spellship: Magitech Chronicles Book 3** goes live?

Sign up to the mailing list!

Check out MagitechChronicles.com for book releases, lore, artwork, and more!

Previously On

Whenever I start the second or later book in a series, I have a dilemma. Do I go back and re-read the first book(s), or just dive right into the latest release?

To help readers with this, I include a summary of the previous books. I try to make these funny, and have done this for all my novels. (I think the *Deathless* recaps are the best, though the *Void Wraith* ones are good, too.)

If you want to know more about the setting, there's a whole bunch of lore, artwork, and other goodies at magitechchronicles.com (including a mailing list). There are also character sheets at the end of this book!

Okay, let's get to it.

In an announcer's voice: *Last time on* **The Magitech Chronicles...**

The story begins with Major Voria, who is arriving at a floating palace over the world of Shaya.

WTF is Shaya, you ask? It's kind of like the word "Smurf," and gets used for a lot of things.

Shaya originally refers to a goddess who got kacked (that's totally a word). Her body is, apparently, a giant hippie tree that crashed on a barren moon. Because Shaya's all magicky, her body created a breathable atmosphere around that part of the moon.

So Shaya refers to the world, and to the goddess herself. Are you smurfing confused yet?

Anyway, now the Shayans live out their lives on her branches or near the roots.

Voria meets with the Tender, a superhumanly beautiful woman whose role, purpose, and powers were left largely unexplained. She's the Guardian of Shaya, a demigod mystically empowered by tree lady to watch over her people.

The Tender told Voria she'd deciphered an augury (totally not a prophecy, and I totally didn't choose *augury* because *prophecy* has been taken) showing Voria's involvement in a war with the draconic Krox.

Clear as mud? Yeah, it's a lot; I know. Now that readers were thoroughly confused, I jumped into another PoV character, a guy by the name of Aran.

Aran wakes up in restraints with a number of other prisoners / slaves.

His captors are a pretty girl-next-door type named Nara, and a muhahaha style villain named Yorrak. Yorrak tells the slaves that they're about to make a run on the body of a dead god, called a Catalyst.

This particular Catalyst, a giant floating head full of very angry tech demons, is called the Skull of Xal. The slaves clash with the demons, who tear most of them apart. Aran makes friends with a man named Kaz, and the two fight their way past the demons. They have a choice: Die, or dive into the scary purple god-light where Nara and the slavers disappear. They choose to brave the light, and enter the mind of a god.

Aran sees Xal's memories, and for a brief instant understands the secrets of the universe (this was my favorite chapter in the whole book to write). He learns Xal was killed by a gathering of gods, convinced by Krox that Xal had betrayed them.

All this god-politics stuff becomes important later, but at this point all we really care about is the fact that Aran comes out of the Catalyst with void magic.

We also learn that magic items can catalyze, too, and Aran's spellblade awakens after touching the mind of Xal. It hasn't yet reached snarky-sidekick-level intelligence, but you guys know that's coming. Although, in this case, the sword is more murderous than snarky.

Kaz survives, too, and also gains void magic. When they come out of the Catalyst, Kaz attacks Yorrak, and Aran helps him.

Yorrak uses a morph spell that turns Kazon into a hedgehog. =O

Right around this point, many readers were like, *WTF am I even reading? A god-damned hedgehog? Are you f-ing serious? The cover looks sci-fi, but there's magic everywhere!* There was a deep-seated fear Kazon would become some sort of stupid comedy animal sidekick.

Spoilers: He didn't.

Aran finishes off Yorrak while Nara and her friends join the mutiny. Together, they overcome Yorrak's guards, but Nara immediately takes over and makes Aran a prisoner. We're shocked (we're not shocked).

The joke is on Nara, though, because Voria conveniently arrives with the Confederate Battleship *Wyrm Hunter*. Nara pilots Yorrak's spellship, but Voria easily catches her and disables her vessel.

Nara begs Aran to help fight, and claims that if the Confederates capture them, they'll mind-wipe them and conscript them into the Marines. Aran agrees to help, because plot.

Voria sends a boarding party of tech mages, under the command of Captain Thalas (aka Dick Sock), who kicks the crap out of Aran. Aran does manage to disarm him first, ensuring that Dick Sock has ample reason to hate him for the rest of the book.

Nara also attempts to betray Aran, and claims he was one of the slavers and she was one of the slaves. Captain Dick Sock is not impressed, and takes both her and Aran prisoner.

It turns out Nara was right. Voria mind-wipes her, destroying her mind and replacing her with an innocent woman with no memories. This raises some very troubling moral questions about slavery, in case you ever need a quick excuse to tell your English professor that *Tech Mage* is totally valid for your book report. Make sure you use the word "themes" when you try to sell it.

Voria spares Aran, though she doesn't explain why. The reader already knows it's because Aran was in the augury the Tender showed her. Aran isn't sure how to feel about this, and of course doesn't trust Nara even though her newly wiped self seems sweet.

Before I go any further, you may notice that Nara is Aran spelled backward. There's a cheesy joke about it. Trust me, there's a reason. You'll find out in Book 3.

Anyway, the wonder twins are introduced to their squad of tech mages: Specialist Bord (the comic relief), Corporal Kezia (a short, pretty drifter who talks like the characters in the movie Snatch, Irish Travelers), and my personal favorite...Sergeant Crewes. Crewes is a badass who brooks no nonsense, and has most of the best dialogue in the book. Love that guy.

Anyway, Aran and Nara get a Team-America-style

training montage (Montage!), where they learn how to use spellrifles, spellarmor, and other basic magic.

Voria takes Aran to a place called Drifter Rock so they can load up on potions, especially healing potions. Thanks to the convenient augury, she knows he will be instrumental in their battle against the Krox, and she uses this as an opportunity to get to know him.

Voria trades her super-powerful, ancient eldimagus (living magic item) staff for every potion the drifters have. This includes a potion the drifters claim can bring someone back from the dead, which was my attempt at sneakily foreshadowing the fact that someone was going to get resurrected. That particular cheat is rampant in *Dungeons & Dragons*, which inspired much of the setting for the *Magitech Chronicles*.

Enter Nebiat, the antagonist (dun dun dun). Nebiat is an ancient Wyrm who likes to spend her time in human form. She uses binding magic to mentally enslave the governor of a planet called Marid, and we're all *gasp*, because that's the planet from the augury.

The Krox invade with a full dragonflight and a bunch of troop transports. They wipe out the defenders, who come from a planet called Ternus. Rhymes with burn us, as in "Shit, these dragons are burning the crap out of us."

At this point, the politics in the book aren't very clear. Ternus is a human world with no magic, and they have the largest technological fleet in the sector. But they suck at defending against magic, and for that they need Shaya. Both Shaya and Ternus are part of the Confederacy, though Shaya is clearly in charge while Ternus is the annoying younger sibling.

To complicate things further, there is a third group

called the Inuran Consortium. The Inurans buy technology from Ternus, and take magic from Shaya, then use both to make spellrifles, spellarmor, and spellships.

Voria needs those weapons and armor if she's to have any prayer of taking down the Krox. Fortunately, the head of the Consortium is looking for Kazon, the guy who got turned into a hedgehog earlier in the book. Kazon turns out to be the son of the Inuran Matriarch, and controls a shit-ton of voting stock she'll lose if he dies.

The *Wyrm Hunter* arrives in-system and we finally get some dragon-on-starship combat. The *Hunter* kills the mighty Wyrm Kheftut (Nebiat's brother), then links up with the Ternus defenders who survived the battle with the Krox.

For those who asked (a surprising number of you): yes, both Kheftut and Nebiat sound Egyptian, and that is a theme for the Krox (woohoo, another one for your book report). And yes, there are subtle links to my Deathless setting, which also links heavily to Egypt.

Voria comes up with a plan, and manages to take back the orbital station the Krox conquered. This plan is a success only because Aran and Nara do an end run and drive the binder off the station, so they're the heroes of the day.

Unfortunately, there's a complication. Captain Dick Sock orders the Confederate Marines to suicide against the Krox position to weaken the binder. Aran, Nara, and Crewes mutiny to stop this. They save the Marines, but Dick Sock wants them dead—especially Aran.

Things come to a head when Voria finally meets with the Inurans. She trades back Kazon (who turns out to be her brother, *gasp*), but Kazon insists they also free Aran, since Aran saved his life at the Skull of Xal.

Dick Sock demands Aran be put to death for assaulting a superior asshole, and has the law on his side. Technically, Voria has to execute him. Or course, technically, she's been stripped of command, and Thalas should be in charge. (Did I not already mention that?)

Shit.

Voria is already in deep. She's been officially stripped of command, but refuses to step down. If she does, she knows her people—and the people on the world below—will die.

So Voria charges Dick Sock with treason, and executes him on the spot. This solves her immediate dilemma, but also creates a whole bunch of problems that (spoilers) she's going to run into in this book.

Crewes steps up and asks Voria to promote Aran to Lieutenant, because Crewes doesn't feel qualified to lead and thinks Aran can. Voria's hesitant, but agrees because of the augury.

The Confederates head down to the planet, and, because Nebiat has bound the governor, it's a trap =O. Hundreds of Marines and thousands of citizens are killed in a surprise Krox raid.

Aran manages to kill two different binders, but pays a high price: Bord is killed. It's terribly sad. I mean, you felt bad, right? Bord was kind of an ass, but he was amusing. He at least deserves a moment of silence, you savages.

The Krox retreat back into the swamp, leaving the Confederates to recover. Voria suspects the governor, but doesn't have proof yet. She heads to the local archives and meets with the head archivist (powerful mage / librarian).

She learns what Nebiat is after in the swamp: some sort of potent *water* Catalyst that appeared during the godswar, when a god's body crashed to this world and formed the crater the city was built in. Voria realizes she needs to get out there, but before they can leave there are a few things she needs to take care of.

She talks to Aran about how terrible it is to lose a man under your command, then she's all *Psych!* She uses the potion they got from the drifters to bring Bord back from the dead.

Cheating, maybe, but I don't like killing characters when I can avoid it. As Rick would say, "We can only do this a few more times, Morty." That means I can't keep doing fake-outs. Someone has to get the axe, or you'll think people have plot armor. Will someone die in this book? Now you'll wonder...*muhahahaha*.

Anyway, Voria confronts the governor, proves he is bound, and has him removed from power. She calls for volunteers, then the Confederates and their new colonial militia allies head into the swamp to find Nebiat.

There's lots of *pew pew RAWR I'm a dragon*, and Aran kills the binder who got away on the station. They find Nebiat's super-secret ritual at the heart of the swamp, and they begin their epic brawl.

It's clear from the start that the Confederates are outmatched. How were Aran and Voria going to beat a much more powerful army of dragons? Many readers began suspiciously waiting for the *deus ex machina*. I mean, I had to have one. There was no other way for them to win.

Things got worse when the Marines finally arrived at the battle with the newly minted militia. They were wiped out to a man, and their bodies were animated and sent to attack Voria and Captain Davidson.

Throughout the book, I kept mentioning the Potion of Shaya's Grace that Aran received as a gift from Kazon (along with his new Proteus Mark XI Spellarmor). Aran pops the potion, which makes him faster and stronger, and gives him the ability to see several seconds into the future.

Aran grabs Nara and the two of them fly up to the summit of the mountain where Nebiat has placed the ritual. On the way up, Aran makes the (not so) casual observation that the mountain looks like it's a real face.

He brawls with a bunch of enforcers while Nara tries to stop the ritual. We've seen her latent true mage abilities manifest several times, so we aren't surprised when she steps into the circle and begins manipulating the spell.

This is the part where I hoped all my little hints paid off. The mountain was actually the ancient Wyrm Drakkon. Minor spoilers, but Drakkon invented the style of martial arts Aran was trained in before the mind-wipe. Drakkon is crazy-powerful, and super-old. If Nebiat enslaves him, the Confederates are screwed, and that's exactly what her ritual is designed to do.

Voria hoped destroying some of the urns holding the magical energy would stop the ritual, but they were only able to blow up the spirit urn. Spirit magic is used in...*drumroll*...binding. (If you want more details about the magic system, I've got a ton of it at magitechchronicles.com, including a video.)

Nara realizes the spell can be completed if she removes the binding portion. The rest of the spell is designed to wake a creature from mystical slumber.

She completes the spell, and the mountain stands up. Drakkon crushes the Krox forces, and Nebiat goes full GTFO. She flees the planet, and doesn't stop running until she reaches her father's system.

Voria, Captain Davidson, Aran, Nara, Crewes, Kezia, and

Bord all Catalyze in a blast of magical energy from the *water* Catalyst.

This provides a glimpse into Marid's mind. Aran experiences the god's death, which happens some time after Xal. Her last act is to create a living spell, one designed to stop Krox even though Marid herself died. That spell is very important in the book you're about to read.

Drakkon (finally) explains the Big Mystery (™) to Aran. Nebiat wanted to enslave Drakkon, because he's the Guardian of Marid. Controlling him would give her an army of drakes with which to assault the Confederacy, and Ternus would fall within months.

Drakkon was vulnerable, because in his grief over his mother's death he went into something dragons call "the endless sleep." Before seeking solace, Drakkon used a potent spell to move the world where Marid died. He put it in a far-away system, where other gods would struggle to find it.

Then Drakkon positioned his body over the wound that had slain Marid. He covered the heart wound, muting the magical signature and preventing primals from all over the sector from being drawn to that world.

Now that he's awake, he's pledged to raise the drakes on Marid, and when the time is right he will bring them into the war against Krox. So, in the end, Voria accomplished her mission. She stopped Nebiat, but sacrificed almost her entire unit to do it.

Aran and Nara lived, but both are missing their past. Aran desperately wants to reclaim his, while Nara is still hiding from hers.

Crewes, Davidson, Kezia, and Bord survived, but everyone else died. The survivors are tired, and they are out of resources...but they are alive.

Now, Major Voria must atone for her actions.
Nara must learn to be a true mage.
Aran must learn who he really is...

Welcome to *Void Wyrm*

PROLOGUE

Nebiat swam through space, spreading her leathery wings and enjoying the torrent of heat and light on her scales. Blue stars were rare in this sector, and she enjoyed the particular mix of radiation and quanta this one broadcast. She basked in that glow, and waited.

She did not wait long.

"Why have you entered this system, spawn of Krox?" a mighty voice rumbled in her mind.

She flipped over languidly, presenting her back to the sun. "I have come in peace, with no deception. I will lower my defenses, and submit to your *seeing* spell."

Khalahk, the great black Wyrm, studied her impassively. He was larger than her, but only by a little. They were nearly the same age, and had been both rivals and lovers over the centuries. "Very well."

He extended a claw, and sketched his seeing spell. The magic washed over Nebiat, binding her will so she could speak no word that wasn't true, nor utilize any illusion or deception. She loathed the need to submit to such a spell, but in this case the truth was her most potent weapon.

"Now then, why have you come? This system belongs to the last dragonflight, and you know it." Khalahk eyed her curiously, swimming closer to the star until he was a mere kilometer away.

"I have come to persuade you to kill a human. This human, Major Voria of the Shayan Confederacy, has slain over a dozen of my brothers and sisters." Nebiat paused. Some believed you should hold your trump card in reserve, but she usually led with it. Put your opponent immediately at a disadvantage, then press them. "Kheftut was among the fallen."

"No!" Khalahk belched a thick bolt of blue lightning at the star. The sun was untroubled by the outburst. "His death was to be mine. Now we will never know which of us was the stronger."

"He was killed by a pack of lowly humans. I want one of them dead—the woman who leads them. You, I think, will seek the death of another." She gave him a draconic smile. "One of Voria's conspirators, the man who delivered the killing blow to Kheftut, is from your world."

"He is an Outrider? That cannot be." Khalahk flapped his wings aggressively, as if challenging another male for dominance.

Nebiat couldn't lie or deceive, so she showed the bored expression that matched her true feelings. "It can be, and it is. Your lost Outrider was mind-wiped and conscripted by Voria, and she used him to great effect against my people."

"One of our own servants, murdering dragons?" Khalahk spoke softly to himself as if he hadn't heard her. Finally, he looked up at her. "He must be put down. We cannot have mortals believing themselves our equals. This cannot be tolerated, or it will spread, as it has in the past."

"I'd hoped you might feel the same way I did." Nebiat flipped again, presenting her back to Khalahk. The move was submissive, and sometimes the prelude to a mating flight. "You can find Voria on Shaya. I've taken the liberty of performing an augury. She will leave the planet in twenty-two days."

"If I kill her in Shayan space, they may take it as an act of war," Khalahk pointed out cautiously. He flapped his wings, as a human might have casually flexed a bicep.

Even knowing who she was and what she was capable of, he still desired her.

Nebiat gave a coy smile. "They could. You'll have to decide if you can live with that." She kept her tone neutral, but the seeing spell forced her to speak. "I would, of course, prefer that you go—both to kill Voria, and because a war between Virkon and Shaya would help the Krox."

"What is the name of this traitorous Outrider?" Khalakh asked. He too began sunning himself, a sign of trust.

"He is called Aran, but his full name during his time among you was Aranthar."

"Aranthar?" Khalahk hurled another bolt of lighting at the untroubled star. He thrashed back and forth, clawing at the space around him. Nebiat found his rage both curious and amusing.

"Who was he?" she asked curiously. That bit she hadn't been able to puzzle out. Someone very powerful had taken great pains to eradicate his former identity. Even learning his full name had taken every scrap of divination she possessed.

Khalahk ignored her question, refusing to share whatever he knew. "You say he'll be leaving Shaya in twenty-two days?" His eyes crackled with power.

Nebiat almost pitied this Aran. Almost. She bowed her neck respectfully. "I am certain of it."

Khalahk flapped again, extending his wings to their full span. "Then, in twenty-two days, the last dragonflight will finally have vengeance upon the man who caused the death of my grandson."

1

THE END

Voria had never been escorted under guard before, at least not by Confederate troops. She held her chin aloft, kept her posture ramrod straight as she took measured steps up the scarlet carpet. The pair of blue-uniformed guards led her into a large chamber with stadium seating sloping down to a stage. That stage probably served for entertainment most times, but today it held three stern-faced judges.

It spoke volumes that the Confederacy didn't possess a proper courtroom, even on the world that had given birth to it. These people didn't take the Marines seriously enough to give them a proper justice system.

But that didn't mean she didn't take it seriously. Let them have their games. She was a Marine, and she'd die one.

She marched briskly down the stairs and stopped before a table with a single chair. The guards stopped a few paces back. She wasn't sure if she should consider the fact that they bore spellrifles an honor or an insult.

"Major Voria," called the judge sitting in the center chair. Hard eyes peered out at her from a chiseled face framed by an ash-colored beard. His uniform was Confederate, but his drawl put him from Ternus. "Thank you for coming. Please, be seated so we can begin. Some of us have real work to be about."

She sat.

"My name is Admiral Nimitz. Colonel Nimitz, if you want my Confederate rank." The admiral spoke slowly and his scowl deepened with every word. "To my right sits—"

"I know who the others are," Voria snapped. She glared at Nimitz. "You say your time is valuable; let's skip the preamble, shall we? Soldier to soldier, Admiral. I, too, have work to be about. There is a war on, as much as you'd like to pretend otherwise."

"Major Voria," snapped the platinum-haired Shayan to the admiral's right—Caretaker Ducius, one of the most powerful nobles on Shaya. "We're here to charge you with murder of Captain Thalas, and to strip you of command. Do you really want to begin these proceedings by further antagonizing us? My son is dead, Voria. Dead at your hands."

"I served with Thalas," she shot back, eyes blazing. "The only reason you're outraged is your family's precious honor. You didn't know your own son well enough to know why I was forced to do what I did, and you certainly didn't feel any pain at his death. Don't presume to lecture me."

"Order," Nimitz roared, slamming a thick book down on the table as a makeshift gavel. "By Ternus, you self-righteous bastards demanded my world send a representative to this farce. I'm here. But if I'm going to preside over this mess, I will damned well follow the laws you magic-loving slits ratified. This isn't a trial. This is an inquest."

"Does the Inuran representative have anything to add?" Ducius asked coldly.

His gaze never left Voria, and she couldn't blame him for

his animosity. She'd expected it. She held her head high, but despite her bold words she couldn't quite force herself to meet the accusation she knew she'd find there. She *had* killed his son—though Thalas had left her little choice.

"I do not," the pale-skinned judge said.

Voria recognized the man, though she'd never met him. Skare was, in a very real sense, the single largest threat to her mother's empire. He was a rarity among Inurans, his face a bit too long, and his eyes set a little too close together. Even his white hair flared out oddly, like some awkward bird's. Her mother found his appearance appalling, especially given how easily he could rectify it with magic.

She read nothing on his face, neither irritation nor glee. If he felt anything about being here, he buried it so deeply not even a glimmer showed.

Nimitz eyed Ducius in irritation. "On my world, a judge with a personal stake as large as yours would recuse himself from the case. You've got a vendetta, and I'm already tired of hearing about it. So how about you shut your smug face, and let me ask the questions, since, you know, I'm the *presiding judge*?"

"Admiral, if—"

"Don't think your parlor tricks will prevent me from punching the smugness out of you," the admiral interrupted.

Ducius frowned, but finally subsided.

"Excellent. Now then, Major, let's talk about your botched operation at Marid, shall we?"

Voria clenched her fists, and her nostrils flared as she fought to contain the angry words. So many people had died on Marid, but they'd *accomplished the mission*. Not only had Marid had been denied to the enemy, but they'd also gained a powerful ally.

She spoke only once she'd tamed the storm. "You've read my report, I assume."

"Yes, and let me begin by saying how much I detested reading it," the admiral shot back, leaning out from his chair as if daring her to protest. "You are one of the most self-righteous people I have ever encountered—and I've had to deal with Ducius, here. That's the level of asshole you are. Your entire report is filled with words like *duty*, and *honor*, yet neither prevented you from breaking your oath."

"Breaking my oath?" she choked out, her gut clenching reflexively. The blow felt almost physical.

"That's right," Ducius snapped. "You were relieved of command before even reaching Marid. That put Captain Thalas in charge, but rather than accept the order, you murdered an officer of the Confederacy in cold blood."

There it was. They had her neatly, by the letter of the law. Nothing she said could alter that fact, and that fact was what they'd hang her with.

"Please, speak again, Ducius." The admiral had turned his full ire on Ducius, and the Shayan Noble at least had the good grace to look embarrassed. "All I need is one more excuse. Don't give it to me." He turned back to Voria. "This inquest will be short, and to the point. We've read the reports. What else can you tell us that might alter our decision?"

"As stated in my report, I executed Thalas because he knowingly endangered my command, and thus all the lives on the planet below." Voria straightened again, meeting his gaze—not defiantly or petulantly, but proudly. "I did something terrible. I murdered a man I respected, because if I had not done so the planet Marid would belong to our enemies. Within a few years, the Wyrms would boil out from that world and overwhelm Ternus herself. I have witnesses to those facts, including the Guardian of Marid, our new ally."

"You've got an ancient lizard, and your heavily biased mother," Nimitz countered, shaking his head. "I don't put much stock in either."

"Pardon me, Admiral," Skare said mildly, his voice barely audible. "May I have the floor?"

"This should be interesting," Nimitz allowed, waving at Skare to speak.

"I understand that you meant no insult to my people, but you've offered one. You just casually dismissed the sworn testimony of an Inuran Matriarch, the major's *heavily biased mother*." Skare frowned, but his voice remained neutral. "I know Jolene well. In all likelihood, it will be one of her assassins that ends me. She would never risk endangering herself or her empire over the welfare of her half-breed daughter. I would urge you to lend her testimony great weight, Admiral. If she is worried about the Krox, then we should be, too."

"Noted." Nimitz turned his attention back to Voria, and she again stood proudly. "I find we have sufficient evidence to move forward with a trial. The charges include inciting mutiny, and murder of an officer during a time of war. Do either of my colleagues wish to add to these charges?"

Ducius smiled cruelly at her. "No."

Skare eyed her impassively. "No, Admiral."

"Major Voria, do you wish to enter an official plea?"

Voria took a deep breath, and ended her career. "Guilty, sir, to both charges."

POLITICS

"Admiral," Voria called as the judges began to leave the stage.

The admiral turned in her direction, but didn't approach.

She took that as an invitation, and crossed the gap between them. "May I have a moment of your time, sir?"

"A moment," he allowed. His face bled suspicion. "What do you want, Major?"

"Sir, may I ask what's going to happen to my battalion?" she asked in a small voice—certainly smaller than she was used to.

"That hasn't been decided," he said. "Your new mages will be given standard training in their respective fields. The rest will likely be given leave until this trial is over. Most likely, you'll never see them again. Since we are being candid, Major, I'd like to ask you a question, off the record."

"Yes, sir?"

"What do you think of the Confederate command structure? Your honest opinion." He folded his arms, watching her carefully.

Voria gave the simple, unvarnished truth. It wasn't a real secret. "I think it is completely ineffective, sir. The Marines are mired in politics and given neither the men nor the material to conduct war. Each regiment or battalion is sponsored by a different noble house or colony, like we're sports teams, not one cohesive fighting force."

"A disgusting practice, I agree. I don't like you, but I'm a pragmatist. The Shayan government is a bunch of preening attention whores with no understanding of how war needs to be conducted. My government has asked me to assess Confederate readiness, and I'm genuinely alarmed, Major. I thought Shayan arrogance was a holodrama stereotype, but it's alive and well in this courtroom."

"Sir, with respect: why are you explaining this to me?" Voria clasped her hands behind her back. It wasn't an ideal habit, but the gesture was less indecisive than putting them in her pockets.

"Because the aftermath of your mission on Marid could spell the end of the Confederacy. You understand that Ternus equipment comes with video recorders, right? The footage playing across Ternus shows dead civilians and dead Marines. Only one officer from Ternus survived the mission, and none of his command." The admiral's voice paled to a near-silent shred of itself. "Our people died by the thousands, and your government doesn't even care. At all. The missives they've released here show nothing but victory. They show dead Wyrms. They don't reveal the carnage— and quite frankly, ma'am, I'm not sure we want to be allied with anyone that whitewashes a mess like this."

"I can't blame you for that, sir, but I'm just a line officer. I don't have the time or energy to follow Confederate politics. It's the men I care about. I felt every death keenly; I still do. Had I any other choice, I'd not have spent their lives, but you have no idea how close we came to defeat. Every life mattered, and we sacrificed nearly everything to keep Marid free." Voria rather enjoyed being this candid, even if the admiral was openly hostile. At least he was honest in his dislike. "Withdrawing from the Confederacy would be understandable, but don't you need allies against the Krox? Make no mistake, they are coming for Ternus. Soon. Marid was a stumbling block, but we have no idea how many minions they're hiding in the Erkadi Rift. When they're ready, they're going to fall on your world. It's only a matter of time."

"We know, and that's the only reason my world hasn't yet withdrawn from the Confederacy. We need you, and you know it. The Krox will come for us first, and they will keep coming until Ternus falls. Even then, I don't think your people will react until the first Krox troop carrier arrives." The admiral shook his head sadly. "It's a real shame. Your people could be leaders."

"They were once, I think. No longer," she admitted. "I'm sorry, sir. For everything. I only did what I thought was best for the planet, and for the sector as a whole."

"I understand, Major. As I've said, I don't like you—I can't, after you killed so many of my Marines. But I understand you, and you're one of the few Shayan officers I can respect."

The admiral turned and walked off the stage. He didn't look back.

MONGREL

The *Wyrm Hunter* gave a low, pained groan as the hull cooled, sounding like an elderly parent sitting down for the last time.

Aran gave the vessel a final affectionate look. Her outer hull was pocked and scored from their recent battles with the Krox, and her keel was cracked in at least two places. He was no engineer, but he doubted she would ever fly again—not without a lengthly and expensive refit.

"Is there any chance they'll repair her?" he asked Crewes.

The sergeant hadn't said much since they landed; his normal sarcastic commentary was conspicuously absent. Aran had no idea what coming home meant to Crewes, but he didn't think the sergeant was looking forward to it.

"Nah." The dark-skinned man shook his head sadly. He looked so odd outside his spellarmor, wearing the same simple blue uniform Aran and the others wore. "She's trash now as far as the brass is concerned. They ain't never gonna give us what we need to win this war. They're too busy bickering over who gets to sit at the big kids table with the Tender."

"What's going to happen to us?" Nara asked quietly. She stood a few paces away, nervously fingering the cuff of her parade jacket.

"Don't you worry your pretty little..." Bord trailed off, his smile wilting as Kezia glared up at him. "What I mean to say is, you'll be fine, Nara. You, too, Aran. I'm not calling you *sir* neither, not until we're reassigned."

"That doesn't answer the question. Kez, what's going to happen to us?" Aran asked the pretty drifter.

Her normal smile was absent. "They'll assign you and Nara as apprentices for training. You'll end up at the war college, and she'll go to the university." Kezia looked up, and her eyes were heavy with exhaustion. "The rest of us will be given leave until they figure out what to do with us. Good thing, too, because I need a break. If the major is cleared, we might be given back to her. More likely, we'll be here for months. Or even longer. The Confederacy doesn't outfit a ship too often. They might even choose to discharge us, though that's rare. I have a cousin that was furloughed for two full years before they called her back up."

Aran had nothing good to say to that, so he said nothing. They were being broken up, and he didn't see a way around it. Depths, he wasn't even sure he wanted to see a way around it. This war college might be able to teach him more about his abilities, which took him one step closer to unlocking his identity.

"Heads up," Crewes called.

Aran followed his gaze and saw a tall woman approaching with incredible grace, her hand resting on the hilt of a slender spellblade. She wore a version of the Confederate uniform, but instead of the jacket the major and other officers wore, she had a simple form-fitting top with a unit patch on the shoulder. Her flowing pants ended just above a simple pair of...sandals? She wasn't even wearing boots.

She walked toward them with deliberate purpose, and her gaze locked on Aran as she crossed the ramp connecting the *Wyrm Hunter* to the starport. The tall woman stopped several meters away and adopted a comfortable resting stance. There was something familiar about that stance, but the place where the memory should have been was as hazy as ever.

"I'm looking for Lieutenant Aran?" she called in a clear, pretty voice.

Every part of her was perfect, from those piercing eyes to her shapely legs. Aran recognized the hallmark of the Shayans, though unlike the other Shayans he'd met, this woman had bright red hair. It fell to the small of her back, but had been tied with several leather cords into a thick ponytail.

He should be attracted to her, and he was, intellectually at least. But he'd already seen enough of the Confederate command structure to be highly suspicious of anyone they sent. Best to keep his guard up.

"That's me." Aran crossed the distance between them. He rested his hand on his spellblade, mirroring her stance.

"I've received orders from a Colonel Nimitz to bring you to the war college for assessment." Her expression soured as she sized him up. "Though I'm not sure why they think a mongrel like you is worth the trouble. Is that a pikey? Does she do your laundry?" She gave a derisive laugh as she nodded toward Kez.

Oh yeah, this lady was a real treat.

He folded his arms and forced an even tone. "That

'pikey' stopped the Krox at Marid. Do you have a copy of these orders? You'll forgive me if I don't blindly follow every stuck up Shayan who approaches me in a starport."

"It's legit, sir. You can tell by the unit patch on her shoulder. She comes from the war college." Crewes shook his head. "She pretty much owns you until we get re-assigned. She's gonna take you back to the college for an assessment, most likely."

"Do you have a name?" Aran demanded, eyes still locked with the redheaded war mage.

"You will address me as Premaster Reekala, and you will only do it when I have asked you a question." Her eyes narrowed. "Is that clear, mongrel?"

Aran had already been through Tech Mage boot camp. He damned well wasn't going to go through it again with this war college.

"Are you an officer in the Confederate military?" he asked mildly.

"No."

"Then you can't give me orders." Aran kept his tone nonchalant, but her expression soured further. "I'm not trying to be an ass, but I want you to understand where I'm coming from. I've watched friends die, seen innocent civilians slaughtered. I'll be damned if I put up with any more abuse from officers trying to break me. You want to take a swing at me? Expect me to swing back."

"If you swing," Nara snapped, "Aran won't be the only one swinging back." She stepped up to stand next to him, glaring up at Ree. "Your people have no idea what it's like out there. Show a little respect. Aran is a hero."

Ree gave a musical laugh, though there was a cruel, brittle edge to it. "You must be the pirate girl I've heard so much about. Is it true you can't even cast a spell without a spellpistol? I thought you were a true mage."

Nara colored. Aran frowned. Ree calling him mongrel didn't bother him. Her insulting Kez and Nara did.

Ree smiled magnanimously, clearly pleased by Nara's discomfort. "I'm not inhuman. I'll give you time to talk with your mongrel friends and your pet pikey. But be swift. I need to make sure you're housebroken before I introduce you to Master Erika."

Kezia's eyes narrowed dangerously, and even Bord balled his fist. He stepped protectively in front of Kezia. "You wanna watch where you throw those insults. Kezia's worth three of you. Probably more."

"Be a real shame if you accidentally fell off Shaya. It's a long way down," Kezia snapped, stepping around Bord. "What do you say, Lieutenant? Why don't we joost toss her body over the side? We can pretend we never met her. No one will miss her. I bet loads of people would thank us."

Ree's smile vanished and her hand tightened dangerously around the hilt of her sword. Aran didn't recognize the stance her feet slid into, but he knew an offensive bearing when he saw it. She was getting ready to attack.

"Think of the paperwork, Kez." He interposed himself between Ree and Kezia, offering Kez an apologetic smile. She gave a tight nod and backed down. Bord led Kezia a few meters away and the two spoke in low tones. Aran turned back to Ree. "You said I could have a minute."

Ree nodded stiffly, and walked back across the narrow wooden bridge leading back the way she'd come. She stopped at the far side, inspecting her nails.

Aran turned back to the company. "I wish we had more time."

He offered a hand to Kezia, since she was closest. Instead

the drifter surged forward and seized his leg in a fierce hug. Bord accepted the handshake, and Nara gave him a weak smile. Crewes snapped to attention, of course, giving Aran a crisp salute.

"Good luck, sir. Now you lot get off him. The LT has work to be about," Crewes barked in his best parade voice.

Kezia released him, and moved to stand with Bord. Aran took a deep breath and gave Nara what he hoped was a reassuring smile. She returned it, but he could see the fear in her eyes—a fear he definitely mirrored.

He turned and followed Ree. She reeked of violence as she stalked back into the starport sprawled across the massive redwood limb where the city lay. They mounted a set of stairs up to a transport platform, this one much smaller than the area where the *Hunter* had been parked.

"Is that yours?" Aran asked. He gave a low whistle as he approached the sleek, wedge-shaped fighter parked near the center of the platform, golden hull gleaming in the sunlight. She might be arrogant and racist, but damned if she didn't have style.

"Don't touch anything, mongrel," Ree snapped. She moved to the side of the cockpit and sketched a single pink sigil. *Dream*, Aran realized. A set of shimmering blue steps appeared one after another, snaking down from the cockpit to the deck.

The way she'd sketched the sigil was nearly identical to what he did with his spellarmor. He wondered idly why that was necessary. It seemed like true magic, if what people like the major did were any indication.

The canopy rose, and by the time Ree had trotted up the stairs she was able to duck inside. Aran followed, but took a moment to appreciate the fighter once he'd reached the cockpit. The inside was spacious, allowing pilots to stand. It had a pair of command matrices, but, unlike those in the *Hunter*, these had a comfortable couch for the pilot to sit in.

Ree had already moved to the pilot's matrix, and began tapping sigils. The canopy started to lower, so Aran hopped inside and moved to the co-pilot's matrix. He buckled himself in as the fighter rose smoothly into the air, flowing in a way that sang to Aran. He *belonged* in a fighter.

They zipped away from the starport, quickly gaining altitude. Aran appreciated his first view of Shaya, which was unlike any world he'd ever been on. The small moon orbited a large blue world, and beyond that hovered a massive yellow sun.

The moon itself was largely barren and empty, except for a single continent. A titanic redwood tree stretched into the sky above them, its branches providing shade for more cities like this one, and some far larger. Magical power pulsed from the tree, a low, subsonic hum that relaxed Aran.

That energy extended outward in a glittering dome covering thousands of kilometers; inside the dome, the moon had been completely transformed into a lush paradise. There was no rock to be seen, only a forest of redwood trees and an undergrowth of ferns and short bay trees.

"You're gawking like a simpleton. Have you never seen a Catalyst before?" Ree's tone was all smug superiority. She plunged ahead without waiting for an answer. "I don't know why a mind-wiped mongrel is to be granted entry to the college, but I follow orders. Master Erika wants you tested. If you perform admirably, she may even order me to take you on officially as an apprentice. I'm not sure I can think of a worse fate than tutoring simpletons."

Aran swiveled the command matrix's chair around to

face her. "Training under you sounds like *loads* of fun, but I think I'm going to pass."

"If you're assigned to me, you'll do what you're told, mongrel. Your only other choice would be to run," Ree snorted. She guided the fighter into a steep climb. "And that, I'd like to see—and I mean that. Try to run, because it will be me they send after you. And I would like nothing better than to hunt you down."

4

OUTRIDER

Ree's fighter glided to a stop atop a landing pad built over the forest floor that had accumulated on Shaya's titanic limb. Now that they were closer, Aran realized these people had erected cities on every available branch, most of which were a kilometer or more wide and several kilometers long. Unlike the smaller, haphazard structures clustered around the base of the tree, the ones on this branch were manor houses, skyscrapers, and what Aran guessed must be the war college itself.

"This is the second burl," Ree said, "where a number of kamiza are housed. Mongrels like you aren't normally allowed this high up."

"Kamiza?" Aran asked. He hated how little he knew, and how much power it gave people like Ree over his life.

"It's an ancient Shayan word. The closest translation might be 'important school'. It's where we all train." She unbuckled herself and climbed the ladder as the canopy swung silently upward. Aran followed her through a wide doorway into a slanted building styled to look like part of the tree. Inside, a dozen students paired off against each other, each armed with a slender spellblade identical to Ree's.

"Take off your shoes," she whispered. Ree kicked off her sandals, and he suddenly understood why she wore them. If you trained barefoot, then they were far more practical than boots. But what did you do in the field? Fight barefoot? That was ludicrous.

He knelt and began unlacing his boots, conscious of Ree tapping her foot impatiently. He set his boots next to her sandals then rose back to his feet.

The teacher guiding the class reminded Aran a bit of the major. She had the same chestnut hair, though her features were more worn. The weight of their gazes, though—that was identical. The woman looked at Aran and he felt the same desire to straighten his posture that he did when Voria eyed him.

Ree cleared her throat. "Master Erika, I've brought the student the Confederacy asked us to evaluate." Ree gave the teacher a deep bow, then moved to the far side of the kamiza. She stood on a training mat, watching Aran with amusement. "Would you like me to test him?"

"Resting position." Erika barked. Her students instantly stopped their sparring, bowed to each other, and sank into a lotus position wherever they happened to have been standing. Erika clasped her hands behind her back and walked to the mat, near Ree. "Does the student have a name?"

"The student can speak for himself," he called confidently, interrupting Erika. She seemed amused, and gestured at him to continue. "My name is Aran. I'm a lieutenant in the Confederate military. We've just returned from Marid, where we defeated the Krox."

There were a few whispers at that, but most of the students didn't react when he mentioned the Krox. Aran licked his lips. How did he want to start off his stay here? The way he behaved would set the tone for his entire relationship with these people.

Shayans looked down on the Confederacy, and on the drifters. He already knew that much. If he wanted their respect, he'd have to earn it, and in a very visible way.

"If you want to test me, fine. I'm happy to wipe that smug look off her face." Aran nodded toward Ree. Maybe he'd get the chance to pay her back for the way she'd treated Nara and Kez.

"Really?" Erika raised an eyebrow. Her tone was mild, and perhaps a touch amused. "Very well, then." Her tone went sarcastic. "You're clearly a *skilled* warrior. If Ree's smug face is bothering you, then do something about it."

Aran studied Erika suspiciously, but the offer seemed genuine. Ree's expression had gone hard, and no longer betrayed any emotion. She was ready for a fight. So the war college's entry test started with a duel, then. Finally, something he could get behind.

"We're fighting with live blades?" Aran eased his spellblade from its scabbard. The weapon thrummed in his grip, but the rhythm had deepened. Whatever energies the blade had absorbed back on Marid had changed it, though Aran didn't yet understand how. "Probably should have figured that part out before getting myself into a fight," he muttered.

"Of course we're using live blades. I am a life mage. If one of you is injured, I will tend to it." Erika walked off the mat, and turned to face her students. "Watch closely, class. I believe an unexpected lesson is about to be administered."

"Count on that." Ree gave Aran a wicked grin. "Consider this the first of many lessons, mongrel."

"You keep calling me that." Aran prowled toward her,

adopting an offensive stance. He couldn't put a name to it, but it felt *right*. "How about—"

Ree's right hand shot forward and launched a blazing orb at his face. Aran hopped backward, but the orb exploded in a blinding flash. He blinked away spots as he desperately sought Ree. He knew she'd be on him instantly. He needed to move.

Aran vaulted into the air and used a trickle of air magic to increase the height of the jump. Ree's blade hummed through the space underneath him, millimeters away. Aran landed in a crouch several meters away, blinking rapidly as he faced the direction the blow had come from.

Ree sprinted toward him, and the tip of her sword began to glow with golden energy. Aran considered his reaction for a fraction of a second, then reached for the water magic within him. Marid's touch was still new—cooler and harder than *air*, and much more elemental than *void*.

He extended a hand, and a jet of ice coated the floor. Ree vaulted it, and Aran smiled as he tracked her trajectory. He channeled a mixture of *air* and *void*, and his blade crackled with purple lightning. Now that she was airborne, her trajectory was predictable.

Aran darted forward and brought his blade up in a whirling strike. The blade whistled through the air, slashing through both of Ree's legs.

Only...the blade met no resistance.

The blow continued onward, pulling Aran off balance. A blade punched into his kidney from behind and burst out of his gut to expose a blood-soaked tip. The pain took him back to Marid, and Aran roared. The screams of the dying echoed through his mind; for just a moment he was back in the battle. Rage flashed through him—the desperate need to survive at any cost.

Aran's elbow shot back, and Ree's nose broke with a loud crack. He rolled forward and her sword pulled free from his back with a nauseating *pop*. He whipped his hand at his opponent, seizing both ankles with tendrils of air. He yanked her off her feet, and she barely retained a grip on her weapon as he dragged her closer.

He summoned more void lightning, plunging his eager spellblade through Ree's shoulder and into the training mat. The violet lightning flowed into her, and Aran knew the agony must have been immense.

But Ree never broke eye contact, and her only concession to the pain was a grunt. She whipped both legs up and kicked him hard in the chest, flinging him backward. Aran rolled with the blow, coming to his feet several meters away. Ree rose with a graceful flip, landing on her feet and beginning to circle. She raised a hand to her bloody shoulder, grimacing as golden light flowed into the wound.

"You can heal, too," he whispered in indignant awe. Talk about an unfair advantage. Any blow that didn't kill you could simply be removed as if it had never been.

"End this," Erika barked, though it was unclear which of them the words were intended for.

Aran glided forward, slashing wildly at Ree. She easily parried the blow, but he was already flowing into the next. He balled his free hand into a fist, aiming for her jaw. As it approached he drew on *water* and a heavy sheath of ice grew around his fist. It shattered Ree's still broken nose, knocking her to the ground.

He seized the hilt of her spellblade with his air tendrils, yanked the weapon from her grasp, and extended his sword until the tip touched her throat. "Lady, I might not remember much. I might be a mongrel. But I am also a depths-damned Marine. You want to look down your nose at me? Fine. Do it with respect."

She glared up at him hatefully, and in the back of his head he heard the major's voice. He'd just won a tactical victory, but lost a strategic one. He should have let her win. That would have been the smart thing, but he just wasn't wired that way. He clutched at the blood welling from his gut, swaying slightly.

"Well done," Erika mused, moving to stand next to Aran. "You've been trained in Drakon Style?" She pressed a hand to the small of his back and warm, golden light flowed into the wound. The pain eased, and he could feel his skin knitting back together.

"Uh...sure." The word triggered a split-second of *deja vu*, but Aran couldn't place it. "What does that mean, exactly?"

"I keep forgetting you've been wiped." Erika extended a hand to Ree and helped her to her feet. "Tell me, little sister, did you understand the lesson?"

She glared at Aran. "Oh, I understand it. Perfectly."

The rest of the students studiously avoided looking in her direction, and Aran couldn't really blame them. He was going to pay for humiliating her, of that he was certain.

"You recognized the style I used," he said. "What is it?"

Erika turned toward him and raised the same eyebrow. "You are new to our ways, and as such I will overlook such disrespect—for now. Ree, you will take Aran as an apprentice. Assess his skills as a war mage, up to and including piloting. Then bring him back to me for remedial instruction."

"You're just going to ignore my question?" Aran forced himself to remain calm.

"Until I deem it worthy of answering, yes. I could tell you of the style you practice. What's more, I can tell you where it originates. I can give you a piece of your past back, apprentice." Erika moved to stand no more than a meter away, then leaned in close. "If you want that piece, then you will do exactly what Premaster Reekala says. You will apply yourself to your studies. Do that—master what she teaches you during the next few weeks—and I will answer all your questions, Outrider."

The word tumbled through Aran's mind, maddeningly familiar: *Outrider*. What did it mean?

5

THE TEMPLE OF ENLIGHTENMENT

Nara had never been so terribly alone as when she stepped off the transport onto the soft forest floor. She clutched her satchel, which contained everything she owned in the world. Well, everything but the spellpistol belted to her thigh. Would they let her keep that?

The wind tugged at her dress uniform, keening. It seemed ever-present at this altitude, and she wondered if it was possible to get used to. The long jacket felt odd, and made her look too much like the major, but at least it kept her warm. She'd never been this high up; it would be a several-kilometer fall if she were somehow blown off Shaya's branch. The branch was easily six hundred meters wide, with a sprawling complex of magically shaped buildings nestled safely between a burl and the tree trunk.

The root-shaped door to the largest structure opened, and a cloud of smoke and brimstone zipped out. It paused, somehow closing the door, then zipped in her direction. The cloud compacted, billowing thickly into a bipedal form. After several moments the smoke dissipated and revealed a girl not too many years younger than Nara.

Well, *girl* might not have been the right word. Her skin was a rich ebony, the color of fresh stone in a lava field. Her hair mesmerized Nara; a thousand tiny rivers of flame rolled down her shoulders, heat shimmers rising from wherever her fiery hair pooled.

She was beautiful in an exotic way and wore a uniform identical to Nara's, though hers had a pair of sigils along the collar. Were those the aspects she'd mastered? *Fire* and *dream*, it looked like.

"Welcome to the House of Enlightenment." She gave a curtsy, flaring her jacket as she dipped. "I am called Frit, and I will guide you to your quarters, Apprentice Nara."

"I, uh...hope this isn't rude, but what are you?" Nara asked, struggling not to gawk.

Frit's features hardened, and whatever friendliness had been in her gaze vanished. "Please, come with me. I'll be punished if you are tardy. I need to get you situated before His Supreme Arrogance calls for you."

"Supreme Arrogance?" Nara ventured.

Frit frowned as she eyed Nara sidelong. "Master Eros. Come on."

Nara followed Frit through the wide double doors, into... paradise. The place was utterly silent except for the whispering of pages turning. High shelves full of books lined every wall, and row after row snaked through the room. A few even floated near the vaulted ceiling, apparently reached by blue translucent stairs. Those contained glowing dragon scales.

Knowledge scales, Voria had called them during the single brief lesson she'd given Nara on their trip back from Marid.

The books whetted a hunger Nara hadn't realized had been building. So much knowledge, and so much power— maybe enough to take control of her own destiny. Finally.

"Come, come," Frit grumbled. She hurried between the shelves, leading Nara deeper into the library. Finally, they stopped at a narrow hallway, and Frit released a puff of smoke from her mouth as she spoke. "Your quarters are the last door on the right, but we're out of time. Drop your satchel on the bed and hurry back. We need to begin your assessment soon, and it will be worse if we make him wait."

Nara headed obediently up the hallway, pausing before the last doorway on the right. There was no door, just an opening into a room with two narrow beds. One side of the room was clearly occupied; a mirror and a small grey book sat on the nightstand. Nara set her satchel on the other bed, and hurried back up the hallway. She could learn more about her new roommate later, but being late on her first day seemed like a terrible way to kick off her apprenticeship.

"This way." Frit wound toward the center of the library, and Nara followed her among the beautiful shelves. She inhaled deeply, smiling at the wonderful, musty fragrance.

They hurried down a trio of steps into an open section of the library about thirty meters across. Deep power thrummed through Nara as she stepped over the threshold, and she gazed around her in wonder. A ward of some kind?

A dozen wide desks fanned out across the room, each with a single mage wearing a version of her outfit. The students had sigils on the collar of their uniform, and many, though not all, had something like a unit patch on their shoulders. Most were the stylized white tree on a green background she'd come to associate with Shaya.

A few were reading, but most were casting some sort of spell. The boy at the closest desk, maybe seventeen or eighteen years old, extended a hand; a wilted flower straightened in a pot. At another table, a girl sketched the final sigil to an illusion spell. A caricature of the boy appeared, struggling in vain to get the wilted flower to straighten. The class laughed, and Nara found herself joining in.

"This is a *library*," roared a long-haired man near the center of the room. All laughter ceased. His frigid gaze swept the room, somehow more terrible given how supremely handsome he was—divinely so, even for a Shayan. His imperious gaze fell on her, and Nara forced herself to meet it. "You're Voria's new discovery, aren't you? Come here, Apprentice."

Nara realized he was talking to her, and quickly hurried to stand before him. She was mindful of all the students watching her, every last one of them younger than her by at least five years. That only made this all more awkward.

"What's your name?" he asked, eyeing her like a dragon beginning its dive.

"Nara, sir."

"I'm no officer. I know you've been wasting time in this Confederate nonsense the politicians dreamed up." He shook his head disapprovingly, and floated over to her, his feet a few millimeters above the ground. "That's over. You're here now, and you'll be here until I deem you worthy of leaving. Judging from the slack-jawed expression, that will likely be years. Now then, let's have a look at you."

He waved a hand and a circular mirror about two meters across floated over to hover next to her. Instead of her reflection, the mirror showed a glowing outline of her body. The energy was dotted with sigils, especially the area over her heart. Some she recognized as belonging to different aspects. Others were smaller but more complex.

Spells, she realized.

"Hmm, yes, yes. Very interesting. You've been to a *dream* Catalyst, but which one?" He bent closer, his face close to hers as he inspected the mirror. "And so many second-level spells. Who trained you, Apprentice?"

"I've been mind-wiped, sir." She realized belatedly she wasn't supposed to add the *sir*.

"Ah, yes, now I remember. The pirate girl." He turned from the mirror and finally looked at her. Nara had been stared at by men many times, but had never seen the casual indifference she found here. He saw her as a *thing*, a puzzle. Not a person; much less a woman. "You will make an excellent case study. Will your morals be overwritten by a new set? Or will your previous nature reassert itself, returning you to a vicious life of crime? Perhaps I will publish a paper with the results."

Nara wilted like the illusionary flower.

"Frit, come over here," the man ordered imperiously.

"Yes, Master Eros?" Frit asked neutrally.

Nara noticed that Frit never raised her gaze from the floor. She also noticed a tiny ring of golden runes around Frit's throat that she'd missed before. Some kind of magical collar?

"Teach pirate girl about the Circle of Eight, and find out which aspects she's proficient with. Compile a missive, and send me the relevant details." Eros turned from them, and strode over to berate another student.

Nara smiled weakly at the flaming girl. Frit did not return it.

"Let's get this over with." Frit frowned at her. "What do you know about magic, and acquisition of spells?"

"I know about the Circle," Nara explained. "A little, at least. I know each of the eight aspects. But beyond that? Not much."

Frit gave a put upon sigh. "Do you even know what a true mage is?"

"No," Nara admitted in a small voice.

"Simply mastering one of the aspects isn't enough to make a true mage. All true mages have learned at least one spell from a Greater Path." Frit raised a hand, quickly sketching a series of glowing sigils. She created a small illusionary Circle, and touched the sigil for *fire*, then *dream*. "When used in conjunction, *fire* and *dream* allow me to cast divination spells. I'm a flame reader, which isn't what most people think. I don't read flames, or I don't have to anyway. I *am* flame, and I read futures. There are seven other greater paths, each requiring two aspects."

"And the only difference between a true mage and other mages is the amount of study?" Nara asked.

"Well, study, and the fact that they need two adjacent aspects on the Circle. If you have *fire* and, say, *spirit*, you can't learn a greater path. You'd need to gain another aspect, one next to either *fire* or *spirit*." Frit scrubbed a hand over her Circle, and the illusion disappeared. "War mages spend their time learning to channel their magic through their bodies, which is both powerful and limited. We learn to manipulate the universe. Their magic is easier and more intuitive. Ours requires decades of study to truly master. Of course, a war mage can't create a solar system. Do you understand now?"

Nara considered Frit's lesson. The part about adjacent aspects definitely made sense. "I think so. I don't remember much, but I know I'm an illusionist." She tentatively sketched an *air* sigil, then a *dream*. She wove the magics together, forming an illusory Circle of Eight that matched the one Nebiat had drawn back on Marid. "I've also got void magic."

Frit gave a low whistle, and a puff of flame shot from her mouth. "If you find a way to master *fire* you'll have access to most of right half of the circle. You could learn divination, or even destruction. Eros is going to love this."

Nara didn't like the way Frit talked about her like she was a thing, but her time in the Confederacy had taught her that people in power often treated others like property, even if they weren't slaves. It wasn't Frit's fault. The fiery girl seemed as much a prisoner as Nara. Perhaps more.

She smiled at Frit. "I'll learn everything you're willing to teach."

And then, after she'd learned everything these people had to teach, she'd use the magic they taught her to find Aran, and escape this wretched world.

6

THE HEARING

Even though Voria's fate was the subject of the trial, she was still pleased the proceedings were held in a much more formal setting than the inquest had been. Since Shaya lacked the courtrooms Ternus seemed so fond of, they'd made use of a small coliseum used for worship of the goddess.

A titanic branch swayed above the open-air structure, shading the proceedings and lending an earthy, clean scent Voria had definitely missed. The stadium itself was largely empty, which didn't surprise her. Shayan nobility weren't interested in Confederate matters, even something as scandalous as a half-breed being tried for mutiny.

"Major Voria." A clear voice rang out from the base of the stairs, and Voria turned to see an unfamiliar dark-skinned man. His height and bearing put him from Yanthara, the very first Shayan colony. "This way, please."

She approached with a dignified walk, taking the opportunity to study the rest of the proceedings. The same three judges sat on the stage, in the same order. Ducius wore his hostility openly, while Skare sat in supreme patience.

Admiral Nimitz looked annoyed at everything, but not at her in particular.

The dark-skinned man indicated a simple chair in front of an empty desk. "Please, be seated."

Voria sat.

"My name is Mercelus Crewes. I am serving as the prosecutor for the Confederate military," Mercelus explained. "My job is to present evidence to provide context for the grievous crimes you've already admitted yourself guilty of. The advisory will digest the evidence, then present their findings to the tribunal, which will render sentencing. Do you have any questions before we begin?"

Voria shot a sidelong look at the advisory. Sixteen men and women sat in a cordoned-off section of the stadium seating. Each member represented a different world—theoretically, at least. All were citizens of Shaya, and had likely been pressed into the trial merely because they happened to have a parent or grandparent from a specific colony. Most looked bored.

Wait, was the drifter...sleeping?

"No, I have no questions, Prosecutor Crewes," she replied mechanically. She already knew they wouldn't provide her with an advocate, a Ternus tradition. Shayans were expected to defend themselves, under the grace of Shaya.

Voria would have preferred an advocate to futile prayers.

"Let the record state that the defendant has already admitted her guilt." Mercelus turned to face the advisory and raised his arms expansively. "The question we're here to determine is which crimes the major is guilty of, and whether or not there are mitigating circumstances that should warrant a stay on her execution."

A white-robed Shayan elbowed the drifter awake.

"The accused has been charged with inciting mutiny, and with the murder of an officer during a time of war," Mercelus explained. He ambled over to Voria and smiled almost fondly. "Yet this woman also saved an entire world. Had she not been at Marid—had she not seized command —the planet would be little more than ashes. What remained would belong to our enemies." His tone bled sympathy.

Voria went cold. She recognized a master strategist at work, though she didn't understand the tactic. He was painting her a hero, building her up. There was only one reason to do such a thing during a trial: the higher the hero, the greater their fall.

"I believe such heroism does indeed merit consideration from our esteemed judges." Mercelus finally turned toward the stage and gave the judges a respectful nod. "Yet that does not change the fact that these crimes occurred. The facts are clear. Major Voria knew she'd been stripped of command, yet still chose to execute the lawful commander of her battalion. She knowingly recruited heavily from an already decimated population. Men, women, and even children followed her into that swamp. How many emerged? How many out of hundreds? Marines, civilians. Nearly all died. Only a handful of mages—her chosen few—survived. So I ask you, is this a woman we should trust in a leadership position? A woman who will spend the lives of her men like credits?"

Mercelus walked over to the advisory. Even the drifter watched him with rapt attention, captivated by his incredible oratory skills. "I leave it to you to decide. The prosecution rests."

"Well, that's a damned relief," Nimitz rumbled. He sat up in his chair, and if he didn't exactly smile, at least the scowl thawed a few degrees. "Ternus trials can go on for days, with each side arguing trivialities. Major Voria, would you like to offer a defense?"

"What defense can she offer?" Ducius snapped. He leaned out of his chair and spat at the ground near Voria's little table.

She flared her fire magic, sketching a tiny sigil, and the spit evaporated before reaching the ground. Ducius glared hatefully at her, and Voria glared right back. She'd killed his son, but his son had left her no choice.

"Yes, Admiral. I do wish to present a defense, though I promise it will be short."

A whisper passed through the advisory. Every last face tilted upward, most slack-jawed.

She followed their gaze, raising a single hand to cover her mouth. "Please, Goddess, no. Anything but this."

Two figures drifted slowly down from the sky above. It was a simple flight spell, but the radiant nimbus of golden power around the couple made them appear divine beings descending to converse with their mortal flock.

The first figure landed near the advisory, and the glow around her faded. It revealed possibly the most beautiful woman in the sector: the Tender herself, Aurelia. Her hair caught the sunlight, dancing in shades of red and gold as she walked toward the judges. Her golden armor radiated immense power, a reminder she was, at heart, as much warrior as caretaker.

"What in the hells is this about, Aurelia?" Nimitz roared. His eyes flashed, and he rose slowly to his feet. His hands shook with rage, and they balled into fists as a vein throbbed in his forehead. "I realize you don't take the Confederacy seriously, but if you were just going to interrupt the proceedings why bother with a trial at all? We're at war, woman. We do not have time for your holodrama antics."

"Apologies for my entrance, Admiral." Aurelia gave a low, respectful bow. The motion was perfect, absolutely oozing grace. "I assure you I am not here to interfere in the trial. Quite the opposite. I have come to offer testimony on behalf of the accused."

"*Relevant* testimony?" Ducius asked.

That was interesting. Last Voria had been aware, the two were allies, at the very least. And they'd been lovers once, though that had been decades ago.

Ducius scowled at Aurelia. "We aren't interested in character witnesses."

The second figure had been largely ignored, which was understandable when a demigoddess walked into the room. Yet Dirk cut an impressive figure as well. He hadn't aged a day since Voria had last seen him, and still appeared to be in his early forties. Grey touched his temples, adding a distinguished note to one of the handsomest men in the sector— and one of the most arrogant. He could have removed the grey magically whenever he wished.

"That much is clear, Ducius," Dirk said, walking to stand before the Shayan judge. "You want my daughter dead, and you'll stop at nothing to achieve it. I assure you: if by some miracle you get your wish, I will end you, you pathetic cur."

A collective *oooh* echoed from the advisory, and the drifter leapt to his feet. "Fight 'em! Do it, Dirk."

"Admiral Nimitz," Voria boomed, in her full parade voice. Everyone fell silent, and all eyes moved to her. "As I was saying before I was interrupted, I do have a defense I would like to offer. Before I call my first witness, if you wish to hold my father in contempt of court I doubt anyone would object." She rounded on Dirk. "You don't belong here, father. This isn't an arena down in the dims. This is a trial in a court of law. Show some respect."

Her father blinked at her, then began to laugh. The advisory joined him. Nimitz put his face in his hands.

Well, if she hadn't been certain she had come home, now she definitely was. All the fighting, and the death, and these people treated her fate like it was a game.

7

FOR GOOD OR ILL

Voria took a deep breath, waiting for complete silence before she began. "I'd like to call Tender Aurelia as a witness." Voria waved at the makeshift witness stand, just another chair near the stage.

Aurelia glided across the floor, each movement a perfect, divine motion. She tossed her hair over one shoulder and sat gracefully. The entire court focused on her, and Voria's stomach roiled when she saw how hungrily her father watched the Tender. Revolting.

"Ask your questions," Nimitz said. He folded his arms, watching Aurelia with distaste. He was possibly the only man in the room not staring in open lust. Even some of the women stared.

"Tender Aurelia, would you tell the court about our meeting on the night before I departed for Marid?" Voria asked.

The advisory's nervous rustling ceased, and they focused on Aurelia's response.

"I summoned you to my palace to discuss the contents of an augury I had spent decades translating," Aurelia began.

She licked her full lips, staring up at the judges. "*I* called the major there, and showed her the augury in question. *I* showed her she would need to go to Marid, and sacrifice nearly everything in order to stop the Wyrm, Nebiat, from enslaving the Guardian, Drakkon."

Voria rose from her chair and clasped her hands behind her back. "And would you explain to the court what the consequences of failing to enact this augury might have been?"

"I believe Ternus would have withdrawn their support. The Confederacy would dissolve, and our member worlds would be conquered by the Krox. In a single human generation, the sector would be overrun. Our mother would be given to their god as a plaything." Aurelia gestured at the tree the coliseum sat on, indicating Shaya herself.

"Objection, Admiral," Mercelus snapped. "This is pure conjecture."

"Overruled." The admiral sighed. "Make this quick, Major."

"I told you my defense would be short, Admiral. Here it is." Voria approached Nimitz, stopping just below the stage. "The Tender convinced me that if I failed to stop the Krox at Marid, everything I've sworn to uphold would be destroyed. Did I retain my command after Confederate high command stripped me of it? Yes. Did I then execute the man chosen to replace me? Yes. I did both, because if I had not, the first obelisk would have fallen. Ternus would have been the second obelisk. Tell me, Admiral, what would you have done if faced with that kind of choice?"

"The admiral isn't on trial," Ducius roared, shooting to his feet. From the corner of her eye Voria saw her father mimic the gesture. At least he didn't charge the stage, or tear off his shirt so he could pound his chest.

"Settle down, Ducius." The admiral eyed the Shayan with disapproval. He shifted back to Voria. "He's not wrong. I'm not on trial. You are. What I would have done is irrelevant. But your point is taken. You did what you did because you believed that to do otherwise would destroy the Confederacy. Prosecutor Crewes, did you have anything you wanted to ask?"

"I do, though not of the Tender herself." He bowed low to the Tender. "I would like to call another witness to the stand. I would like to ask the major herself to explain certain actions."

"Very well. Major, take the stand."

Aurelia rose from the chair, giving Voria's shoulder a sympathetic squeeze as she passed. Magical warmth spread into Voria, driving away a bit of the stress. She frowned, smoothing her uniform as she sat in the chair the Tender had just vacated.

Mercelus moved to stand before her. "Thank you, Major. We appreciate your heroism, if not the manner in which the incident occurred. Your reasoning behind retaining your command is clear, as is the reason you executed—"

"Murdered!" Ducius snapped.

"—murdered Captain Thalas," Mercelus smoothly corrected himself. "But there is an issue that remains unclear to me. In your report you state you acquired a potion of resurrection. Is this correct?"

Voria's heart sank. "Yes."

"You are aware how incredibly rare such potions are?" Mercelus asked. He folded his arms, giving a friendly smile that never reached his eyes.

"I am."

"And you were aware that you could have used this potion to restore Captain Thalas to life, thereby mitigating your greatest crime?" The question was delivered mildly, but it stilled the entire courtroom. Even the wind seemed to die.

"I knew the potion would restore him to life, yes." She braced herself, already knowing what the next question would be.

"Then why didn't you use it? Why spend that potion to resurrect a—"

"A goddess-damned gutter rat pikey!" Ducius roared.

Nimitz slammed his makeshift gavel several times. "Damn it, Ducius. If you do that again, I swear I will thrash you right here, in front of everyone. Calm yourself, man. At least try to pretend you're an adult."

Ducius's hateful glare shifted to Nimitz, and he sat again with a curt nod.

"I chose to resurrect the *gutter rat* because he was the only tech mage in my unit who possessed life magic," Voria explained, drawing everyone's attention once more. "I had already seen the augury, and I knew he was supposed to be alive at the final battle. But I will be honest—that isn't the only reason I chose to use the potion on Specialist Bord. I did it because I knew Bord could help us win, and Thalas would only try to further weaken us. He was blinded by his own hatred for Lieutenant Aran. You've read my report. You know he lost his objectivity."

"So," Mercelus said quickly, overriding Ducius's choked response, "you allowed a noble—an officer—to die in favor of a lowborn tech mage. You ignored the gravity of your previous decision, so much so that you decided to double down on it. That's what we're hearing, isn't it, Major? You held the captain's abilities in low esteem, and you found dealing with your first officer's legal and legitimate insubordination difficult. So you murdered him, then made damned sure he stayed dead."

Voria's jaw snapped shut. She didn't want to answer, but there had been a question in there, and she was honor bound to answer it. "That's precisely what you are hearing. Thalas would have gotten us all killed, and we'd have lost the battle for Marid. I killed him, and chose not to bring him back. I'd do the same thing again."

She knew the words had damned her, but at least she could still look herself in the mirror every morning. She'd told the truth, and damned if it didn't feel good. She'd have preferred to die on the battlefield, but having her career die in a courtroom wasn't so bad.

"Very well," Mercelus began, without a touch of smugness or animosity. "I have no further questions, your honors."

"Major?" Nimitz asked.

"No further questions, Admiral."

"Thank the bloody gods." Nimitz rose to his feet. "Does the advisory wish to offer counsel?"

Most times the advisory did, as anyone could stand and speak. Perhaps it was the admiral's grim face, or simply the fact the Tender was there, but not a single advisory member spoke—in defense or accusation.

"All right. The judges will retreat for a short recess. When we return we will render judgement." He rose, and walked through the curtain at the back of the stage. Ducius and Skare followed a moment later.

Voria moved back to the chair she'd been given at the little table and sat, resting her elbows on the table. For good or ill, the dice had been cast. Her gut told her that everything was about to change, regardless of the outcome here. She hated the uncertainty, the knowledge that all her careful habits and routines were about to be obliterated as her life fell once more into chaos.

"Voria." Aurelia approached the table and sat lightly on one corner. She brushed a perfect lock from her perfect face. "I have deciphered another augury, and to be truthful... it frightens me. I was hoping—"

"Really? You want to do this right now?" Voria snapped. "My career is about to end from the last augury you delivered. Can you wait until this is done before beginning the next crisis?"

"I—of course, Major. How insensitive of me. Please, deal with your...situation, and come seek me out when you have time." Aurelia rose and retreated to sit next to Voria's father. Their hands clasped, and Voria looked away.

She sat proudly at the table, and waited for her fate to be delivered.

8

THE SENTENCING

Voria had composed herself by the time the judges filed back onto the stage. Ducius looked troubled, which surprised her. They had plenty of rope with which to hang her, so why wasn't he his usual smug self?

The admiral's expression was unreadable, and to Voria's surprise, she realized Skare's angular face bore faint amusement, the most emotion he'd yet demonstrated.

The admiral sat heavily, and waited for the other judges to sit before he spoke. "Getting these two to stop dithering took longer than expected, but this court has settled on a sentence. This sentence required some...stipulations. Major Voria, in your report, you recommended Lieutenant Aran for the Silver Starburst, the Sun Cross, and the Golden Arrow itself."

"Respectfully, sir. He killed three adult Wyrms, one of those in a one-on-one fight. His team foiled Nebiat's ritual. Without him, victory wouldn't have been possible." Voria knew honesty killed careers, but she'd be damned if she'd let them slander her men, and that was *exactly* where this was going.

"You will amend your report to reflect the following facts," the admiral said, clearly uncomfortable with the words. "The hero of Marid was Captain Thalas, and Thalas will be posthumously awarded the Golden Arrow for his extreme valor. Lieutenant Aran did nothing worthy of special note, and will not be awarded a medal. He will, however, be allowed to keep the field rank you bestowed."

Voria folded her arms, almost forcibly holding in the words she really wished to fling. She settled for tact instead. "What makes you believe I can be convinced to lie on my report in such a way?"

"Because," Ducius called. The smugness had returned, full force. "If you do otherwise, I will cast the deciding vote to have you executed. You say you believe in this war, Major. Just how committed are you? Victory, at the expense of your honor—a small price, really. My son dies with the honors you denied him, and you get to live." He glared hatefully at her, all amusement gone.

Voria considered her response carefully. If she agreed to this, Aran might never know—but that wasn't really the point. He'd *earned* those medals. He'd distinguished himself. It didn't feel right to keep that from him.

But if she did not agree, her role in this war ended. She died, and if the new augury the Tender had deciphered was as important as the last...she wouldn't be there to stop the Krox. Honor didn't win wars; in this instance, she simply couldn't afford it.

"I will amend the record to reflect the facts," she said, "as they have been stated in this proceeding. Lieutenant Aran was worthy of no special merit, and Captain Thalas was the hero of the day."

Each word came harder than the last, and her eyes shone by the end—shone, but didn't loose a single tear. She'd be damned if these bastards saw her cry.

"Very well." Nimitz straightened uncomfortably. "Then this court now renders final judgement. On the charge of inciting mutiny, you are found not guilty. On the charge of murdering an officer during a time of war you are found not guilty. Finally, on the charge of gross negligence leading to the death of enlisted personnel...you are found guilty. You are to be demoted to the rank of captain, and you are officially stripped of command. You are to be placed on a period of administrative leave for no less than eight weeks, after which you will be assigned to a more experienced officer for guidance."

"Sir," Voria called weakly. "What about the *Hunter*, and her crew?"

"Captain Davidson will be given temporary command of the *Hunter*," Nimitz allowed. Ducius shot him a venomous look, but Nimitz continued. "He'll oversee the decommissioning prior to being reassigned. As for the rest of your mages, they'll be placed in appropriate units as assignments become available."

That blow was almost too much. Survival was pointless if she possessed neither a ship nor a crew to go haring off on whatever mad quest Aurelia's augury had in store for them.

"This session is adjourned." Nimitz pounded the gavel, and the judges filed off the stage.

Voria sat, unable to rise. She had no idea what came now, no idea what to do next. Eight weeks of administrative leave? What did that even mean? What would she do?

"Ria," her father called, crouching to give her a hug. She grudgingly admitted it felt good to be wrapped in his arms. "I'm sorry, little one. I know how hard this must be for you."

"Don't call me that." Voria stood up and slipped from his grasp. "I'm not your little one any more. I'm a officer without a ship, and with no way of remedying that. I have no funds, Father."

Aurelia glided up, delivering a smile. "I cannot aid you directly, but your father can. Come with us, Voria. Watch the augury, then we will begin planning. The days ahead may be difficult, but we will face them together. You are not alone."

"Yay," Voria muttered sarcastically. "I get to hang out with my father and his paramour. Won't this be fun."

9

SPELLFIGHER

Aran sat up with a groan. One day had blurred into the next, each day harder than the last. Today was the twenty-first, and theoretically final, day in his testing. Those days were long, too. Twenty-six hours instead of the sector standard of twenty-four. Two more hours of training, with the same amount of sleep.

The previous days had been endless drills, sparring, and running. So much running. He'd honestly believed he was in good shape, but the last week especially had taught him how painfully wrong he'd been about that.

At least the bed was comfortable. Aran was pleasantly surprised by the quarters he'd been provided. Instead of the bare-bones barracks he'd grown used to on the *Hunter*, he was given a spacious apartment complete with a stunning view of the rolling hills and valleys far below the branch of Shaya on which the manor sat.

The room came with a wardrobe of silken uniforms identical to those Ree had worn—minus the patch on the shoulder. He guessed he'd probably have to earn that, but that was fine with him. If the Confederacy wanted to train him to be a more effective killer...well, that would just make it all the easier to escape.

He was more and more sure that was the right path. These people were oblivious to the war, and to the threat the Krox posed. They were utterly incapable of dealing with someone like Nebiat. They played their war games, but what would they do when a real dreadlord showed up?

Besides, the casual racism Ree and the other nobles showed toward Kez and her people, and to humans, wasn't exactly endearing. These people were arrogant and out of touch. They made the perfect target for someone like Nebiat, and he didn't want to be around when that inevitable hammer fell.

He'd committed to fighting the Krox, but he didn't see anything saying he had to do it for a military that cared nothing for the lives of its soldiers, or even their own citizens.

Aran walked onto the balcony and stared down at the city. Most of the lower buildings were squat and ugly, clustered between the roots. Many areas had colorful tents arranged haphazardly, like flowers in a wild garden.

He heard a whine from above, and looked up to see Ree's fighter descending. It didn't slow until the very last moment, snapping to a halt no more than a meter from where Aran stood. He held his ground and glared at the opaque canopy. Ree probably had the scry-screen active.

"I take it we're going somewhere?" he asked dryly.

The canopy slid upward and Ree's face appeared over the side. "Get in."

"Should I bring anything with me? My spellblade is inside."

"I can see that," Ree snapped. "Never, ever take off your spellblade. Sleep with it. Bathe with it, mongrel." She added the most force to the last word, making it an insult. "Now run and fetch it."

"Yes, Mom." Aran trotted back inside, shaking his head. He scooped up the spellblade and buckled the scabbard around his waist, then headed back outside. He climbed the shimmering blue steps and leapt into the cockpit. The vessel began moving before he'd reached the co-pilot's couch, and he had to strain to grab the stabilizing ring as the fighter entered a steep climb.

"Today we're testing your piloting skills," Ree explained. She seemed amused by his struggles, and gave a disappointed sigh when he finally buckled the harness and locked himself into the matrix. "Being a war mage isn't just hand-to-hand combat or manifesting spells. Our spell-fighters are the first line of defense for Shaya herself. You might be a passable duelist, but that's far less important than what you can do with a fighter."

"Well, keep your expectations low. I've never piloted one of these things, at least not that I know of." Aran watched the scry-screen appreciatively as the planet fell away beneath them.

"Is the vessel familiar, at least?" Ree sighed.

"Yeah." Aran ran a hand lovingly along the silver ring rotating around the command couch. "She's familiar."

"I don't know what backward world you came from, but I'm guessing even they trained their war mages to be pilots. They'd be foolish not to, if they wanted to defend their skies."

The fighter rumbled briefly; the rumbling stopped as they burst through the protective dome of life energy sustained by Shaya. They entered open space, and Aran smiled at the void. This he knew.

"We both know I'm pretty ignorant. The mind-wipe saw

to that. I know you enjoy lording that over me, and I'm fine with that...as long as you give me answers." Aran pivoted the chair to face Ree as they departed the moon's gravity. "Pretend I'm a child. What is a war mage? I've heard *war mage*, and *tech mage*, and *true mage*—but I don't really understand the difference between them. Can I become a true mage? Can they become war mages?"

"Our children learn this in their first-year classes. I supposed it isn't really your fault." Ree blinked, more surprised than combative, for once. "Very well. Before we begin, I will answer your questions. It is, after all, my responsibility to somehow turn you from an ignorant mongrel to a proper Shayan war mage."

Aran noticed she said *Shayan*, not *Confederate*.

"I'll use small words so you can understand." Ree guided the fighter toward the dense patch of asteroids ringing the azure gas giant that Shaya orbited. "Anyone who possesses even a single aspect of magic is a tech mage. It requires no training to pick up a spellrifle and fire it, just the magical spark to power the weapon. So anyone who goes to a Catalyst is automatically a tech mage, assuming they gain magic and not simply a magical adaptation of some kind."

The fighter zipped into the asteroid field, winging nimbly around a rock the size of the *Hunter* as they approached the center of the field. The asteroids were more dense here, and avoiding them required deft handling. Aran was impressed, though he certainly wasn't telling Ree that.

"War mages learn to channel magic through our bodies. Instead of using sigils to construct a spell externally, like a true mage, we manifest it directly. This means many of our spells can't be countered, but it also limits the types of spells we can cast."

Ree's face, the smugness softening, was lit by the planet

below as the fighter whipped around another asteroid. Aran could tell she loved piloting, which was at least a little common ground.

"Okay," he said, "that makes sense. I've used a number of abilities, and I've wondered why I didn't need to cast like Voria does."

Ree's face darkened at the mention of the major. "True mages, like the traitor who conscripted you, spend years learning magical theory. This allows them to access powerful spells, provided they have the right aspects to fuel them." The fighter slowed, and Ree guided it to a graceful landing atop a floating ball of ice that almost qualified as its own moon. "Is that clear enough for you?"

"Can war mages learn to be true mages?" Aran asked.

"Yes, if they invest the time. But right now it's your abilities as a war mage that I care about. Impress me, mongrel —or wash out. I'm fine with either, really." Ree tapped several sigils on her command matrix, and the rings began to slow.

"Wait, you want me to fly us out of this?" Aran glanced up at the scry-screen. Thousands of asteroids rotated around them, and a massive hunk of iron slammed into a ball of ice not far off their starboard side. Both exploded spectacularly.

"Are you telling me you can't do it?" Her smugness overwhelmed any reservations Aran might have had. So much for common ground.

"No." Aran tapped the same initiation sequence he'd seen her use: *fire, fire, air.* "I've got this."

He guided the craft into the air, amazed at the difference from piloting the *Hunter*. Flying the battleship was like moving a mountain. The fighter responded instantly, zipping in whatever direction Aran wanted, quick as thought. He flew low over an icy mountain, then zipped up into the asteroid field.

"Woo*hoo!*" Aran yelled, pouring magic into the drive. The fighter accelerated, and he whipped it between a pair of rotating asteroids. The level of control was heady, and it touched something deep in the back of his mind. He'd done this...many times.

Aran poured void magic into the spellcannon, instinctively. A void bolt shot into the asteroid blocking their path, boring a smooth hole directly through the center. Aran guided the fighter through the hole, shooting out the other side.

He whipped past more asteroids, pouring on even more speed. Fewer and fewer asteroids flitted by, until the fighter finally burst out of the field and into the open void. Aran guided the craft to a halt, then turned to face Ree. "Not bad for a mongrel, eh?"

Ree shrugged, unimpressed. "I've seen better. But I've also seen worse. Tomorrow, we'll try something a bit more difficult."

10

ICE AND ROCK

Aran sat up in bed with a groan. The silk sheet slid from his chest, exposing the mass of bruises.

The twenty-first day had been worse than the previous twenty put together. After his fighter training, Ree had spent the rest of the day kicking his ass in the kamiza. He'd never again gotten the drop on her as he had during their first meeting, and suspected he might never again. She'd adapted quickly to his style, and for some reason he struggled to adapt to hers. The longer they sparred, the faster she ran him through.

A chime came from the entry hall, and Aran fished his rumpled uniform from the floor. He hadn't quite reached the door when it slid open and Ree stepped inside. She eyed him appraisingly as he slid on his shirt, but didn't say anything until he'd finished dressing.

"You have a package outside," she finally said.

"Okay."

Her uniform was immaculately pressed, her hair perfectly styled. She crinkled her nose at him. "You are a slob, even for a mongrel. We gave you a dozen clean uniforms. Why are you wearing that one?"

"Ree—can I call you *Ree*?" Aran asked, buckling on his spellblade.

"No."

"Ree, you're clearly used to having all the advantages in the world. Me? The Confederate Marines didn't give us squat. When I fought on Marid I didn't have a second uniform, or even a change of socks. Not that you people even know what socks are." Aran moved to the door, and met Ree's gaze without flinching. "You want to train me to fight? Fine, I'll learn. You don't get to tell me how to dress."

"You *want* to look like a mongrel? At least the Caretakers will see you for what you are without you needing to open your uneducated mouth." She stalked past him and climbed the glowing steps to her fighter. Aran moved to join her, and she held up a hand. "I'm taking the fighter. You're not."

"Then how do you expect me to follow you?" Aran demanded, expecting another painful lesson.

"I told you, you received a package." She nodded toward the front door of his apartment, and Aran realized there *was* a package. A familiar black crate. The same crate that had delivered his spellarmor, back on the *Hunter*.

The canopy closed and Ree's fighter moved into the air. Her voice boomed from the external speakers. "Make it quick, mongrel. I have more important things to do than teach the unteachable."

Aran took his time walking to the crate, slapping the familiar red button. The casing retracted into itself, exposing his Proteus Mark XI spellarmor. He grinned at the midnight armor, "Oh, I definitely missed you."

To his surprise, the armor quivered in response.

He blinked. "I'd forgotten. Marid must have changed you, too. I wonder what you can do now?"

Aran sketched the *void* sigil before the chest and slipped inside the armor. It solidified around him, and he grinned at the familiar comfortable interior. It was the first time he'd used the armor since they'd clashed with Nebiat.

He willed a bit of *void* from his chest into the suit, and she shot into the sky. Her handling was still beautiful, but she was also noticeably faster than before. A new icon had appeared on the screen showing what appeared to be a miniature glacier.

A missive request appeared in the bottom of the screen, and Aran acknowledged it. A view of Ree's face appeared on the corner of the HUD, basically a tiny scry-screen. That was definitely new. Part of what Marid had done?

"Head into the asteroid field. You have thirty seconds to hide. Once you are hidden, I will hunt you. Your goal is to survive as long as possible." She delivered the words without her usual rancor, just the ever-present conde-scension.

"You want me to pilot a suit of spellarmor, and you're going to hunt me in a fighter? We both know how this ends. It isn't a fair fight. What's the point?"

"Were the Krox fair on Marid?" she growled, her eyes flaring with their own inner light on the corner of his HUD. "The point is to teach you to follow orders, and to survive in un-winnable scenarios. Now, can you follow orders, or must I report your training a failure so soon after it has begun?"

"I can follow orders," Aran growled right back, but he flew up through the atmosphere, toward the asteroid field.

The truth was, he needed to know the things she could teach—or, rather, what Erika could teach. If that meant swallowing his pride, he might have to learn to do that.

Tomorrow, maybe.

He flitted between the asteroids at the edge of the field. The suit was even more mobile than the fighter—the only real advantage he'd have against her. Not that it mattered. He could evade her, but his spellrifle wouldn't so much as scratch her hull, even if he fired a third-level spell.

That didn't mean he couldn't try. He opened a vertical slash in the air and withdrew his spellrifle. The barrel, enhanced by Marid, was longer now. Theoretically, that might enhance the range of his spells, which could prove useful.

He whipped around in midair, staring between the suit's legs out at the empty space where Ree's fighter still hovered. "So we're clear, what's the victory condition here?"

"Victory? Disable my craft." The way she said the words showed just how likely she thought that was.

"All right." Aran zipped between asteroids, trying to anticipate where Ree would enter. She'd be gunning for him quick, he suspected. But how could he turn that against her?

Her fighter streaked into the field, and her spellcannon loosed a beam of pure golden energy. It punched through not one but many asteroids. She vaporized a path into the field, homing in on his location as if she were a diviner.

How is she following me? he wondered, kicking off an asteroid and flying deeper into the field. His smaller size made that easier, but Ree had a massive advantage in speed.

Another cannon shot punched through the asteroid next to him, peppering him with debris. He altered direction, zipping around another asteroid, one large enough to withstand a shot from Ree's cannon. He wound through a low canyon, circling to the far side of the city-sized hunk of ice and rock.

Moments later Ree's fighter whipped into view. The nose dipped, bringing the cannon into alignment with his armor.

"Oh, shit." Aran whipped his rifle up and drew from his void magic. He flipped the selector all the way to three, and sighted down the scope at Ree's cannon. He had no idea how to counterspell, but she was using *life* energy. Perhaps that could be countered with *void* energy.

He waited until her spellcannon filled with golden energy, then fired his void bolt. It shot out, directly into the path of the beam of golden energy. His void bolt disappeared within the blinding golden glow, with no visible effect. The golden energy continued on, slamming Aran into the canyon in a spray of ice and rock. Red spots bloomed all over the paper-doll representation of the armor.

"What in the depths was that?" Ree taunted through the missive pane, frowning at him. "You could have dodged that."

"I was trying to counter your spell," he admitted.

Ree laughed musically. "Oh, mongrel. It doesn't work that way. It is possible for an equal amount of *void* energy to cancel *life*, but your bolt wasn't anywhere close to equal. Why didn't you use an actual counterspell?"

Aran was silent.

"You don't know how, do you?" She wore her smugness like armor.

"No, I don't." He shot up from the ground, zipping out of the canyon and back into the asteroid field. "So how about you teach me, rather than mock me?"

"Remedial training is not my job, mongrel. I believe Master Erika will be quite amused by the...gaps in your knowledge." Her mouth slid into a mischievous smile. "Now hide again. We're not done here."

"I'll show you gaps," he muttered, and flew around

another asteroid, trying to guess the route she'd take after him. Around that big one, almost certainly.

Aran sighted down the barrel, aiming for a jagged crack that ran through a battleship-sized hunk of ice. He fired a level-three void bolt, then a second, and finally a third. Using that much magic made him dizzy, but he shook it off and zipped up to see what his spells had done.

The bolts sped into the crack, slamming into three separate sections of ice. The asteroid shuddered after the first, and cracked after the second. The third sent a dozen fighter-sized hunks of ice spraying out into space, directly into the path of Ree's fighter.

She flew around the big asteroid...and slammed into a hunk of ice. Then another. Her ship tumbled end over end, falling toward the big asteroid. At the very last instant she regained control, and flipped the fighter back in his direction.

"That was clever. This is blunt." Her cannon warmed up, the golden glow building.

Oh, crap.

The beam shot into his armor, knocking him into an asteroid. The paper doll went entirely red and a soft warning chime sounded within.

"Oww."

Ree laughed again. "Take heart mongrel, you've amused me today. I've never met a mage over the age of twelve who couldn't counterspell."

11

HONESTY

Aran followed Ree into the kamiza, grateful for the warmth as they left the chill wind. This late at night it was empty, save for Erika, who sat against the far wall, a sweaty towel draped over her shoulders.

She looked up as they entered, and raised a water bottle in greeting. "How did the orbital assessment go?" She stood with a groan.

"Aran isn't a total waste, but his inability to counterspell is a definite weakness." Ree eyed him emotionlessly. Whatever her feelings, she'd mastered them. "He showed impressive tactical initiative. I wasn't able to adequately test his strategic capabilities."

"Excellent, if my suspicions about him are correct." Erika rubbed her hands together then placed them against her neck. Waves of magical heat rose from the hands and she sighed contentedly. "And your final assessment? Sum up the last few weeks of training."

"There were some easily rectifiable deficiencies. He's out of shape, but a few more weeks will cure that. Aran is skilled, but dangerous to himself and to others. Because he doesn't understand what he knows, he uses his abilities instinctually. This can lead to some impressive feats, but ultimately makes him both predictable and unusable in battle. I'd recommend sending him back to remedial training. Have him learn again from the ground up." Ree watched him the entire time. He expected to find her usual smugness, but he read something different there. Regret, maybe? Pity? It was gone too quickly to be sure. "I can have him in a cockpit in a month, and in two years he'll be the best war mage to come out of this kamiza since Dirk."

Erika took a swig from her bottle. She eyed it with intense consideration, as if the bottle were far more important than his own fate. Finally she looked up at him. "And you, Aran? How do you feel about this assessment?"

How *did* he feel about it? It sucked being told he didn't cut it, but was Ree wrong? It stung, but nothing she'd said was untrue.

"I—well, the first part is accurate. I can't counterspell for shit, and half the time I don't even know why I do something. That makes improvisation difficult, because I don't really know what I can do. I'm always reacting to things, which puts me at a perpetual disadvantage." Admitting it was difficult, but lying to himself or to Erika wasn't going to help him improve. And he *needed* to improve. "I don't know what's entailed in starting my training over, but I'm willing to try."

Ree eyed him as if seeing something terrible and inexplicable at the same time. "You're...agreeing with me?"

"It's really, really simple. I got my ass kicked on Marid. I don't want to get my ass kicked next time. The only way I do that is learning from my mistakes. You people can teach me, so...do it. I'll be a willing student. I'll toe the line, if you'll help me improve." Aran folded his arms. "I'll even call you Premaster Reekala, if you want."

Erika laughed. "Thank you for your report, Ree. Why don't you get some rest? I'd like to speak to Aran alone."

"Of course, Master." Ree's tone made no attempt to hide the hurt. She turned gracefully and walked from the kamiza.

"She doesn't like me." Aran shook his head sadly.

"Her issue isn't with you personally. She doesn't like what you represent." Erika took another swig from her water bottle. Her breathing had calmed, the last stage of a workout. "Has anyone taken the time to explain to you what the Confederacy really is?"

"No, I guess they haven't," Aran realized aloud. "I mean, I get that it's a government with a military, but I don't really understand how the different member worlds play into it. It seems like Shaya does whatever the hell it wants, and it doesn't seem to much value the Confederacy."

"That's what you're encountering with Ree." Erika walked deeper into the kamiza, toward the door that led further into the building. Aran followed, and she spoke again once he'd fallen into step beside her. "The Confederacy was the brainchild of Tender Aurelia, though you won't find her name officially attached to any part of it. Before it was founded sixty years ago, each world in the sector stood alone. Some, like Shaya, had colonies. Most were single worlds, because interstellar travel is prohibitive, in both time and cost. It takes a standard Ternus vessel three years to cross the sector from end to end."

"But...we crossed a large part of it in less than a week." Aran shook his head as they entered a small kitchen.

Erika moved to a counter and plucked an apple from a bowl. She drew a knife from the block and expertly sliced the fruit into wedges. "Apple?"

"No, thank you. The Umbral Depths are even more important than I thought. Any world with void mages can move about quickly, striking behind enemy lines, or delivering supplies." Aran finally understood just how important Nara's run on the Skull of Xal had been. They'd gained incredible power. The implications were staggering.

Erika popped another wedge into her mouth, chewing thoughtfully. As she swallowed, a warm golden glow suffused her eyes. "So you can see your importance. Whoever earns your loyalty will gain a powerful weapon, one that will only grow in strength over the decades. Ree worries you'll choose to stay with the Confederacy."

"Do I have a choice?" Aran asked. "I thought I had to serve a four-year term in exchange for my 'crime.'"

"Your term can be bought out. Fifty thousand credits for each year, and you're a free man. If you have a wealthy patron, you're free to do as you choose."

The news sent Aran reeling. He leaned against the counter, heart thundering. He could be free. Free to make his own decisions. Free to pursue his own destiny.

"You'll receive many offers in the next few seasons." Erika ate another wedge. "War mages are rare. Very few people have both the magical power and the manual dexterity to learn to fight as we do. It requires years of training to really master—but somehow, somewhere, you've already done that."

"You recognize the style I use. You could tell me about my past." Aran eyed her sidelong.

"I could. I won't. Not right now, anyway." Another wedge disappeared. "Ree believes—correctly, in my mind—that putting a man of your talents in the Confederate Marines is a maddeningly stupid waste of resources. In a decade, you could be one of the most feared men in the sector. You could help alter its fate. Heroes are not just legends, Aran. They are forged, here, in this kamiza."

"But not if I die in the next battle with the Krox. If I were just a tech mage, then no one would really care. I'd have potential, but that potential is meaningless without years of training and dedication." Aran cocked his head. "I'm still not one hundred percent clear on the difference between a war mage and a tech mage. Is it just training?"

"All magic requires study of one form or another, though tech mages cheat by outsourcing that study to the person who crafted their weapon and armor." Erika finished the last of the apple and wiped her hands on her loose pants. "In our case, that training allows us to manifest spells directly through our bodies. They're nearly impossible to counterspell, unless we're firing a ranged spell. We're close-range fighters, though some war mages dedicate themselves to killing from a distance."

The door to the kamiza opened again, and footsteps pounded closer. Ree sprinted back into the room holding a golden disk with runes around the outer edge. A missive.

"The trial has been decided." She set the disk down on the counter. "Voria has been stripped of command and demoted to the rank of Captain."

Aran moved to a stool and sat heavily. What did that mean for his future? For the fight against the Krox?

"Was there more?" Erika asked with minimal interest.

"A little." Ree paused, and Aran looked up to find her staring at him. "The official record is being altered. Voria put Aran up for several commendations. Those commendations have instead been posthumously awarded to Captain Thalas. They're calling him the hero of Marid."

Aran started to laugh.

"You think this is funny?" Ree blinked at him.

"No, I think this is typical," Aran said. "Thalas treated Marines like pieces on a game board. He wanted to waste their lives, pointlessly. He's everything I hate about Shayan nobility: arrogant, racist toward drifters." That drew a sniff from Ree. "He put his own honor and petty need for revenge over the welfare of the battalion. If he'd been in charge instead of Voria, not only would we all be dead, but that planet would be, too. And they're giving this guy a medal?"

"So what are you going to do about it?" Erika asked him, with the same apparent disinterest.

Aran rose to his feet and stalked toward the door. "This is bullshit. I'm going to find Voria, and we're going to make this right."

12

WHEELS WITHIN WHEELS

Nebiat inhaled slowly, turning in a slow circle and smiling up at the city around her. The smallest house could easily be called a mansion, and the biggest houses could be considered towns in their own right. The amount of Shayan wealth on this single branch rivaled that of all the others combined.

She walked up the thoroughfare, a wide path lined with bark that had been crushed to mulch by the passage of endless feet. A raven cawed in the distance, and several deer trotted boldly across the path ahead. They'd never known a predator.

The Shayan nobles who dwelled here had no idea how much they resembled those deer.

She followed the path to a ring of redwoods. Six mighty trunks grew close together; only a few narrow gaps remained between the arboreal giants. Nebiat slipped through the largest, into a small clearing. These trees were children of the Shayan's stupid tree goddess, and their latent magic served as a sort of ward—the kind of ward that would shield casting from prying eyes.

Nebiat raised a delicate finger and traced a *void* sigil. She built the Fissure spell quickly, opening a three-meter gap into the Umbral Depths. Nebiat added an *air* shield over the gap, to prevent the atmosphere from being sucked into space.

Within moments, the first enforcer had climbed out. The enforcer's brothers and sisters quickly joined her, filling the little clearing. When the last had arrived, Nebiat closed the Fissure.

"Get into position, little ones," she instructed with an absent wave.

The enforcers scrambled up the trees, their scales darkening to blend in with them. They disappeared into the canopy above, each training a spellcannon down into the clearing. At best they'd prove a distraction, but she'd take every advantage she could get given who she'd come to meet.

Mere moments after the last enforcer had vanished a woman stepped between two of the trees. Not just any woman, or even any war mage. This was a true master. She moved with deadly grace, and her hand rested confidently on the hilt of her spellblade. Her chestnut hair had been bound into a simple ponytail, keeping it out of the way in a fight.

"Ahh, you must be Master Erika," Nebiat crooned. She didn't offer a hand in friendship, or any other greeting. There was no sense pretending a false civility. If this woman had been properly bound, then she'd do as Nebiat wished. If not, she'd cut Nebiat down, regardless of what she said or did.

"You already know I am." The woman glanced over her shoulder, then back at Nebiat. "We need to make this quick. We cannot afford to be seen together."

"No pleasantries then. How efficient." Nebiat gave a subtle gesture, the wave meant for the enforcers above. They'd stand down, unless she was attacked. "Given that you haven't drawn that blade, I take it your rumored allegiance to my father is true?"

"Yes." She frowned. "What do you want, dreadlord?"

"How long?" Nebiat demanded.

"Eighteen years," Erika snapped. Her eyes narrowed dangerously. "The wording of my binding is very specific. I can't kill you. I can kill the six enforcers above, and I can do it before even the fastest is aware they're dead."

"Very well, throw your temper tantrum if you must. I'll wait." Nebiat inspected her fingernails for several moments. Erika made no move to attack. "I guess you really are in a hurry. You were told to obtain a specific magic item, and to bring it. Do you have the eldimagus?"

Erika reached into a satchel attached to her belt and removed a small golden bracelet lined with impossibly tiny sigils. The power pulsing from the item prompted Nebiat to take a step backward. Erika laughed. "If I wanted to use it on you I already would have."

"And what would have happened if you'd snapped it around my wrist?" Nebiat whispered. She didn't know what the thing did, only that it was powerful and that her father was certain she could use it to neutralize Eros himself.

"The bracelet appears benign to magical scans, because its power is harmless enough. It stores the next spell a mage casts." Erika took a cautious step closer and offered her the bracelet.

Nebiat accepted it gingerly, holding it up to study the enchantment. "It looks like that spell can be tapped into later, to be used by the caster. Even if I tricked Eros into wearing it, couldn't he merely cast the spell into the bracelet, then use the bracelet to fire the spell at me?"

"That is the genius, really." Erika folded her arms, her mouth going sour. "This bracelet is broken, or intentionally mis-designed. It can't actually hold a spell. Every time a caster tries, the spell dissipates."

"So, this will effectively counter any spell that a mage casts?" Nebiat slipped the bracelet into her own satchel.

"Precisely. And once donned it cannot be removed without a full nullification. Your father commanded me to acquire it several years ago, and I've been holding onto it since. Now I know why."

If the betrayal bothered Erika then she certainly didn't show it. "Well done. I will relay as much to my father. But I also have a task for you."

"Are you certain you wish to jeopardize my place here?" Erika asked cautiously. "I am the most highly placed spy your father has access to. If you cost him that, I doubt even you will enjoy the results."

"I understand, but this warrants the risk." Nebiat reached into the satchel and withdrew a vial of sickly green fluid. Black motes swam sluggishly through the liquid. "I've heard rumors that you and Dirk were once lovers. Is that true?"

"It was." Erika nodded, her face an unreadable mask.

"Rekindle that relationship, and when the time is right get Dirk to sleep with you. On that night you will throw an extravagant party. Drinking. Sex. Whatever you think Dirk wants." Nebiat handed Erika the vial, and the master took it. "When he is vulnerable, you will slip him that."

"What is it?" Erika asked as she held up the vial for inspection.

"A rather nasty poison. It removes the subject's ability to

use magic, and lasts for many hours. This is how we will turn Dirk." Nebiat smiled. The idea of converting Voria's father to her cause made her positively giddy.

"And what's the point of all this? I've heard nothing worth risking my cover." Erika's frown was nearly undetectable.

"Why I'm going to kill the Tender. I have a vial for her, this one so rare even she isn't aware it exists." Nebiat didn't show the vial. She enjoyed the occasional risk, but that one wasn't worth even contemplating, much less doing. The poison was irreplaceable. "You aren't quite ready to know the full scope of the plan, but I will contact you when I am ready."

13

FRIT

Nara sketched another sigil in the notebook, the ink flowing easily from the magical pen. She already missed her scry-pad, which was far faster and allowed her to search for specific data. While she loved books, they seemed needlessly primitive, but over the past three weeks she'd not seen a single piece of technology in the university. Even tech-magic devices were forbidden.

Frit suddenly plunged through the door, throwing herself onto her bed. Nara glanced at her from the corner of her eye, trying to decide if her reluctant roommate needed time to be alone. She could gather her things and head for the library, though she hated how everyone watched her—especially the younger boys. It creeped her out.

"Do you want to talk about it?" Nara finally asked.

Frit sat up, wiping a fiery tear from her cheek. The magical sheets on the bed resisted her flames, but the frame had already warped from constant heat.

"I'm sorry for the drama. His royal assholeness is particularly bad today, and it makes me miss home is all. And my people." She pulled her knees up to her chest. "My people are taken from the Heart. It's a blazing ball of light and flame, brighter than any star. We gather around it, bathing in his brilliance. Shayans know this, and capture my people as slaves. Those of us who survive initial training are sent to the Skull of Xal to acquire void magic. Most don't survive. The tech demons there are terrible."

A single memory flashed through Nara's mind, a quick image of a three-meter-tall demon carrying a spellcannon. The memory wasn't attached to anything, but Nara sensed that it related to the Skull.

"What happens to those who survive?" Nara asked. She set her pen down and moved to sit on the edge of Frit's bed. From here the heat was pleasant. Any closer, and she suspected it would grow painful.

"We're trained to be war mages or true mages. We become weapons, expensive pets for Shayan nobles." Frit blinked away the last fiery tear, and looked sidelong at Nara. "It's nothing like what will happen to you. You'll be married off, and given a life of luxury."

"Excuse me?" Nara blinked, then she laughed. "I promise you no one is going to marry me off. I'm only here long enough to learn. If they try to marry me—or do anything else I'm not comfortable with—I'm gone."

"Gone?" Frit looked at her directly. "Where would you go?"

That took Nara aback. Where *could* she go? Aran was involved in his own training. Voria was still on trial, so far as she knew. She wasn't close enough to Crewes to ask him for help. Kez would take her in, but the drifter had her own troubles.

"I don't know," Nara said. "It's a big galaxy. I'm sure I could find something to do."

"Well, you've already mastered illusion. Some of the

richest entertainers in the sector are illusionists. And you're pretty. I bet nobles all over Shaya would come to see someone like you perform." Frit extended a smoldering hand as if to touch Nara's hair, but withdrew it suddenly when she realized what she was doing. "I'll never get to entertain. I exist to kill."

"So do I. Before we came here, my unit fought the Krox. A lot of people died, and a few more fireballs on our side might have kept people alive. We'd have been thrilled to have you fighting with us." Nara pulled her knees up, too, mimicking Frit. "I don't know much about Shaya, or about the people who live here. But I know one good Shayan. Major Voria—"

"—is half-breed trash," came a harsh voice from the doorway. Nara looked up to see Eros enter the room, his too-handsome face locked into a scowl. "If you are wise, you will disassociate yourself from her immediately. You don't want to go down when she's stripped of command, which I assure you will happen this afternoon. She's a pariah, and we're well rid of her."

"She's twice the mage you'll ever be," Nara snapped, leaping from the bed. "While you're hiding here under your big tree, she's out fighting the Krox. Marid is free because of what we did there—what you were too afraid to do."

Behind her, Frit gasped.

Eros watched Nara impassively for an eternity and a half, then raised a delicate eyebrow. "I see we have a great deal of misinformation to correct. Leave us, Frit."

Frit leapt from the bed, skirting Eros as she sprinted out of the room. Nara stood defiantly. She'd be damned if she was going to roll over for this bastard.

"Your exploits on Marid were impressive," Eros admitted. He picked a piece of lint from his sleeve. "Yet much of that victory was luck and instinct. You were untrained. You didn't understand how to utilize your magic. You didn't know the right spells to save your companions, and people died as a result. You could have saved them, had you received the kind of training we teach here. Right now, you're little more than a jumped-up tech mage. Imagine what you could be if you spent five years mastering your abilities. You could be a terror on the battlefield, cloaking a kill squad as you eliminate enemy mages. Tell me, child: do you understand why I hold Voria in such contempt?"

"No." Nara stared defiantly back, still wondering what his motive in all this was.

There was some merit to his words, even she could admit that. Making mages into more powerful tools made a lot of sense, but what was the point if those mages never entered the battles that really needed them?

"Because she isn't a fraction of the mage she could be. She could become a force for change on this world. She could found her own house. Instead, she's locked in a mad battle with a superior foe. A battle that will get her, and anyone who follows her, killed." Eros sat next to Nara and took her hand in both of his. He turned it over, showing her the palm. "If you give it a chance, this can be the most powerful weapon you've ever been given. You don't need that spellpistol, and you don't need someone like Voria giving you orders. Learn to think for yourself." He closed her hand into a fist, then rose. "I'm told your studies are progressing extremely well—faster than Frit initially promised. There is so much you can learn here, if you try. Don't be distracted by petty politics, child. What you do in these next few weeks will determine your future for decades. You owe Voria nothing."

Nara considered his words, and hated herself when she

realized she couldn't find fault with them. Did she owe the major? Or should she be looking out for herself, and her own future?

Eros rose from the bed. "Now, come with me. It's past time you learned how to duel."

14

DUEL

Nara stepped hesitantly through the wide doorway into the dimly lit room. In each corner, a magical flame hovered in midair. The flames gave off heat, so they weren't illusions. A golden ring covered most of the floor, with tiny white sigils lining the edge of the metal.

"Join me." Eros pointed to the far side of the ring, opposite him. He didn't speak again until she stepped over the ring, into the circle. "This is a dueling circle. We use it to dampen our magic and prevent accidental death. Move to the far side, and we'll begin."

"I feel like this is going to be a very short fight," Nara pointed out.

She reached instinctively for her pistol, but Eros's hand flashed. He sketched a quick trio of sigils, and a crackling void bold shot into her sidearm. The weapon disintegrated with a *pop*, its particles dissolving as Nara stared in horror.

"My pistol! That was my only weapon."

"No!" Eros snarled, stalking closer. "That was a crutch, used by tech mages who don't fully understand magic. You no longer have the luxury of crutches. Now you stand on your own, mage. You want to punish me for destroying your toy? Good. Do it. But do it with a spell."

Nara's hand rose up like a cobra, and she instinctively sketched a single dark sigil. The void bolt zipped from the air over her shoulder, aiming unerringly for Eros's irritatingly perfect face. He raised a single finger, and sketched a counterspell. Her void bolt exploded into magical shards mere millimeters from its target.

"A good beginning. You're in a magical duel. You've probed your opponent's defenses with a void bolt, and found him prepared for it." Eros prowled around the edge of the circle, watching her. "Now what? Do you take the offensive, or settle into a defensive pose to see how he'll react?"

Nara tensed, trying to decide what the correct course of action was. Eros had been a true mage longer than she'd been alive, if the rumors around the university were true. So how could she possibly win a duel with him?

His finger twitched, and a beam of golden light zipped into the floor at her feet. It exploded upward, each shard slicing painfully into her. She staggered to the side, but caught herself after a step. The circle had blunted the impact of the spell.

"Right now you are hesitating out of indecision, not tactical awareness." Eros stopped and frowned reprovingly. "You're afraid. Afraid I'll hit you with a spell you cannot defend against. Afraid of the pain. Afraid of the humiliation."

He sketched a single sigil. Something invisible wrapped around her hair, yanking her toward him; he lunged, pulling a dagger from his boot and pressing it to her throat. He released her instantly, and the dagger vanished back into its sheath.

"That fear makes you predictable," Eros explained. He

stalked the edge of the circle. "The purpose of the dueling circle is to remove that fear."

"Bang-up job so far," Nara shot back, touching the bead of blood on her throat.

She raised her hand again, sketching a quick series of pink-and-white sigils. A cloud of pink particles blasted out in a wave before her, but Eros hopped nimbly out of the path.

"There! Anger. That is another option, though certainly not the best for true mages." Eros raised a hand, but didn't cast. "Anger overrides fear, making action possible during stressful situations. However, anger only allows you to access certain more primitive parts of your brain. It limits you, forcing you to familiar, well-worn reactions. That, too, makes you predictable. You fall back on your training, and a wise mage understands how their opponents have trained."

"So what's the answer then?" Nara pulled back to the edge of the circle. She hated that her voice sounded sullen, but it was maddening not to understand any of this. She'd trained furiously for weeks, but she was trying to make up for years. Why couldn't he just teach her?

"Calm." Eros lowered both arms and took a long, deep breath. He closed his eyes, then opened them with a smile. "War mages rely on anger. It suits them, and it does transform them into lethal weapons. But we do not possess that luxury. We must be calm at all times, able to react in the most appropriate manner in all situations. That can mean a counterspell, or it can mean pressing your opponent with a quick flurry of void bolts. The goal is to never be the one reacting. If you cede the initiative to your opponent, you may never recover it."

Nara considered casting another attack spell, but settled for circling the edge of the ring. "But I've seen Major Voria do that. She counters every spell her opponents throw, until she finds an opening. It's always seemed a solid strategy to me."

"To begin with, it isn't a strategy. It's a tactic. You need to learn the difference." He crooked a finger, beckoning her to assault. "Regardless, there is a critical flaw in Voria's logic. What do you do if your opponent throws a spell you cannot counter, like a disintegrate? What if the spell is too powerful, and the counterspell doesn't work?"

Eros sketched a *dream* sigil, then an *air*. The spell completed almost instantly—an illusion of some kind. She couldn't see anything different. Eros still stood there, in the same position. There was nothing different, so what had the spell done?

"So you're saying pure offense is more effective?" She sketched another void bolt, flinging it at his face again.

This time Eros didn't dodge. The bolt rippled harmlessly through him—that was the illusion. Nara began to spin, but it was too late. Eros's dagger pressed to her throat once more. He shoved her forward, toward the center of the ring. She staggered but caught herself.

"I'm saying that a single, perfectly calculated strike your opponent doesn't see coming is the best way." Eros gave her the first genuine smile she'd seen. "You're an illusionist, pirate girl, not a battle mage. There is no reason your opponent should ever have the opportunity to strike at you. Nor should they see your attacks coming. You kill them, fast and deadly, then you teleport out before their companions can react."

Nara raised a hand to her throat; it came away with more blood. "You make a very convincing argument."

"The first of many, I hope. You have a great deal of potential, pirate girl. Houses from all over Shaya will court you, all in the hopes of marrying you into their family." Eros walked to the edge of the ring and picked up a towel. He tossed it to her, and she was surprised to realize she was coated in sweat. "You must decide what it is you really want. Power? Money? Fame? Glory?"

"Magic," she gave back without hesitation. "I want to learn it all. If I can unlock the full circle, I'll understand the universe."

"So power, then." Eros gave a grim smile. "You remind me a great deal of myself at your age. The endless thirst for new knowledge. It must be especially challenging after your mind-wipe."

"Is there any way to...reverse the spell?" She wasn't even sure she wanted to, but she had to at least know whether it was possible. Besides, perhaps she could help Aran regain his own memory.

"I've heard legends of gods rebuilding minds, but I've never seen any practical proof of such a thing. There is no recovering the memories, so far as I know." He frowned. "It's not a life you have any business wanting to remember, pirate girl. Come at me. Again."

Nara tossed the towel to the ground outside the ring, and prepared another spell.

15

DARKNESS

Voria moved to the balcony, staring down at the goddess's swaying branches. The view was breathtaking, a marvel any number of citizens would eagerly vie for, yet today it brought her no peace.

It was the same view she'd had the last time she'd visited the Tender, though this time she'd been given her own quarters. And, much as she hated to admit it, she needed that generosity. She had nowhere to go, and no real resources to speak of.

Every scale and every credit had gone into the war effort, and the Confederate script she'd been paid with was very nearly worthless on a planet like Shaya. She couldn't even afford decent accommodations, or daily rations.

"More wine, Ria?" Her father crooked a finger and the crystal pitcher floated down. He allowed it to refill his goblet, but she covered her own. "Don't be so stoic. You're alive. Celebrate that."

"You'll forgive me if I'm not in a celebrating mood, Father. Not all of us can hide here on Shaya flitting from party to party. Some of us still have a war to fight." Voria tightened her hands around the goblet, wishing they were wrapped around her father's neck instead. "You have so much influence, so much respect from these people. You could convince them to rally against the Krox, to help the Confederacy win this war. But you do nothing."

Her father plucked an apple from the bowl next to him and took a large, crunchy bite. He chewed thoughtfully, and his eyes glowed a soft gold as he consumed the life-imbued fruit. "Ria, I'm proud of who you've become, but I'd remind you that you are very young. You have just passed forty, and are in the throes of your first war. I understand that everything is urgent and new. You think failure here will mean the end of everything. But after you win this war, there will be another. And another. And always another. It will go on for decades, and when you pass your first century you will realize there is no end to the cycle. I'm tired of war, little Ria. I've done my part."

"What about the Tender?" Voria demanded. "Does she feel the same way?" She refused to believe that the *de facto* ruler of Shaya would abdicate her responsibility to protect her people.

Aurelia's voice came from the entryway to the room. "No, I do *not* feel the same way." She glided inside, still wearing her golden armor. "In fact, I agree with you, Voria. I've long chastised your father for wasting his abilities, but he refuses to leave the capital.

"Perhaps if you stopped sleeping with him, he wouldn't have a reason to stay." Voria meant it playfully, but cringed at her own words. *Poor taste.*

"Perhaps." Aurelia smiled at Dirk. "Sooner or later, you are going to need to accept your responsibilities, Dirk."

He shrugged, sipping his wine. "Maybe."

"Tender, I apologize for being a forward guest, but you

said there was a second augury. I'd like to see it as soon as possible." Voria shifted her weight, peering up the hallway toward the room where Aurelia had shown her the first augury. "May we use the Mirror of Shaya?"

"I thought you might like time to relax...but if you are ready, of course we can view the augury. This one is not so terrifying as the last, though it does raise a number of very troubling questions."

Aurelia followed the balcony to the far side of the room, then walked up a short marble hallway that ended at a pair of double doors covered in tiny dragon scales. The last time Voria had been here, they'd shown Shaya, but now the scales showed unbroken blackness. It was a minor but disconcerting difference.

"Dirk," Aurelia said, "perhaps you should wait out here."

It wasn't a suggestion. Voria's father nodded and gave a graceful bow, then retreated a few steps. His petulant frown made it clear he felt excluded. The doors parted silently, and Voria stepped into a darkened chamber that smelled of sulfur and other reagents commonly used in ritual casting. Such reagents didn't aid the spell, but they often aided concentration.

The doors slid shut silently, and the ritual flames sprang to life. Each danced over the corresponding aspect, giving life to the ritual circle surrounding the Mirror of Shaya. That mirror showed impenetrable darkness now, the same as the door had shown.

Voria took a step closer, peering into those inky depths. "Tender, this may be answered by the augury you're about to show me, but why are both the door and mirror black?"

"I don't know," Aurelia admitted, "and it terrifies me." She joined Voria at the edge of the circle. "That's part of why I've been so frantically deciphering this augury. The mirror went dark three days ago—the door, two days. I don't understand the magic at work here, but we are not alone. Flame Readers all over Shaya have complained that their fires show nothing. Something powerful enough to dampen all divination is obscuring our collective vision."

"I see." Voria folded her arms, shivering.

"Watch." Aurelia sketched a *dream* sigil, then a *fire*. More joined the first pair, building a complex divination spell. When Aurelia had completed the spell, the mirror flared, and a shape appeared in the darkness.

"I can't quite make it out," Voria mused.

"It's a planet." Aurelia pointed at the curvature along the bottom.

Voria leaned closer, but there was almost no light in the augury. "Why is it so hard to see?"

"That part took me a while to verify. The planet is so dark because it lies within the Umbral Depths."

Voria turned to look at Aurelia, whose features were lit by the flames. "I thought the depths were empty?" she said slowly. "I've never heard of anything in there—not a single world. I know Ternus tried to establish an outpost, but we all know how that turned out."

"The depths are far too vast to be completely empty," Aurelia countered. She nodded back at the augury. "Look."

The perspective shifted, and they were on the surface of the planet, zooming through canyons. Many-legged shapes moved through the darkness, their flat, black eyes glinting at her from the shadows.

"What am I seeing?" she whispered. Light glinted off the creatures' skin in a familiar way, the same way it might glint off a...dragon.

"They're called arachnidrakes. An offshoot of the original dragons. They're larger, tougher, and nearly impervious to magic. Like the Krox, they begin in a bipedal form, similar to an enforcer, but eight-legged." Aurelia shuddered in distaste. "They're reputed to be less intelligent than standard Wyrms, but given the level of intellect, they might still be smarter than unaugmented humans."

She trailed off as the augury shifted again. It showed a massive stone temple, an entire mountain carved to honor some long-forgotten god or goddess. That mountain stood alone in the center of a flat plain, easily visible for hundreds of kilometers. An infernal glow came from within the temple covering the summit and surrounding slopes. It represented potent magic, perhaps a full Catalyst.

Sudden darkness billowed from the temple, obscuring the augury. The flames winked out around them, smothered by magic that sucked the warmth from the air.

"What just happened?" Voria asked in a small voice.

"A part of the magic. I believe there is more to the augury, but whatever that temple is has somehow snuffed it out." A golden light sprang up around Aurelia, illuminating her features. "Now you've seen it, and why the matter is so urgent."

"I'm not sure I agree. What's so urgent here, and what do you expect me to do about it?" Voria shook her head. "This isn't a battle with the Krox. This is a glimpse of a world in the one place no sane captain would lead her crew. And it isn't even clear why someone would want to go to that world, or what they'd do when they arrived."

"If we could see the rest of the augury, those questions would be answered," Aurelia pointed out. "Unfortunately, I haven't yet discerned a way to do that. All I have are premonitions. I believe that world is vital to our survival, and someone left something for you to find there. A weapon of some kind. Powerful magic that we can use to resist the Krox."

"That's your takeaway?" Voria blinked as she followed Aurelia from the chamber back to the bright area around the balcony. "I didn't see myself, or anyone I recognized. What could possibly make you associate that with me?"

"A feeling."

"A feeling? You want me to fly into the Umbral Depths because you have feelings?" Voria began to laugh—timidly at first, but it grew quickly. Before she knew it, tears streamed from her eyes. "Following you got me stripped of command, got my vessel taken away. And now...now you want me to somehow fly into the Umbral Depths because... feelings." She laughed until she wheezed.

"Please." Aurelia walked slowly to Voria and took Voria's hand in both of hers. Warmth flowed into Voria. "Shaya comes to me sometimes as I sleep. I see her thoughts, and her memories. In this instance, I'm seeing a memory, a very old one. She knew you'd be going into the Umbral Depths. She helped craft the spell that hid a world there. You, and your friends are meant to do this. In the dark you will find the strength needed to resist. You will be shaped, whatever that means."

The words knocked Voria back a step. When a goddess spoke—even a dead goddess—wise mortals listened. "Let's say I was willing to listen to your mad plan. How would I even get there? I don't have a ship."

"Now, that," Aurelia said, delivering a dazzling smile. "Is something we can fix."

She gestured, and the doors opened to reveal her father sheepishly eavesdropping.

16

WHAT'S A TEXAS?

"This is your idea of a ship?" Voria demanded. "She's not even space-worthy—and even if she was, she's a simple Ternus frigate. She doesn't even have a spelldrive. How would we open a Fissure?"

Voria surveyed the long, rectangular frigate. She was lined with Ternus Gauss cannons—an imprecise weapon, but one that could be fired as many times as needed. Then Voria noticed the hastily welded cannon along the bottom. A spellcannon, from the looks of it.

"Father, I know you tried, but are you certain you want to trust your daughter's fate to...this?" She touched the side of the hull, and orange rust flaked off.

"She has a full spelldrive, and she has the most important quality a vessel can have, Ria." Her father leaned closer, tousling her hair as he had when she was a child. "She's free. You're broke. This is what you have. Deal with circumstances—"

"—as they are, not as I wish them to be." Voria frowned. She hated that axiom more than any other, but she also admitted that learning it early had saved her a great deal of heartache over the course of her life. "The ship will do nicely. Thank you, Father."

"There is another option." Dirk smiled suddenly. "Why not ask your mother?"

"You know as well as I that she wouldn't even return the missive." Voria rested a hand against the frigate's hull. "Does she have a name?"

"Her name is *Big Texas*," her father supplied with an affectionate grin. "She's not much larger than my first ship."

"What does it mean?" Voria asked. "What's a Texas?"

"It's a regional designation from ancient Terra. One of the Ternus colonies is called New Texas. Maybe there's some relation."

"Well, she certainly isn't very big." Voria tugged at the airlock latch, and the door reluctantly rumbled up into the ceiling. "Let's see what she's got."

They entered a narrow cargo bay. A metal catwalk led over it and into the central portion of the ship. There were no proper quarters, just eight individual bunks. Beyond the bunks lay a tiny kitchen, a head, and the cockpit of the ship.

"It's...cozy."

"Thank you," called a muffled voice from the cockpit.

"Excuse me?" Voria said, quickening her step. She pushed through the mess, into the cockpit.

A pair of legs poked out from under a console, wearing a standard set of Ternus overalls. "Hey, there." The small man attached to the legs wheeled out into view. He had unruly red hair, and his thick glasses made him look like some sort of studious waterfowl. "Name's Pickus. You must be the new owner of the *Texas*. You got a name?"

"Voria. Ma—Captain Voria," she supplied, offering a hand. Pickus took it, and she helped haul him to his feet. "What is your role here, Pickus?"

"I'm a mechanic. Well, an engineer, technically. But these days I mostly just fix stuff. I come with the ship. You want her to keep flying, you need me to keep eating." Pickus gave a sly grin. "I ain't even asking for pay. You just gotta give me a place to berth, and the stuff I need to fix the ship."

"Well, it appears I have a crew, if a small one." She turned a smile at her father. "Thank you. This is exactly what I needed to get started."

"What will you do now?" Aurelia asked.

"If I'm going to head into the Umbral Depths I need a crew, and not just any crew. I need Aran, and my tech mages. I need Nara."

Each of them had filled a role, and all would be needed to attempt something as mad as this.

"And how are you going to secure them?" Aurelia asked. "You've been relieved of command."

Voria smiled. "I've got an idea about that. All Marines are entitled to leave after an extended campaign, which means they can get up to four weeks off. I can't officially command, but I could take some friends on a pleasure cruise into the Umbral Depths. I just have to convince them it's worth it."

"Wait, we're going where now?" Pickus adjusted his glasses. "The Umbral what?"

"Is he serious?" Voria asked, looking to her father.

"He's from Ternus, and has next to no experience with magic." Her father shrugged. "At least he can keep this tub flying. Now then, is there anything else you need from me? If not, I'd like to get back to my, uh...*studies* with Aurelia."

"Ugh." She crinkled her nose. "Every time you make a little headway, you intentionally say something to nauseate me."

"We all need a hobby." Dirk winked at her, and started walking back to Aurelia's shuttle.

The Tender waited until he'd departed the ship before she spoke. "You will face loss, Voria; of that I am certain. I don't know how you intend to persuade them to follow you, but it's unlikely they will survive the darkness."

"I am so glad I have no idea what you are talking about." Pickus laid down on his wheeled cart and slid back under the terminal.

"I'll find a way. It's all I can do." Voria hung her jacket from a torn panel in the wall. "At least we have a ship."

Aran guided the fighter into a smooth landing atop the Tender's floating palace. The landing struts clicked down with a whir, and the canopy rose, exposing him to the howling wind outside. This high up, the wind must be ever-present.

He climbed from the cockpit, quickly surveying the landing area. A pair of guards in golden Mark X spellarmor flanked a door leading below. Both carried ornate spears, and Aran could feel their magical strength from thirty meters away. He did not want to tangle with these guys, especially since his spellarmor was still back at the kamiza. Erika had balked at the very idea he might bring it.

"I've come to speak with Major Voria," he roared over the wind. He approached with his hands raised high, hoping the Tender's guards hadn't been instructed to kill intruders.

"Are you expected?" asked the guard on the right, a woman with the clipped accent of Shayan Nobility. She sounded a good deal like Ree, though older.

"I should probably have sent a missive. I'm willing to

wait here, if you'll take word to her that I'm here." Aran settled into a comfortable resting stance.

Both guards reacted instantly, flowing into combat stances.

"Whoah, easy." He raised his hands again, standing perfectly still. "What triggered that?"

"When an Outrider of Virkon settles into a centered stance, wise warriors strike first," the woman growled. "Sentinel, go inform the Tender we have a guest. Ask her for instructions on how best to...conduct him into the palace."

The second guard opened the door and slipped inside, leaving an awkward silence. The woman hadn't lowered her spear. She stood motionless, as still as a statue. He had no doubt she could impale him instantly, so he tried to stay as still as possible.

"Can I put my hands down?" he asked after several minutes.

"Slowly, yes. But keep them away from your spellblade, or I will remove them." The words were friendly—cheerful, even.

"Okay." he lowered his hands. "Listen, I know you're guarding and all, but can I ask you a question?"

"You may ask. I might answer."

"You called me an *Outrider*. That's the second time I've heard that term. What does it mean exactly?"

Her spear didn't waver. Not even a millimeter. "Now that is a very curious question. How is it you know Drakon Style, but don't know what an Outrider is?"

"The short version? I've been mind-wiped." He offered a smile, though he couldn't tell if it moved her at all, since she was encased in that golden armor. "And, as you can imagine, I'm a little curious about my past. So can you tell me about these Outriders?"

The door opened and the second guard returned. "He's allowed below, with no escort."

"The Tender said that?" The woman slowly lowered her spear. "Very well. Head down those stairs and take the first entryway on the right. You'll find Voria on the balcony there."

"Thank you." Aran gave a grateful nod as he headed below.

He could have pressed for details about the Outriders, but that would put the guard in a difficult position. He had a name now, and could ask Erika directly. If she refused to tell him, he could start asking around until he found someone else who knew about these Outriders.

The walls were all carved from a reddish-golden wood that Aran assumed must come from Shaya herself. Potent magical energies radiated from the walls in waves—even from the parts that bore no runes. He followed the stairs gradually down, and they spilled him out onto a balcony wide enough to house a full company.

Several golden couches floated throughout the room, and three were occupied near the center of the room. Aran recognized Voria instantly; her posture was ramrod straight despite sitting in an opulent chair designed for relaxation.

The man to her right had similar features—a bit more angular, but in a boldly handsome way. He was the type of guy that drew every eye in the room, unless he happened to be sitting next to an even more beautiful woman, which he was.

Aran had had no idea what to expect of the Tender—but whatever he'd imagined, this wasn't it.

She wore a smaller set of golden spellarmor, very similar to her guards. It left her face bare, and framed by brilliant hair. At first, he thought it was scarlet, but as she turned it became almost blond. The hair wasn't what caught his attention, though. Her face was—perhaps literally—divine. It had the kind of beauty that inspired artists to devote their lives to capturing it.

Aran straightened his posture, settling into that instinctive stance again. He approached them at a walk, moving directly to Voria's couch. "Major, I—"

"It's *Captain* now," she corrected.

"Voria," Aran started again. Her eyes widened at the use of her name, but he continued. "I heard the outcome of the trial, and I came to hear it from you. Is that how we're being rewarded for what we did on Marid? They're demoting you and whitewashing the story so Thalas comes out the hero? Do you even realize how that will play on Ternus? They already know the truth."

"Father, Tender...allow me to introduce Lieutenant Aran of the Confederate Marines. He is—was—one of mine." She arched an eyebrow, and Aran reluctantly extended a hand to Dirk.

The man's grip was firm, but not enough to suggest he had anything to prove. He added a respectful nod, which Aran returned. The man's posture was relaxed, but he radiated danger. Aran might not remember how, but he recognized the presence of a master.

The Tender simply nodded at him, so he nodded back. Dirk's jaw fell open, and Voria gave a delighted little laugh. The sound was even more terrifying than a Wyrm's wingbeats.

"It's a pleasure, Lieutenant." Aurelia sized him up, and he couldn't tell whether he met her unspoken standard. "You are welcome in my home, so long as Voria will have you."

"Thanks, but I've got my own place. I just came to talk to

Voria, then I'll be on my way." He turned back to Voria. "Tell me you're not going to take this lying down."

"The demotion? Aran, since we're apparently on a first-name basis, let's be candid. I don't give two shits about the Confederacy, or Shayan politics. I care about Confederate citizens—lives, Lieutenant. Near countless numbers of innocent lives, all trying to survive in a sector overrun by demons, or Krox, or Wyrms. So yes, I'm going to take this lying down. I won't fight it. Instead, I'm going to sail into the Umbral Depths, and I'm going to find the world that Marid left for us to find. It's there, not here, that we'll find the tools to fight this war. And since I know the Confederacy won't support my mission, I'm not even going to tell them about it."

"And you want me to go with you." Aran gestured at a floating carafe, and a goblet materialized in his hand. The carafe filled it with a sweet-smelling golden liquid. Might as well enjoy the perks while he had them.

"You're going to fight me on this?" Voria gave a sarcastic laugh and rolled her eyes. "This is simply brilliant. My ship is a floating can, and my first doesn't want to go. That's saying nothing of how hard it will be to get Nara on board. Eros won't release her easily."

"What about Crewes? And Kez and Bord?" Aran asked.

Voria didn't answer. Dirk and Aurelia both avoided his gaze uncomfortably.

"Oh, this is rich. You want *me* to get them on board, don't you?" It was Aran's turn to laugh. He should have expected this. "And the worst part is...you already know I'm going to do it, don't you?"

"I'm sorry, Aran. Before we go any further, I ask you to consider something, just for a moment. I am no more interested in journeying into the depths than you are. I don't want to go. I don't want to die. I want to clear my name, and see you properly honored." She leaned forward in her chair, stabbing a finger in his direction. "Don't assume this is *my* mission. You want to be equals? Fine, we're equals. I'm just as tired of this as you. If you want to be angry with anyone, it should be her." She nodded her head in Aurelia's direction.

"She's not wrong," the Tender admitted. "I did show her the first augury, and this one."

That put things in a new perspective. In a way, Voria was as much a victim of circumstance as he was. "All right, I'll see if I can get Crewes and the others on board."

He had no idea how he was going to do that. Let's fly into the Umbral Depths with no support, no material, and oh yeah on a ship that seemed to be coming apart...well it didn't exactly make for a winning pitch.

18

UH OH

Nara chewed the wooden end of her pen, then finally added a notation to the spell she'd been researching. It combined *void* with *illusion*—well, theoretically at least. She didn't even know if that was really possible. She looked up and considered heading back out to the stacks to locate a couple more reference tomes.

She decided to be lazy, instead, and turned back to the previous page, surveying with pride the list she'd made. She'd identified seven distinct spells in her aura, four first-level and three second-level. There were several more spells unidentified, but she remained confident she could puzzle those out as well.

1st Level
Shift
Icy Armor
Sleep
Void Bolt

2nd Level

Instant Growth
Paralyze
Invisibility

"Nara." Frit hurried up to her desk, drawing the attention of several other students. Frit lowered her voice. "You said you knew Major Voria, right?"

"Yeah, why do you ask?" Nara's heart sank as she rose from the desk.

"Well she just walked into the library." Frit pointed back through the rows of shelves. Sure enough, Voria had just strode into the library. She wore the same uniform, but the patch on her shoulder had been replaced with captain's bars.

"Depths, I think she was demoted." Nara hunched low against the table as the major—the captain now—strode by.

"Why are you hiding? I thought she was your commanding officer." Frit blinked flaming eyes in puzzlement.

"She is...or was. But I was conscripted. They didn't give me a choice. And Voria isn't very friendly. She's never liked me, I don't think." Nara breathed easier once Voria's path had taken her across the library.

"It looks like she's here to meet with Eros." Frit stared after Voria as the captain disappeared into Eros's office.

"That can't be good." Nara sat on the edge of the desk. "She's here about me, I know it."

"What do you think she wants?"

"If I had to guess, she's got yet another mission she expects me to tag along with." Nara frowned. She liked Voria, but knew the sentiment wasn't returned. To Voria—to many people—Nara would never be anything but a reformed pirate. At least when Eros called her pirate girl she got the sense he was inspiring her to be something more.

"That doesn't sound so bad. I'd love to get out of this place and go do something that matters." Frit's words were bitter, and brought Nara up short.

"I guess I really do take my freedom for granted." She looked at the collar of sigils around Frit's neck. "Does that thing control you?"

"Yes." Frit nodded sadly. "My people are all fitted with one as soon as we're captured. When we're sold, our new master is given the control unit. Fortunately, Eros has never used it on me. But he's also never allowed me to take it off."

Eros's door crashed open, and his head poked out of the office. "Get in here, pirate girl. Now." He disappeared a moment later.

"Uh oh," Frit said sympathetically.

"Yeah, definitely *uh oh*. I'll let you know how it goes." Nara steeled herself and headed for Eros's office.

19

CHOOSE WISELY

Nara straightened her posture before rapping at the door to Eros's office. She knew Voria would be watching.

Eros's muffled voice came from within. "Enter."

She opened the door and slipped inside. Eros sprawled across a golden couch that floated a meter off the ground. A crystal goblet full of a dark red liquid floated within easy reach. He looked, as always, supremely relaxed.

Voria was his opposite in every way. She stood ramrod straight, her hands clasped crisply behind her back. She eyed Eros with clear distaste, and Nara noted the emotion reflected in the eyes of her new mentor.

"Took you long enough, pirate girl," Eros said, without looking at her. He pointed to another floating couch. "Sit."

Nara looked to the couch, then at Voria. The corners of Voria's mouth twitched down, just a hair. Nara moved stubbornly to the couch, sitting comfortably. Eros preened as if she'd brought him a present, a clear sign they were fighting —over her, she guessed.

"*Captain* Voria has come to ask you to accompany her

on a mad quest into the Umbral Depths," Eros explained. He gave Voria an amused look. "She's citing an obscure law from the ratification of the Confederacy. Any soldier who exhibits exceptional valor may request an extended leave when the battle is done. Apparently, this was used for them to make a pilgrimage home to thank Shaya for their victory. But she wants you to use this time to commit suicide."

"Sir?" Nara asked, turning to Voria; her face hadn't aged, exactly, but her weariness gave that appearance. "What happened at the trial?"

"I was stripped of command." Voria's mouth firmed into a tight line. "The *Hunter* will likely be decommissioned, and we will be divided up piecemeal and given to whatever unit or house bids the most credits for us."

"But, after everything we did..." Nara trailed off. She balled her hands into fists, her head snapping back up. "So let me see if I've got this straight. You want me to leave my training here to follow you on a mission for the Confederacy, even knowing the Confederacy is responsible for stripping you of your command? Why would I do that?"

"Because this is bigger than either of us." Voria's hands fell to her sides, and some of the hardness left her face. "The Tender herself showed me an augury. Something is happening in the Umbral Depths. There's a world there, a world we're meant to discover. Aurelia believes that we'll find the weapons we need to fight the Krox. I can't do this without you, Nara. I need you, and so does Aran."

"Has he agreed to go?" Nara asked coldly.

Voria nodded. "He has. Nara, please. You were on Marid. You saw the same things I did. If we don't undertake this mission, if we don't find whatever is hidden on this world, then Nebiat will. The Krox will. You know what will happen if they gain an even bigger advantage than they already have."

Voria's voice lacked conviction, and hit Nara harder than the words themselves. She was at the breaking point—attacked from all sides, including her own. Nara stowed her own anger, reaching instead for empathy. "I'm sorry, Captain Voria. I want to help, but I'm not strong enough yet. Give me some time to train, then call on me whenever you like. But right now? I've just begun my training. There's so much for me to learn. I need time."

"I see Eros has already begun to work on you." Voria turned a baleful eye toward the handsome Shayan.

"Is he wrong?" Nara protested. "I need time to master my abilities. I could be really strong one day. Maybe stronger than you."

"Maybe." Voria's face softened, torn with indecision. "If you don't want to go, I obviously can't force you. I wouldn't ask if the matter weren't urgent. Crewes, Aran, Kez... If they're going, they need that backup. I can't be the only true mage, Nara. I need help. I don't mind admitting that. I'm no illusionist, and you've already saved us all once."

Nara looked to Eros, who studied her silently. "Master Eros, what do you think I should do?"

"You're at a crossroads, pirate girl. If you believe Voria, then going with her could save lives. More likely, they're going to die, and going with them simply ensures you'll die, too." He leaned forward on his couch, sneering at Voria. "I've seen many good apprentices die at her feet, pirate girl. I'd hoped that tradition had come to an end."

"She was right on Marid," Nara admitted. "She could be right here, too. I can't risk ignoring her. But make no mistake, Captain. I'm coming of my own free will. I don't work for you anymore."

Voria looked taken aback. Nara thought maybe she should be, and straightened proudly. She wasn't going to be anyone's doormat.

"Are you going to send her into combat unarmed?" Voria asked Eros. She raised an eyebrow. Eros looked embarrassed for some reason. "You just claimed to be her master, didn't you? You know the ancient laws as well as I."

"You and your obscure laws. Pirate girl indeed. I should have expected this," Eros said wearily. "If you are going to go I am honor-bound to arm you. Take a staff. Whichever you think best fits you. Consider it repayment for the destruction of your spellpistol." Eros waved a hand, and the illusionary wall covering one side of his office winked out of existence.

Several staves hung from the wall, each distinct in its own way. The one on the far right was largest, a full three meters—too impractical to carry around. The next topped two meters, and was still longer than she'd prefer. The third and fourth weapons were more the right size, with one much more elaborate than the other.

The elaborate one had several emeralds rotating around the tip, each pulsing with clean, cool energy. The haft was golden—some sort of magical alloy, though not one Nara was familiar with.

The last staff was simple. A two-meter length of silvery feathersteel, with a single dark onyx set in the tip. That onyx had a dark nimbus of faint power, but the staff was otherwise unremarkable.

She raised an eyebrow at Eros. "I can take one of these? And I get to pick which one?"

"Think of it as an investment," Eros said. His couch drifted closer, and he scowled at her. "If you somehow survive the journey to this world, you will encounter the

Catalyst from the captain's augury. Yes—didn't know I'd already seen it, did you, Voria? When you encounter this Catalyst, the staff you take with you will grow in power. Use this trip well. When you return, be ready to to study, pirate girl."

"Yes, master." Nara sketched a bow, and moved to inspect the staves more closely. She had no idea what the wisest choice would be, and her attention shifted from staff to staff as she struggled to decide.

"Which will you take, and why?" Eros asked.

"I like the one with the feathersteel rod as the base." She studied the smallest staff, particularly the onyx at the top. "It's lightweight, strong enough to break bone, and able to hold at least three catalizations. I can fight with a weapon like that, so I should pick one that will enhance my offensive capabilities. Its power will grow with me, and I can forge it into the weapon I need."

She touched the nimbus of dark energy around the tip. It was cold, but not painfully so. "This one is the youngest, but if I understand the little I've learned of enchantment, that also gives it the most potential to grow. If you want to invest in me, then this is the one I should take. I will bring it back to you someday, a full eldimagus."

"I've no doubt of it. And remember: you are my apprentice, not hers." Eros gave the smuggest look anyone had ever given to Voria's annoyed face. "Fight well, pirate girl. And return safely. I have a great deal to teach you, and I can't do that if you are dead."

20

POSTURING

Voria waited for Nara to exit the room, then rose and moved to the door. "May I?"

"You may." Eros waved absently as he settled back into his chair.

He removed a pipe from his jacket, and lit it with a spark of flame from his finger. He puffed several times, then blew the cloud out over his head. The heady scent of dried fern filled the room. Voria knew she'd be a giggly fool if she spent more than a few minutes in here with the door closed.

Eros offered her the pipe. "So, how do you want to do this?"

"Can we skip the posturing?" Voria asked, refusing the pipe with a shake of her head. She sat on one of the couches, and sank into it like it was a sponge. They were maddening, and it was impossible to retain proper posture.

"We can keep it to a minimum, at least. I'll start. That girl has more potential than you ever showed, Voria. I show her a spell once, just once mind you, and she's mastered it. I've never seen anyone so driven to learn, or so apt an apprentice. If I can ensure that her moral compass isn't permanently broken then she could be the finest mage in a generation. She's far more important than you, in the long run." Eros enjoyed another puff, exhaling it above him again. His eyes had gone glazed, and a boyish smile graced his face. "If you are the end of her, I will travel back in time and kill you in this very instant. Don't come back without her. There, how did I do?"

"Marvelously. Here's mine. You're a pathetic worm, *Master* Eros. You hide in here wasting your enormous power, even though you could be out there making a difference. If you'd been at Marid, then Nebiat wouldn't have escaped. We need you, and you're here training children? It's madness. I'll take Nara with me, and if we need to die to fulfill this augury, then so be it. The galaxy is greater than your new star pupil." Voria frowned at that last part. She'd been the star pupil at one point, and seeing him lavish his attention on another stung—even if he was right. "Can we talk about Nara now?"

"Your posturing was excellent. You're sure I can't tempt you?" He offered her the pipe again, but she declined. She already felt like someone had stuffed cotton into her head. "The girl knows far too many spells, especially second-level spells. Why haven't we heard of her? She has to have apprenticed to someone significant, and there aren't that many mages who could have trained her in illusion."

"That's my worry," she sighed. "Aran caught the mage's name: Yorrak. I've been able to learn nothing. I don't know who he is, or who he works for. Even if I did, I suspect he was just a tool for someone else. The way he disposed of Aran and Kazon—or attempted to—was too sloppy to be the work of a true master."

"You spent time looking into this? I thought you were consumed with your quest for Krox?" Eros asked mildly.

The rebuke was there, though. "This isn't the same threat, or I doubt it is. This is something new."

"I don't have the time or willpower to deal with a new threat, so I'll leave that to you, Eros. We need to know more about where Nara came from, and who she worked for. No one likes losing an apprentice; if Yorrak was part of something greater, they might come looking for her. Even if they don't, I'd still feel more comfortable knowing where she comes from." She paused. "Did she tell you about Aran?"

"I was wondering when you'd bring that up." Eros sighed heavily. "You know better than anyone how I feel about romantic entanglements. I mean, your father is the worst slut in the sector. Possibly multiple sectors. You have more siblings than Shaya has limbs."

"That wasn't very nice, but it was accurate." Normally Voria would have been upset at a comment about her parentage, but for some reason she felt entirely mellow about it. "I don't think you need to worry. Nara and Aran care for each other, but it isn't love, though it could one day become that. They're battle-brothers. They trained together. They were wiped together. If she trusts anyone, it isn't me— or you, I'm betting. It's him."

"The war mage." Eros crinkled his nose distastefully. "Well, at least she has someone to confide it, and at least that trust is built through combat. A true mage can't afford attachments. We don't get to rut around like pigs in heat. Make sure she's aware of that, but do it delicately. And don't tell her I'm behind it."

"If you want to tell her who she can sleep with, you go right ahead. I won't be a party to that kind of nonsense. We're all going to be dead in a few decades, even if we win every battle we ever fight. People should find happiness where they can." Voria felt she'd made an excellent point, and grinned drunkenly at Eros as she began to laugh. "You know, you have an absurdly handsome face, but you really are the most arrogant prick I have ever met." The laughter grew. "Oh, I can't believe I said that."

"Whatever would your soldiers think?" Eros laughed, too. It lasted just long enough for them to realize they were sharing a moment, then they stopped at nearly the same instant.

"Well, then." Voria rose shakily to her feet. "I'm off on my suicidal quest. Do try to learn more about whoever Yorrak is, and who trained him."

"Tomorrow. Today I'm just going to stare at the ceiling."

Voria left the chamber feeling better than she had in days—in weeks. And not just the drug-induced euphoria, though that was rather pleasant.

No, it was the knowledge that she wouldn't have to face this alone. Nara would be there, and Aran. Maybe, just maybe, they could do this.

21

CHOICES

For a single moment Aran considered taking the spellfighter and leaving Shaya. He had void magic now. He could open a Fissure.

But as alluring as the idea was, he simply couldn't do it. It wasn't that the others needed him—though the idea of Nara dying because he wasn't there horrified him.

It was the fact that they'd been selected as the only possibility of the sector outliving the Krox. He couldn't live with the scale of the death that would occur if he walked away. Not to mention the fact that he didn't have any navigational charts for the Umbral Depths, and if he entered, odds were good he'd never emerge again.

He cruised down to the ninth branch, more than three kilometers below the Tender's floating palace, about midway down the tree. Apparently Crewes had an apartment here. Aran had a hard time picturing the sergeant in any environment other than combat. He couldn't even picture Crewes outside of his armor, despite having seen him in a normal uniform just a few weeks back.

He landed next to a trio of battered transport ships in

what amounted to a parking lot, though redwood trees had been planted haphazardly to make it look more like a park. All it did was make it more difficult for ships to land, so far as he could tell.

Aran headed for an oblong building that curved around a stretch of mossy grass. Half a dozen children of various ages ran and played. A few threw light missiles at each other, making the kids who lacked the ability to cast them visibly jealous.

"Hey," he called to a boy he'd guess was around sixteen. "Do you know where Sergeant Crewes lives?"

"Sergeant? I know where *the* Crewes lives, if that's what you're asking. Apartment 4B, right over there. But I gotta warn you, if you're here to give him trouble, that little spell-blade ain't gonna do shit to save you." The kid gave Aran a dismissive laugh.

Aran shrugged and headed up the stairs to the second level. Orchestral music came from Crewes's apartment. Aran sketched a *fire* sigil on the door, and a bright light flashed in the apartment.

Footsteps sounded inside, and the door opened. The music blasted out, overpowering the woman's words. She gave an exasperated sigh, and disappeared back into the apartment.

The music stopped, and she returned with a frown. "What do you want?"

"I'm, uh, a friend of Crewes's. I was hoping to speak with him."

"Turrreeeen!" she yelled over her shoulder. "You've got a visitor. Come deal with him, so I can get back to my holo-drama. It's bad enough you gotta cramp up my sewing room. Couldn't you have stayed with your brother? He's got a lot more space with that fancy job of his, and you two need to spend more time together."

Crewes hurried into view, and for a moment Aran thought it had to be someone else. The sergeant wore a simple t-shirt and a pair of jeans, the mass-produced kind peddled by Ternus. Aran could accept that, but the sergeant's demeanor was...wrong.

"I'm sorry, Ma. You know I can't stay with Mercelus. He's prosecuting my CO. It ain't right." He bent down to kiss his mother's cheek. "I'll get the LT here out of your hair. Why don't you go sit down, and I'll bring you some hot beer?"

"I know I'm just a wipe," Aran offered, "but I don't think you're supposed to heat it."

"I know that," Crewes snapped in a low voice, "but she drinks it that way, and you aren't going to tell her any different. Now what the depths are you doing here, LT? This is my private life. The Confederacy don't get to intrude on that."

"Voria sent me to—"

"The major sent you? Let me get my coat." He turned and grabbed a leather jacket from the hook near the door, then yelled over his shoulder, "Ma! I'll be back in a while." He turned to Aran and lowered his voice. "Come on, let's get out quick before she figures out I'm not making her that beer. We'll have to spend the rest of the evening hearing about how great my brother is, and how I need a real job."

Crewes closed the door, and hurried up the walk toward the parking lot where the ship was parked.

"You're not even going to ask what Voria needs?" Aran asked as he finally caught up.

"Man, it's weird hearing you call her that. I forget the major's got a real name. Don't matter what she needs. I'm so ready to get out of that house. I don't care if the major wants us to fly into the frigging Umbral Depths. It's better than here." He stopped and turned to Aran. "I gotta be honest, LT.

You heard my mom talk about my brother's fancy new job? He's a prosecutor. Guess which case he just finished? So yeah, let's get the depths out of here."

"Yeah, about that," Aran said, moving to his fighter. "The major's taking us into the depths. Not through them to go somewhere else. We're trying to reach a world *inside* the Umbral Depths."

"Shit." Crewes looked briefly back at his apartment, considering. "You know what? It's worth it. Let's get out of here. You got my armor squared away?"

"The major talked to Davidson, and he looked the other way while she smuggled it off." Aran kept his voice low, though he doubted any of the toughs eyeing them cared.

"You talked to Bord and Kez?"

"They're next on my list. I figured seeing you with me might make them more likely to come."

"It's gonna be a tough sell. Kezia's got family here, and she don't get to see them often. Asking her to risk her life again this soon for no pay? I don't know man." Crewes shook his head. "Can't hurt to ask, I guess."

Aran sketched a *dream* sigil, and the blue stairs descended from the cockpit. Did he even have a right to ask Kez to go? She hadn't been mentioned in the auguries, or when they'd met with Marid. Only he and Voria. Maybe her saying no wasn't such a bad thing.

The fighter rumbled to life and zipped away from the branch. Aran guided her around the tree, aiming for the sprawl around the roots. *The dims*, they were called. The closer they flew, the more details leapt into focus. These people lived in hovels, cobbled together largely from mud and discarded refuse. It was a marked contrast to the opulence on the branches above. Even Crewes's lower branch had it far better than these people.

They landed outside the stretch Voria had indicated. By the time they'd exited the fighter, several dozen tiny drifter children had gathered hopefully.

"Does anybody here know where Kezia lives? Pretty drifter with blond hair." Aran fished one of the infused apples he'd taken from the Tender's palace out of his coat. He held it aloft, the light catching the bright red skin. "This came from the Tender's palace. It's the tastiest, sweetest apple you will ever eat. The first person to find Kezia and ask her to come here gets two."

The children stampeded back toward the settlement in a chorus of cheers and cat calls. They all moved in the same direction, a large stack of wooden crates that had been fashioned into a makeshift apartment for a large family.

There was a rapid exchange of completely unintelligible gibberish. After several moments Kezia's head poked out from a crate on the third level. "Bord, look—it's Crewes and Aran." She hopped down excitedly, hurrying over to offer Crewes a hug. The big man returned it awkwardly.

Bord emerged a moment later, a beautiful grin splitting his face. "Did you bring Nara with you? I bet she missed me real bad, and just had to come see me." His face fell when he saw only Aran. "Oh. It's you. Welcome, I guess? Where's Nara? Don't encourage him, Kezia, he'll think we want him here."

"Don't be jealous, Bord. It's unattractive." Kez stuck her tongue out at him...flirtatiously?

"So," Bord said, "what brought you down to our little— very little—corner of the world? Do you know what they call me here? Big fooker. How great is that? These people think I'm tall." It came out all in a rush, just like the drifters.

Aran cleared his throat uncomfortably. "Voria wants us to follow her into the Umbral Depths."

"Wow, you don't sugarcoat anything, do ya?" Bord shook his head and eyed Kezia. "I'm waiting to see what she does before I make a decision."

"That's because you know I'm smarter than you are. Of course, so's that post over there." Kezia gave him a wink. Her joy ebbed when she looked to Aran. "It's good to see you, and you're welcome to stay for dinner, but this is a big ask. The major wants us to joost give up our lives here, and risk it all again? Joost like that? How is she planning to even pay us?"

"I don't think you should go," Aran said, a little surprised by the words. Where had those come from? Then he realized where, and he embraced it. "You guys have something here. A family. We're sailing into darkness, and we may not come back. You guys know what it's like. Don't go."

"Do you mean that?" Bord looked confused. "Don't you need us?"

"It ain't about need," Crewes added. "I agree with the LT. It's about knowing that, no matter what happens to us, you guys are out here living the life. That make sense?"

"I think I get it." Kezia's face fell. "But...what if you die, because we weren't there to save you?"

"What if we bring you, and we all die anyway?" Aran shrugged, and gave a quick laugh. "Voria wants to do this. I'm part of it, like it or not."

"And I ain't got nothing better to do," Crewes added. "You two do. So get to 'em. If we survive, you owe us the first round."

22

GOODBYES

A ran hesitated for only a moment before stepping into the kamiza. He'd spent the brief flight considering what to say after he'd dropped off Crewes, but was no closer to an answer. The sounds of combat rolled over him, as they had often during the last few weeks of training.

A dozen apprentices sparred, this group more advanced than the first Aran had seen. They all used spells in their attacks—most of them light-based, with *light* a subset of life magic. That was common, given their proximity to Shaya. A few students used fire bolts, including a girl with hair of living flame. Only one student, a middle-aged man with a little extra weight around the middle, used a void bolt.

Erika disengaged with the class, leaving them in the care of the middle-aged man. She smiled warmly as she approached, wiping sweat from her cheek with the sleeve of her shirt. "That took longer than I expected. She roped you into something, didn't she?"

"She did," Aran admitted. "I can't say I'm thrilled about it, but I agree with her assessment. There's a lot more at stake here than my ability to fly a spellfighter or handle a blade. If we don't pursue this augury, our enemies will."

"They lurk in the shadows. Always." Erika gave a sudden sigh. "I wish it were otherwise. I wish we didn't have to constantly deal with endless threats. I wish we could give our people the proper time to train. Can you tell me anything about this augury? Or where you're going? I promise I'll keep it in confidence."

"I've been sworn to secrecy," Aran said, shrugging. He hadn't been, but he didn't think Voria would appreciate him telling someone about the augury, not even Erika. The fewer people who knew, the more likely they'd survive to reach the place.

Ree emerged from the back room. She started as her eyes fell on Aran, then they narrowed and she cut a path through the room, eyes locked on his as she approached. "You're leaving, aren't you?"

"I'm taking a leave, yes," he countered, "but I'll be back."

Ree's frown deepened. "Voria's not in command any more, mongrel. If you tie your career to hers, it will probably cost your life. Even if it doesn't, you're making enemies— powerful ones." She shook her head. "You have so much potential, but you're squandering it. You're throwing your life and your career away, for a woman who wiped your memory and conscripted you into service. Do you understand what you're giving up? Your children's children will want for nothing if you marry into the right house."

"I'm not doing this for Voria, and I don't care about finding a rich wife." Aran rested a hand on the hilt of his spellblade. "I care about *this*. I'm going because I have the ability to. Because if I don't, then we cede the war to the Krox. Sacrificing myself—or some imaginary career— doesn't matter, not at all. All that matters is stopping these things. I mean, you've both seen into the mind of a god, at least once right?"

"Many times," Erika murmured.

Ree merely nodded.

"I don't know what you saw, but what I saw terrifies me. *Monsters in the dark, primordial past* kind of terror. I don't know what Krox is, but he had super novas for eyes. His whole goal is to control literally everything in our galaxy, and that's just a warm-up so he can go do the same thing to every other galaxy he can get his cosmic hands on. Someone stops this thing, or we all pay." Aran offered Ree a hand. "I know you don't agree with what I'm doing, but I'm asking you to trust me. It's necessary. I'm sorry I have to leave, but I will be back. There's a lot you can teach me, and trust me when I say I want to learn it all."

Ree shook his hand, but her expression was coldly neutral. "Find me if you survive."

"I will." He smiled at her.

She did not return it. Instead, she turned and headed back into the kitchen.

"She handled that better than I expected." Erika gave a chuckle. "But then, you presented a compelling case. I don't know what you saw in that augury, but I trust your judgement. Tend to this. Survive. Do so, and we'll be here when you get back."

"Master Erika, you know I probably won't make it back." Aran eyed her pleadingly. "I'd like to die knowing about my past. I've learned a little about the Outriders of Virkon, but just a name really. Who or what are they? And do you really think I'm one of them?"

"That's fair. You've worked hard, for a few weeks now at least. I can't do much, but I can give you this." She pulled him into a fierce hug, then released him a moment later and cleared her throat. "Now, then. The style you practice is distinctive. It is, so far as I know, the oldest of all styles. It was created by a Wyrm, who trained human disciples. They were deadly, living weapons. That culture continued for hundreds of millennia, an unbroken empire covering many sectors, until that empire fell, as all do."

Erika's eyes had adopted a faraway look, as if peering into memory. "One world remains, and I've seen it. It's a world—the only world—where humans and dragons work together. They call themselves the last dragonflight, and they train their Outriders as war mages. Typically an Outrider is assigned to a Wyrm with a team of other Outriders. They roam the galaxy looking for Catalysts. Some claim they're after power, but that's not the impression I got. I got the impression their Wyrms were scared, and trying to find the bogeyman they know is hiding in one of the shadows."

"And you think I'm from this world?" Aran asked, numb from the revelation. It was so much to take in. A whole new past—or part of it, at least. If he could find this world, he might even find people who'd known him before his mind had been wiped.

"I'd stake my reputation on it. You're an Outrider. You fight like one. You move like one. The style is all predatory, like a dragon. It's always *pounce, maim, kill*. By far the most aggressive style."

"Doesn't that kind of style leave you open to counterattack?" Aran asked. It sounded foolish not to prepare a defense.

"It can, but you'd be amazed how often it works. You overwhelm someone, and all they can focus on is defending themselves. They no longer think about attack, and they fight the battle purely on your terms." She shrugged, then grinned. "Of course if an Outrider tries that garbage with me, I'll shit a lightning bolt down the hole I tear in their face. You come back to me, and I'll fix that particular gap in your knowledge. No one will ever take you apart in a fight like I have, ever again."

Aran returned her grin, then gathered her into another hug. "I definitely like the idea of not getting my ass kicked as frequently. If I live, I'll be back. Thank you, Erika."

23

HELLOS

"Hello?" Nara called hesitantly. There was no answer.

She ducked inside the hatch, clutching her new staff in a death grip. Was this the right ship? Part of her hoped not. Rust flaked from the walls, and unless this thing had some real surprises, she wasn't sure it could even break orbit.

The interior was dimly lit, so she paused to give her eyes a moment to adjust. The corridor stank of ozone, grease, and less pleasant things.

"Wow." An unfamiliar voice came from her left, and Nara instinctively reached for her spellpistol. Some habits died hard.

Only when she realized it was gone did she raise her hand and prepare to cast, like a proper mage.

The man seemed harmless enough. He wore a set of grey overalls covered in dark stains and reeking of sweat. A mop of thick, red hair covered his forehead and drooped over a thick pair of glasses. He had, if it were possible, even more freckles than she did.

"I, uh, wow. You are about the prettiest thing I've ever seen. I'm really sorry for sounding like an idiot, but...wow. I'm, uh, Pickus." He extended a trembling hand, then withdrew it a second later. "Wait, you're carrying one of those magic sticks. You're not gonna turn me into anything, are you?"

Nara gave a delighted laugh. She offered her hand, and the man took it. His face lit up as he pumped it furiously about a dozen times before releasing it.

She wiped her hand on her jacket, leaving a greasy streak. "I'm Nara. Is this the *Big Texas*? I'm supposed to meet Captain Voria here. I hope I'm in the right place."

"You are most definitely in the right place. Course, I'd have said that even if it weren't true, just to keep you around for a couple minutes. Where are my manners? Come on, I'll take you to the mess and fix you some lunch. The captain should be back soon. There's another guy here, too. Big dark-skinned guy—like a mountain, but talks less." Pickus waved at her to follow, and started deeper into the ship.

She noticed he left the panel he'd been working on open, with exposed wiring. Nara closed it as she passed, then followed him into a small mess.

Crewes's massive form was squeezed into a small seat at the only table. "Nara." He rose with a sudden grin. "Man, am I glad to see you. Captain wasn't sure you'd come along on our little, uh, excursion." He approached her and put a hand awkwardly on her shoulder. "Listen, I don't really do this emotional shit, but since she probably won't say it, I will: thank you. For coming."

"Yeah, thanks, Nara." Pickus dropped into a seat at the table, removed a small device with a glowing screen from his pocket, and began tapping at it. It wasn't all that dissimilar from her scry-pad, though she sensed no magic emanating from it. Pickus didn't look up at her as he spoke. "So what do you do, exactly? I'm guessing Crewes kills bad guys, and Voria gives orders."

"I'm a true mage." It was the first time she'd ever said it aloud.

"There's different kinds of true mage, right? What do you do?" Pickus set his device on the table and looked at her with keen interest. "I don't know much about magic, but I'd love to learn."

"I'm an illusionist. I can cast other spells, too, but that's what I'm best at." Nara raised a hand and sketched *air*, then *dream*. An illusionary image of Frit appeared, as lifelike as Nara was able to create.

"Wow. Beautiful *and* talented. If you tell me you're also intelligent and happen to like galactic archeology, then I think I'm in real trouble." He grinned up at her, and Nara found herself grinning back. She liked the mousey little mechanic.

Aran spoke from behind her. "Oh, Bord is definitely not going to like this guy. He's way too charming."

Nara spun to face him. She hadn't seen him in weeks, and drank in the sight. His lean frame had put on muscle, and he'd let his stubble grow into a full beard that hugged his jawline. His dark hair had been cut short, balancing the beard.

She smiled. "You look good."

Aran crossed the room in three steps and seized her in a fierce hug. She hugged him back, burying her face in his shoulder.

"I missed you," he whispered.

"You realize we don't have bedrooms on this tub, right?" Crewes groused. "If you two get all mushy, the rest of us get sick. Not cool, people."

Aran released her, then moved to hug Crewes. "So you want some, too? Is that what I'm hearing?"

"If you touch me, I'll burn that sad excuse for a beard right off your too-pretty face." Crewes grinned. "Uh, sir."

They all laughed, and Aran moved to sit next to Pickus. "Hey, we haven't met. I'm Aran."

"Pickus." The redhead pumped Aran's hand enthusiastically. "So you've got a sword? I'd heard people still use those. Listen, man, I don't want to offend you, so you tell me if I'm being too forward. You do know they've invented guns right? Like those are a thing here?"

Aran sketched a *void* sigil and a vertical slash appeared in the air. "I'm a war mage. We use the right tool for every job. Sometimes that's a spellblade." He reached into the void pocket and withdrew his sleek rifle. "And sometimes it's a spellrifle."

"Whoah. Can I hold it?" Pickus held out both hands, and Aran handed the rifle over.

Nara heard footsteps coming up the catwalk, and glanced over her shoulder in time to see Voria enter the room. Her eyes looked a little glassy, and she moved slower than usual.

Wait, was she...relaxed? Her shoulders were slumped. Nara had been positive the woman had surgically added an iron rod to her spine.

"Sergeant, I'm pleased to see you came, and I can see you've all met Pickus." Voria gave Crewes a respectful nod. "Where are Bord and Kezia?"

Nara smiled at that, looking around. She'd missed both of them, especially Bord. His endless persistence made the little man rather endearing.

Aran's face drained of emotion, and he tensed as if

preparing for a blow. "They aren't coming. Kezia has family she needs to see to, and Bord decided to stay with her."

Voria's mouth fell open, but no words came. It was the most telling reaction Nara had ever seen the woman display. She stood there for several seconds, unable to summon any sort of response.

"Well...that's their decision, I suppose." Voria cleared her throat and wiped at the corner of her eye. "We'll just have to make do with what we have." She took a deep breath, regaining some of her composure. "As you all know, we're heading into the Umbral Depths. Supplies have already been loaded. Aran, you have the command matrix. Crewes, you're on offense. I will handle defense."

Voria moved to her matrix, slipping between the rotating rings. Aran and Crewes moved to their own, leaving Nara standing there, ignored. Her fists clenched. Voria had made a habit of underestimating her, but this was going too far.

"Captain, I am the only other true mage in your command. Is there a reason you haven't assigned me to a matrix?" She folded her arms, and tried to adopt the kind of sternly confident pose Voria always used.

Voria turned to her with a frown. "You're the only one capable of handling all three matrices, which means you can stand second for all of us."

"Of course," Nara said. Maybe she was being too defensive.

Thankfully Aran saved her further embarrassment. He tapped a series of sigils, and the spelldrive rumbled to life. The vessel lifted into the air with a great deal of shuddering.

"Don't worry too much about the shaking." Pickus shot her a grin. "She doesn't do too well in atmosphere, but once we hit post-atmo she'll settle down."

24

WORST HANGOVER EVER

Nebiat glanced up at the glittering transport as it left Shaya's atmosphere. Voria had left on her quest. Regrettably, Erika had been unable to learn more about the augury Voria had received.

Not that it mattered. The instant they left atmosphere, Khalahk would be on them. There was no way their battered little frigate would survive the encounter.

Nebiat almost wished she were there to see the look on Voria's face, but she had more important work to be about. She smiled as she landed gracefully on the balcony. Several empty wine bottles lay scattered about, and a plate of piksa dust. Erika had done her job well, it appeared. Nebiat strolled into the sitting room. Several women slept wherever their drug-induced frenzy had expired. None stirred as she passed.

She entered the master bedroom and saw two figures in bed. Erika was already awake. She sat on the side hastily pulling on clothes. Her spellblade lay close at hand.

The other figure stirred groggily, but didn't rise. He gave a low groan. "My head. I haven't partied like that in decades.

And it's been even longer for you. Why the sudden change of heart?"

Dirk raised his head, grinning at Erika as she finished buckling on her spellblade. Only then did he realize they weren't alone. He glanced curiously at Nebiat, as if trying to understand her sudden appearance.

"You have no idea who I am, do you?" she asked, with a delighted laugh. "You still don't realize what's going on."

"Erika?" Dirk asked cautiously. He slipped from bed, naked. Rather than move for his clothing he went straight for his spellblade, yanking it from its scabbard. His eyebrows knit together as he reached for something, then his head cocked to the side. He tried again, then his eyes moved to Erika. "Why can't I feel my magic? What did you do to me?"

Erika hung her head. "I'm sorry, Dirk. I don't often say this, but in this I truly had no choice."

"You've been bound," Dirk whispered. He turned back to Nebiat, and this time his eyes made it as high as her face. "You're a dreadlord."

He charged. Denied his magic, and suffering the effects of exhaustion and heavy drug use, he still behaved like a living weapon.

Nebiat sketched a binding and flung it at him.

He raised a hand to counterspell it, then lowered the hand in frustration. The spell slammed into him, arresting his forward momentum. Dirk came up short, eyes going glazed as he fought the spell.

Erika moved to stand in front of Nebiat, ready to shield her if Dirk resisted her magic. He groaned and fell to his knees, then blinked up at her hatefully, unable to rise without Nebiat's permission. She'd won.

"Well done, Erika. We'd never have been able to take

him in a fair fight, but Dirk is as flawed as any other man."
Nebiat smiled cruelly at him. "And now we're going to use
you to kill the abomination you call the Confederacy."

25

EYES

Voria settled into a comfortable stance inside the command matrix's slowly rotating rings. She'd missed being in a matrix, even a misshapen one bolted onto a Ternus vessel never designed with any sort of arcane use in mind. The layout was all wrong, preventing them from adding the correct alignment of sigils necessary to create offensive or defensive runes.

They could fire spells, and even counterspells—but if anything got through, this ship would come apart at the seams, the way her career had come apart. Even a single direct hit would likely be lethal.

The *Texas* rattled and whined as they pushed into the upper atmosphere. Voria licked her lips, glancing over at Pickus. "This ship can survive a climb like this, yes?"

"Course she can," Pickus called from one of the torn leather seats against the cockpit wall. "Just give it a few more seconds. We're leaving the atmosphere. See? She's leveled out. Smooth as silk up here."

The shaking slowed, then ceased. Voria slowly exhaled; once she'd composed herself, she finally turned to Crewes.

"Sergeant, put up a view of the planet's umbral shadow on the scry-screen."

Crewes tapped a *fire* sigil on the silver ring, then frowned up at the unfamiliar display. "Uh, I can't, sir. It ain't working."

"Pickus?" Voria asked. The eternally distracted mechanic had his face buried in his little pocket device, staring at the glowing screen.

He looked up. "You need something, Captain?"

"Why isn't the scry-screen working?" she asked with as much patience as she could muster.

"Because it isn't a scry-screen? It's a monitor. Attached to a camera outside the ship. I can point it wherever you'd like though." He held a finger poised over his device.

"The umbral shadow, if you please." Voria already hated the vessel. She hated the fact that two of the crew she'd assumed most loyal hadn't shown up at all, and those who had...well, they'd only done it reluctantly. None of them had followed out of faith, or even duty.

What did that say about her abilities as a leader?

The scry-screen zoomed in, very slowly. It went out of focus, but when it came back it showed the region of space around the umbral shadow. Hunks of rock floated between them and their destination, but not so numerous they couldn't be easily avoided.

"Lieutenant, guide us to the shadow and open a Fissure, please." She rested her hands on the stabilizing ring. She was about to ask Nara to relieve her when she spotted a flash of movement behind one of the larger asteroids. "Pickus, get the camera on that cluster of rocks to the left side of the screen."

The camera jerked, and showed a large spinning asteroid surrounded by several smaller ones. A pair of crackling white-blue flames hovered in the shadows above the asteroid. Eyes, she realized. They winked out an instant after she spotted them.

"Aran, circle wide around that asteroid. Keep as much distance between us as possible." She pursed her lips, considering. "Nara, please relieve Sergeant Crewes."

Crewes ducked out one side of the stabilizing ring, while Nara entered from the other. Voria turned her attention back to the primitive monitor, with its woefully pathetic camera. Her kingdom for a simple divination spell.

"Sir?" Aran asked. The ship shuddered briefly, then moved in a wide arc away from the asteroid she'd indicated.

"Nara, ready a void bolt for the cannon. Aran, stand by for evasive maneuvers."

Voria prepared for a counterspell, hoping this was all simple paranoia.

A Wyrm materialized only a kilometer from the ship, already banking in their direction. A bolt of blue-white electricity shot from its mouth, crossing the distance almost instantly.

Almost.

Voria completed her counterspell, which burst from the cannon as the lightning licked the outer hull. The lightning shunted into a nearby asteroid, obliterating it. A smattering of pings came from outside as the debris rebounded off their hull.

"Captain, why not have Nara cloak us?" Aran asked.

The ship canted suddenly, faster than the inertial dampeners could compensate for. Voria's stomach lurched, but the maneuver now screened them from the Wyrm with a large asteroid.

"That thing is a hell of a lot faster than we are," he said, "and there's no way I can get there and open a Fissure before it finishes us off. If a single one of those lightning bolts gets through, we're toast."

The asteroid behind them exploded, and the Wyrm burst through the debris.

Voria prepared another counterspell, waiting for the beast to close. "That Wyrm is breathing lightning, so it's not a Krox. Air mages are illusionists and enchanters. It will therefore expect illusion, and likely be prepared to deal with it. It's been lying in wait for us, giving it plenty of time to prepare. We must assume it's using a potion of *pierce invisibility*. No, I have a different use for Nara's abilities. Nara, hit it with the most powerful void bolt you can fire."

Nara didn't reply, but her mouth firmed into a determined line. She sketched a spell, and Voria frowned when she recognized *air* and *dream*. She was using an illusion, not a void bolt. A purple-pink bolt shot from the cannon, and the Wyrm batted it aside with a casual counterspell.

Nara had already begun her second spell, fired on the wake of the first. A fat void bolt shot from the *Texas*, blasting the dragon in the shoulder where the ringbone was attached.

"Uh, Captain?" Nara's voice was a bare whisper. "Why didn't my spell do anything?"

"The Wyrm possesses enhanced magic resistance, probably from an eldimagus it has created. Air Wyrms are some of the most dangerous, especially ones this old." Voria judged the gap to the umbral shadow. They weren't going to make it, not unless she could come up with another solution. "Nara, I want you to cast a support spell. The next time the Wyrm fires I want you to blink our vessel closer to the umbral shadow."

"I've never teleported an entire vessel, just a couple suits of spellarmor."

"Find a way, or we're dead." Voria's words were matter-of-fact, and she quickly turned to the next phase of the plan. "Repeat that each time the Wyrm closes. Once we're into the shadow, Nara, I want you to open the Fissure. That will leave Aran free to pilot, and I can continue to counterspell. It's the only way we'll reach the Umbral Depths."

"Won't the Wyrm just follow us?" Aran pointed out.

The ship rolled between another pair of asteroids, and something heavy pinged off the hull. The Wyrm poked around another asteroid, loosing a bolt in their direction. Voria resisted the urge to counterspell it, instead waiting for Nara. Nara had gone pale, but she calmly raised her hand and began tapping sigils.

A wave of vertigo passed over them as the ship suddenly appeared a thousand meters closer to the umbral shadow. The bolt passed harmlessly through the space they'd just occupied.

The Wyrm vanished again.

"That really seems unfair," Pickus called, his voice high and panicked.

Aran, his fingers flying across sigils on all three rings, shot Pickus an encouraging smile. "Get used to it. Everything we deal with is unfair. Sir, I'm flying as erratically as I can, but that thing is going to be able to unload point-blank, and there's nothing I can do about it."

The ship moved with a surprising amount of grace, a testament to his piloting skills.

"Nara, if you could—"

The Wyrm appeared, directly underneath their vessel. The crackling bolt left its mouth, slamming into the hull before Voria could complete her first sigil. Sparks exploded as a conduit tore itself loose from the wall, raw arcane power spewing into the air from the end.

The sharp stench of ozone washed over the bridge, making Voria light-headed for a moment. Her matrix stopped spinning, and the sigils went dark. She rounded, relieved to see that both Nara's and Aran's were operational.

Nara tapped the last sigil in her spell, and their vessel teleported another thousand meters. The camera spun to face the Wyrm, showing an alarming amount of metallic debris around it. How much of the ship had they just lost?

"Pickus, can you tell me how much damage we suffered?" she asked, as calmly as she could muster.

"Nothing vital, just atmosphere in the cargo bay. We won't be able to access anything other than the mess and the cockpit until we can set down for repairs."

"Noted. Aran, cease all evasive maneuvers. Nara, this comes down to you. Trust your instincts, and teleport us as you think you should. Try to anticipate the dragon."

Voria had no idea if her instructions mattered at all, and badly wish it were her in the matrix instead of Nara. If Nara's timing was off even slightly, the Wyrm would finish them. Voria seized the stabilizing ring with both hands, hating the loss of control. She should be part of this battle, not relegated to the rearguard, yet the practical part of her knew that the two most qualified mages were right where they should be.

Her role was command, and she needed to accept that.

A shape materialized off their starboard side, but Nara had already begun casting. The dragon's head reared back, a deep glow building in its throat.

They jumped into the planetary shadow.

"This will have to be close enough. Open the Fissure, Nara. Aran, I want us through the instant it's wide enough."

The camera focused on the Wyrm, who grew larger every moment.

26

DESPERATION

Aran poured another wave of void magic into the ship. The vessel responded sluggishly—nearly as sluggishly as the *Hunter*, despite the fact that this ship was a fraction of the size. "Piloting a brick against the most devastating killing machine in the sector seems like a great start to this trip. I was hoping we'd at least make it out of the system before dying."

"You didn't really expect anything else, did you?" the major shot back. She barked a short laugh. "I can't believe a god would go to all the trouble of making an augury only to have us die here."

"I'm opening the Fissure." Nara began tapping sigils, and a large chunk of violet energy passed from her hands into the matrix. It flowed into the ship, and a moment later the sky split before them.

The Wyrm appeared behind them again, and Aran used his gravity magic to yank the ship violently out of the way. The bolt of lightning crackled past, tearing off part of the aft hull but leaving them otherwise unscathed. Aran poured on more speed, forcing the vessel into the still-opening Fissure.

"It isn't wide enough!" Crewes roared, an octave higher than normal.

Aran centered the vessel, threading it through the eye of the needle. He passed perfectly down the center, flying with the instincts that had so recently re-awakened. The pulsing violet energies at the edge of the Fissure warped the view on the camera, but seemed to have no adverse effect beyond that.

Then they were through!

Aran piloted them deeper into the depths, then whirled to face Crewes. "Nara, drop the Fissure spell. Sergeant, I want you to relieve Nara for a moment. Nara, don't go far—we're going to need you in a minute."

The Fissure winked shut in their wake.

"Lieutenant, care to share your plan?" Voria demanded.

Aran continued to tap sigils. "I can do or explain, Captain. Pick."

"Do it," she gave back instantly.

Aran was mildly surprised by how readily she turned over command. "Sergeant, I want you to light us up. Broadcast as much heat and light as you can. Make sure everything can see us from as far away as possible." He tapped another pair of *void* sigils and dumped more power into the vessel. He was already tiring, though this was easier than it would have been a few weeks ago. He'd gotten stronger.

The outside of the hull began to glow, blasting light and heat in all directions. All that light revealed nothing but blackness, of course. But anything capable of detecting light had seen them, for millions of kilometers.

Behind them, another Fissure appeared; a moment later, a furious Wyrm clawed its way through. Its hateful gaze fell on their ship, and Aran poured yet another wave of *void* into the spelldrive. "I have no idea if this will work, but I don't see another way to escape this thing. Crewes, keep the light going until that thing closes with us. When it does, turn the matrix over to Nara. Nara, I want you to cloak us when the Wyrm attacks."

"That won't stop it," Voria snapped. "We've already been over this. What's your plan? Explain—quickly."

Aran took a deep breath. They had a moment and he did owe her an explanation.

"The depths are inhabited, though we don't know by what. I'm praying something will come to investigate all the light. And, while the dragon can see through our illusions, I'm hoping whatever shows up won't be able to. Ideally, they'll keep the Wyrm busy, and we'll slip away in the chaos."

Voria gave an approving nod. "Bold."

"And maybe stupid. Guess we're about to find out." Aran held his breath as he watched the monitor. The dragon was closing fast, despite his efforts to coax every bit of speed from the *Texas*. "If I'm wrong, and that thing kills us...uh, sorry."

"It's not as if I have a better plan." Voria walked to stand before the matrix. "Either this works, or we die. As I said, I cannot believe that Marid, or some other god we've yet to meet, would go so far as to make an augury only to have it end like this. I choose to believe we will live."

Aran admired that about her: her courage in the face of death. It inspired him to offer the same level of courage. "Here it comes."

The dragon breathed another bolt of lightning, but to Aran's surprise they teleported out of the path. He glanced at Nara, who shot him a wink.

"I imagine that thing must be getting pretty pissed off." Nara leaned heavily on the stabilizing matrix, a bead of sweat trickling from her forehead. She stood next to Crewes, the pair of them barely fitting inside the spinning rings.

The entire ship lurched forward, sending the crew flying. Aran caught himself against the stabilizing matrix, as did Nara and Crewes. Voria tumbled forward, sliding into the far wall. She seized the loose strap on a harness, arresting her momentum as the ship righted itself.

"What in the depths hit—" the sergeant began.

An enormous claw punched through the ceiling, and Aran flung himself out of its path as it sliced into the floor near his matrix. The ship loosed an agonizing groan as the dragon began to tear the hull apart.

"Sergeant, drop the light," Aran ordered. He rose to his feet, taking slow, shallow breaths as he prepared to cast again.

"Done." Crewes stumbled from the matrix, dropping into the chair next to Pickus. He quickly buckled himself in.

"Nara, you have one more 'port in you?" Aran asked.

She looked exhausted, but she nodded. "Hold on."

The ship warped again, and they appeared a thousand meters away from the Wyrm. The sudden removal of the claw exposed them to space, and their atmosphere rushed through the hole, sucking out anything not locked down.

Aran barely seized the stabilizing ring, fighting desperately to avoid being sucked out into space.

"Cloak us," Aran roared over the rushing wind. He extended a hand at the hole in the ceiling, pulled at the reservoir of water magic within him, and poured out a spray of water, which froze well before reaching the hole.

The ice thickened, building in layers. At first, chunks of ice were sucked through the hole. Then, a large piece stuck, slowing the flow of air. More ice built, until the rushing stopped as the hole was finally plugged.

He gave a relieved sigh, glancing up at the monitor. The Wyrm was closing again, its features twisted with rage. Aran guessed they had maybe five or six seconds, then it would finish them. He tapped the *void* sigils again, pouring the last of his magic into the spelldrive. They accelerated once more, leaving a trail of debris in their wake as they rocketed away.

Something massive slammed into the Wyrm from the side. Aran saw dozens of slimy black tentacles, but had no idea what they were attached to. He didn't want to know, not really. They swarmed the dragon, wrapping around both wings and its legs.

"Do you think it will kill the Wyrm?" Nara asked in a small voice. She leaned heavily on the stabilizing ring.

"I don't know." Aran grinned, ducking out of the command matrix. "But we've gone dark, and thanks to your spell we're cloaked. By the time this fight is settled we'll be long gone, and hopefully we'll never see that thing again."

"Well done, Lieutenant. I am impressed yet again. Nara, that was some incredible spell work." Voria gave her a respectful nod, and Nara responded with a pleased smile. "We're left with a question, one we don't have an easy answer to: why was this Wyrm waiting for us in the void? Why did it attack the instant we left the planet? Wyrms don't hunt this close to Shaya. This thing was here for us."

Aran frowned. "I'll bet you anything I can guess who sent it."

27

REPAIRS

A ran ducked from the matrix and extended his hand toward the dense patch of smoke clogging the top of the room. He waved his hand, swirling several air tendrils. They gathered the smoke into a tight little ball, encasing it in a bubble.

"Pickus," Voria said, clearly back in command, "looks like we're still getting smoke from fires in the ship's interior. How do we deal with that?"

"Uh, I guess we could have the guy with the sword magic up a wall of ice. If he can block off that panel, any fires inside will go out almost instantly. You just have to seal the seams, really." Pickus moved over to the panel and stretched out a palm toward the metal. "Holy crap, that's hot. This is the central static motivator. After the fire is out, I'm going to have to replace it. Until that's fixed, we're basically drifting."

"How long?" Voria asked.

Aran summoned ice around the smoke he'd gathered, letting it fall to the deck with a thunk. "I'll start with the fire." He pressed his hands onto the panel, firing off jets of ice. It boiled away to steam, and the metal buckled from the sudden change in temperature. He poured more water magic into the spell, and a thick coat of frost grew across the panel. After a few more applications, it solidified into two-centimeter-thick ice.

"Perfect. I can probably get her up and running in a few hours. For now, she won't impede our progress. We're already on the right course, so as long as we don't have to turn or maneuver we should be fine." Pickus adjusted his glasses, turning to face Aran. "That was some slick work with the tentacle thing. How did you know it would come?"

"I didn't," Aran admitted. "If I'd been wrong, we'd be dragon lunch. We got lucky."

"Yeah, well, I'll take it." Nara used a towel to mop sweat from her face. "It's nice being alive, but this place is cramped and reeks of smoke."

Pickus looked uncomfortable. "The oxygen scrubbers needed to be changed before we left. After that much fire? They'll never recover. And, uh, we don't have much in the way of spare parts. We have to live with this until we get home."

"We'll make do." Voria reached into her satchel and removed a book. "Presumably you don't need me for repairs. I'm going to study some of the materials I brought. We need to understand what this planet we're journeying to is, and who or what might control it. Aurelia has been vague about exactly what we're supposed to do there, other than a vague premonition that we will receive the power we need to stop the Krox."

"Did you want some help?" Nara asked hopefully. Aran's heart went out to her.

Voria seemed indifferent to the plea. "Eventually. For now, I need some time to think." She walked off into the mess, leaving a wilted-looking Nara in her wake.

"Are there other tasks we can help with, Pickus?" Aran moved over to Nara and squeezed her shoulder. She smiled up at him, then looked away.

"Probably not. You magey types don't know shit about our tech, and I don't want you accidentally frying a circuit board." He turned to Crewes. "You look like you're from Yanthara. You guys buy a lot of Ternus stuff. Do you know how to solder wires?"

"Yeah, I can do that. I don't even need a soldering iron." Crewes held up two fingers, and a bit of flame appeared. "You just show me what you need done." He followed Pickus out of the mess and into the cockpit.

"Guess being useless at repairs means we have five minutes to actually sit down." Nara moved to one of the chairs along the side of the cockpit, sat heavily, and began massaging her own neck. "Battles are short, but they knock me on my ass."

"Yeah." Aran shook his head, taking the seat next to her. "I don't get it. I mean, the Ternus Marines can keep firing forever. We're wiped after a couple skirmishes. I know we'll get stronger over time, but I feel like we're only using half the tools in our arsenal. We really should carry more tech around, to supplement the magic."

"I'm taking the opposite route." Nara extended a hand and a silver staff appeared with a *pop*. "I'm relying more on magic, and less on tech. Eros disintegrated my spellpistol, and I didn't have time to bring another."

"I'm sure Voria will loan you one," Aran offered.

"I almost asked her, but honestly? After working with Eros, I think it's smarter to rely on my magic. He talked a lot about habits and muscle memory during my training." She stopped massaging her neck and looked up at him. "So what do you think we'll find on the planet?"

"Sunshine and rainbows, definitely," Aran replied with a laugh. "There's no way it will be a total clusterfuck, and I'm sure we'll have all the resources we need at our disposal."

"Huh, so this is you on sarcasm." Nara punched him in the arm, though she was smiling. "Stick with the tall, dark, and deadly thing. It's definitely hotter."

28

THE SPINNER OF DARKNESS

Voria looked up from the tome she'd been studying, nodding at Nara as the young woman dropped into the seat across from her. The table was tiny, barely holding the two stacks of books she'd brought with her.

"How can I help?" Nara asked, brushing a lock of dark hair from her cheek. Her eyes roamed the books on the table hungrily—a hunger Voria shared. They might not agree on methods, but that hunger was something she and Nara had in common.

"We'll start with the augury itself." Voria removed the golden plate from her satchel and set it atop one of the stacks of the books. "I'll let you see why we're here."

She played the augury, the flames licking upward as it began to display the same images Aurelia had shown her. When the darkness seeped outward, Nara leaned back in her chair, away from the augury. Her gaze remained steady, and that subtle flinch was her only concession to fear.

Nara looked up at Voria. "What do you think it means?"

"Obviously there's a planet here in the Depths, but

beyond that? We know little." Voria hated admitting her own ignorance, but the only thing worse would be pretending she knew more than she did. "I've done some basic research trying to locate a god powerful enough to do what we're seeing here. I've turned up nothing. There's no god known to dwell in the Umbral Depths, or any god reputed to use darkness to obscure divination, certainly not on this scale."

"Hmm. This is the Codex Divinia, right?" Nara picked up one of the thickest tomes. "Why don't I start here? I'll see if I can find anything we can use. There are a lot of myths in here about darkness."

Voria smiled and turned the page in the volume she was studying. "You're efficient. An admirable quality. I will continue reading the first account of the Umbral Depths. Maybe there's a scrap of legend here."

The pair read in silence for some time, with the sound of pneumatic drills and other power tools in the background. Voria had no idea what Pickus was fixing, and she didn't care, so long as he kept the vessel airtight and flying. She did her best to tune the noise out, perusing chapter after chapter of what amounted to unsubstantiated fairy tales.

The odor of smoke never abated, but true to Pickus's word she noticed it less. The human mind really could adapt to almost anything. She tried to focus on the page, but her mind kept wandering back to the assault by the Void Wyrm.

If Nebiat had indeed sent it, did that mean the dreadlord was back on Shaya, even now? She could wreak havoc if able to work in secret—binding powerful politicians or warriors. It was a bold move for a dreadlord, one that left her vulnerable should Voria find a way back from their current quest.

"Major? I think I may have found something relevant." Nara turned the book she'd been reading and slid it over in Voria's direction. "That page talks about something called the Weaver—the spinner of darkness. She's said to know all things. Only a rare few seek her out, and most never find her. She hides in the cracks between worlds, always evading her enemies. It isn't much, but this picture is all I could find."

Voria stared down at it. A monstrous spider perched in darkness, its eight eyes peering at the reader over a set of vicious fangs. "I believe you're on to something. The arachnidrake from the augury could certainly be the progeny of that thing. See what else you can learn of this Weaver. Perhaps we'll find something useful."

Nara immediately bent back to the book, her eyes shifting back and forth as she scanned the contents. Voria smiled into her hand. The girl was coming into her own, and the longer Voria spent with her, the more certain she was that Eros was right.

Nara would eclipse them all, some day.

29

SHIT, MEET FAN

"Let's hope this works." Aran stepped into the newly repaired defensive matrix and channeled a bit of air magic into the gold ring.

Nothing happened.

He tried the silver. Nothing. "You're sure it's connected?"

"It's connected, but I had to jerry-rig some stuff. Are you familiar with how electricity works? The concept of resistance?" Pickus pushed his glasses up his nose. The question was genuine, without a hint of sarcasm or judgement.

"I have no idea what that is," Aran admitted. "I mean, I know what electricity is, but I've never heard of resistance. Can you dumb it down for me?"

"Uh, sure. Not all the magic you put into the matrix actually makes it to the ship. It's like a hose with multiple leaks. You lose a bunch of water, so you need to pour in extra to compensate. It looks like nothing's happening, but if you pour in more magic, the ship should respond."

"Okay, that makes sense. That's more than what we had. Nice work." Aran stepped out of the matrix. It wasn't much, but it meant one more mage could help defend the ship, even if their spells were weaker. "We should be arriving any minute. I'm going to slow us down. Can you go get Nara and Voria?"

"Hey, Nara!" Pickus yelled.

Aran winced. "I could have done that."

Nara and Voria strolled into the room and dropped into the seats next to the wall. They sat with knees angled toward each other, like friends, or colleagues at least.

Aran smiled as he reached up to tap the bronze ring. "We're about to arrive, and I can't see anything on the monitors. How will we know we're in the right place?"

Voria smoothed the sleeves of her jacket. "The augury might be vague in many ways, but it was very specific about the coordinates for this world. It will be there; I know it."

Aran ducked back into the command matrix and fed a bit of void magic to the ship. He exerted gravity, slowing their speed by about twenty percent. "Okay, we're hitting the coordinates in three, two, one...this is the place." Aran killed the thrust, and the *Texas* slowed to a halt—not that there was any visible reference to show them their speed had changed.

Voria's hands tightened on her armrests. "There's nothing here."

Silence weighed heavily over the bridge as they all stared at the monitor. The unbroken blackness sat there, taunting them. Aran took a deep breath. Had they come all this way for nothing? That seemed too cruel, even for a god.

"I have an idea." Nara's face took on the excited half-smile she wore when figuring something out. "If I were going to hide a world, especially for millennia, I'd want to take precautions to make sure no one found it, right?"

"Doesn't putting it way the depths out here already do that?" Crewes asked as he stepped into the cockpit and dropped into a chair on the opposite wall. The circles under his eyes were large and dark. "Man, I hate this place. It gets under your skin. Like an itch you can't never scratch."

"Hiding a world out here is a start," Nara said excitedly. "But if you're a god, you don't leave it to chance. I'd make an illusion, so even if someone passed directly through the system where you'd hidden the world, they'd have no idea it was there. Aran, guide the ship forward slowly. I'm betting if we continue on our current course, just a bit further, we'll break through their illusion."

"Worth a shot." Aran willed *void* into the matrix and the ship crept sluggishly forward.

They waited for what felt like hours. No one spoke, knowing if Nara's plan didn't work they had no backup.

An eternity later the view on the monitor rippled, and a planet suddenly appeared below them. The screen displayed it in shades of green and black, though Aran doubted that was the real color.

He turned to Pickus. "How are we able to see the planet? There's nothing but total darkness. Where is the light coming from?"

"That's not light. The ship is using a kind of a sonar system. It fires a ping, which maps the terrain, then bounces back to the ship. The image we see is a composite of dozens of pings. Because of the planet's distance, it probably took several minutes to collect the data." Pickus cocked his head, then turned to look at Voria. "Wait—if you guys don't use sonar, how do you see in the dark?"

"There are several magical methods," Voria said, "but now isn't the time to enumerate them." She walked into the defensive matrix, and after a moment Nara stepped into the offensive. "Shall we approach the world and see what we can learn?"

"It's not a big planet," Aran said, "but that's still a lot of ground to cover. Where do you want me to set down?" He coaxed the spelldrive to greater life, and it carried them toward the tiny planet.

Voria grabbed the stabilizing ring with both hands as the ship rattled. "We know what the temple looks like: a large, pyramid-shaped mountain in the center of an empty plain. We'll circle the world until we find it, then set down as close as possible."

"Looks like a breathable atmosphere," Pickus mused, his face bathed by the glow of his little pocket screen again. "But it's cold down there. We're going to want to dress nice and warm."

"Our spellarmor is still in the hold," Aran pointed out, "and we can't reach it until we land." He hated being without it, but right now it was out of reach. "The instant we touch down, I want everyone into their armor. Arm up. We have no idea what's down here."

He focused on the monitor, guiding the ship closer. It jerked as the planet's gravity caught, dragging them down. The rattle increased, and a high-pitched whine came from somewhere in the cargo bay.

"If we lose the hold, we lose the spellarmor." Voria said. "Nara, perhaps cushion our re-entry with ice through the defensive matrix?"

"Good idea." Nara tapped the *water* sigil on each of the three rings, and deep blue energy rolled out of her in waves, into the ship. The monitor showed ice beginning to form, but it melted to steam as full re-entry began. "I don't know if it's helping, but I can keep this up for a few minutes at least."

Pickus patted the wall next to his seat. "The worst of it

will be over in less than a minute. The *Texas* will hold. She's been through far worse."

As if to put the lie to his words, a flaming hunk of magma—like those the sergeant used, but far, far larger—came streaking up from the planet. It slammed into the side of the ship just behind the cockpit, punching a hole through the hull on the aft side of the mess.

Wind screamed through the breach, ripping away Voria's words as she tried to yell something at Aran. He thought swiftly. If he left the matrix, he might be able to seal the breach, but then no one was flying the ship. And, judging from the tortured shriek of metal on metal, this ship wasn't going to survive the landing no matter what they did.

Unless they had access to their spellarmor.

Aran ducked out of the command matrix, and whipped a tendril of air around Nara's matrix. He used it to pull himself closer, fighting the immense gravity as the ship plunged deeper into the atmosphere.

Another hunk of metal ripped loose from the impact point in the mess, and two of the bunks tore off and streaked away from the ship. The whole thing would come apart long before they hit the ground.

He strained to lean closer, pressing his mouth to her ear. "Teleport us to the cargo bay!"

"What?" she yelled back.

"*Cargo bay!*" he roared, pointing at that part of the ship.

Nara's eyes widened in understanding. She seized him around the waist with one hand and sketched a *void* sigil with the other. It was the first time he'd seen her hard-cast the spell, instead of soft-casting it through a spellpistol.

Reality spun and twisted, and suddenly they appeared in a river of flame. Aran roared, flinging himself atop Nara and pinning her to the deck. The heat baked his exposed skin, but moving out of the direct flame turned what could have been third-degree burns into a memorably bad sunburn.

Aran rolled off Nara, and she flipped over onto her hands and knees. They crawled under the torrent of flame bisecting the room, rushing from an exposed electrical conduit on one wall straight out an enormous hole in the side of the ship.

He was still holding his breath, and black spots danced across his vision as he crawled closer to his armor. He stood for the last few meters, staggering to the suit, and seized it with one hand, then sketched the *void* sigil in front of the chest with the other. He threw himself at the armor, sinking inside.

A moment later the HUD came to life and the armor settled comfortably around his skin. Cool air flowed into the helmet, and he sucked in several greedy breaths. Nara had reached her armor as well, and was now carrying the staff he'd seen earlier.

He spoke into the new comm system. "Can you see me?"

Nara's face appeared in a little window in the corner. "Yeah, I can see you. Fancy."

"Do you have a way to slow down the ship? We can try guiding it in with our suits, but I don't know what to do about it breaking up on re-entry." Aran extended a hand, willing his void pocket to open. He retrieved his spellrifle, breathing past the pain in his back as his armored hand settled around the grip.

Nara's face shifted to a frown. "I don't have any brilliant ideas. I guess let's get outside and see what we can do."

30

ANY LANDING YOU CAN WALK
AWAY FROM

The ancient cockpit shuddered again, and the monitor went dark. Lights died all around them, leaving them in relative darkness except for the hellish glow of re-entry heating the hull.

Voria took a single deep breath, then acted. She snapped a hand up, sketching a *fire* sigil, then a *dream*. She added several more, and the spell resolved into a hole in reality. The scry-portal looked down on the planet from above the ship, showing her not only their flight but the terrain below, as if it were lit by a bright moon.

She could see their destination in the distance, a single looming mountain several hundred clicks from where she estimated their landing site would be. That would take days to cross—days they didn't have.

"Sergeant Crewes, I have a task for you," she ordered, her attention still focused on the scry-portal, a complex third-level spell she rarely needed to cast.

"Sir?" Crewes responded. His dark skin had been pale the entire trip, and she knew the depths wore on him even more than the rest of them.

"I want you to move to the starboard side of the ship. Find an existing hole or make a new one; I don't care. I want you to fire every spell you have, one after another. Push the ship's course. Angle it that way, to the southwest. We need to come down near that mountain, as close as you can get us."

"Uh, sir, my spells aren't going to do shit to move this tub. It's too big."

She considered, but only for an instant. "Then we'll need to reduce our weight. Detach the rear. That part of the ship is already heavily damaged. Finish the job, and we'll be light enough for your spells to manage."

"I got two problems with that, sir. First, Nara and Aran are back there." The sergeant unbuckled his harness. "But more importantly? *My armor* is back there. I blow the ship, and that armor is toast. Half our squad is toast."

"If you don't blow the ship, *we're* toast. Sergeant, you understand we are not crashing because of a malfunction, yes? Something hostile fired on us from the surface. They're going to come after us the instant we touch down, and this is their territory. They know it far better than we." She unbuckled her own harness, and wove toward what remained of the mess. She caught herself against the wall near the door. "I'm sorry about your armor, but *this is necessary*. Besides, Aran and Nara are far more likely to survive the crash than we ourselves."

The sergeant didn't reply.

Voria seized the bulkhead, and focused on the span of metal joining the mess to the rear of the ship. It was torn and battered, and the heat had stressed it further. In all likelihood it would tear free soon of its own accord; she just needed to hasten the process.

Her hand shot up and she sketched a third-level void

bolt. It shot into the bulkhead, hitting the already damaged section. A two-meter hole punched through that area, and the ship split instantly. The rear segment plummeted toward the planet below, while their section was flung spinning the opposite direction.

"Sergeant, our lives are in your hands," she roared, fighting the vertigo as the ship spun. "Stabilize our flight and get us falling in the right direction. I'll do what I can to soften our landing."

Crewes moved swiftly to her position, grabbing the bulkhead next to her. "You know, sir, sometimes I really hate the way you do things." He extended a tree-trunk arm, the muscles bunching as he aimed his spellcannon carefully away from them.

He fired. Their rotation slowed.

He fired again. The spin became lazy, and she could see the mountain now. The vertigo abated slightly, though if she'd had breakfast she was sure she'd have lost it.

The wind howled around them as the cockpit section fell toward a deep valley below. She sucked in a breath, and yelled into his ear, "If you see a body of water, try to aim for that."

His cannon kicked again, then two more times in quick succession. Voria could feel the immense magical energy pouring through the sergeant, and Crewes used it to great effect. Their flight was an even arc now, aimed toward a rippling lake near the center of the valley.

"Let's get buckled in." Voria clawed her way back to the closest seat, which happened to be next to Pickus. His freckled face was buried in his hands, and he was whispering quietly to himself.

Crewes made it to the chair across from them. He

buckled his spellcannon into the chair next to him, then buckled himself in. The howling of the wind dropped an octave.

"We're below the mountains now. Brace yourselves!"

She winced, wishing she could see how close they were. There was no way of—

Voria was slammed into her restraints, her head rebounding off the foam cushion behind her. The ship was still for a moment, then began to list.

"We're sinking. Let's go. Move, now!" Voria unbuckled her harness, then turned to Pickus. Blood flowed freely from a gash on his forehead. She grabbed him with both hands. "Let me take a look. It's superficial. You'll be fine, assuming we survive the next few minutes. Get it together, Pickus. I need you on your feet and moving."

"Yes, uh...yes, sir." He nodded, then picked his glasses up from the floor. "Just tell me what to do."

"We're going to have to swim." She pushed him gently toward the area where the mess used to be, which was already submerged. "Swim hard for the shore."

"What if there're monsters in the water?"

"Then our day is about to get a whole lot worse." Voria stripped off her jacket and tied it tightly around her waist. She couldn't have it impede her, but she also didn't want to lose it. She'd want it later.

Voria dove into the water, gasping out an air bubble as the icy shock hit her. It was far, far colder than she'd assumed. Were it not for the resistance Marid had given her, she'd probably already be hypothermic.

Pickus would never make it. She sketched a *water* sigil, then added a *fire*. The water pushed back in all directions, creating a bubble. She swam toward Pickus as he entered the water, then pushed him into the bubble. The bit of fire would keep him warm, but would also burn oxygen.

Voria willed the bubble upward, and swam next to it as they moved in what she hoped was the direction of the shore. With no source of light, it was impossible to know. She considered taking the time to cast a divination spell to aid her vision, but decided to save the magic. Using it might draw the attention of whoever waited on the shore, and she was absolutely positive whoever had shot them down would be there as quickly as they were able.

It took another few minutes to reach the shore, and Voria's entire body had gone numb. She climbed wearily onto the shore, giving a half-smile when she heard Pickus cough a few meters away.

He groaned, pulling himself to his feet. "Let's not do that again."

"Be silent," she hissed. "We have no idea what's out here, or how close. Hold still a moment."

She cast a starlight spell, imbuing herself and Pickus with magical vision. Its range was limited, but they could see fifty meters as if it were a night under a full moon.

She breathed a little easier when she spotted no immediate threat. "Follow me. We're going to circle the shoreline until we find some sign of Crewes. Look for anything, and let me know if you spot him."

"I—It's r—really cold." Pickus's teeth chattered and he clutched his arms around his sodden overalls.

"Walking will warm you." Voria started up the shore, keeping low to the group, and scanning the rocky cliffs above. Her own teeth chattered, but she'd long ago grown comfortable with such rigors.

There was no vegetation she could see, which made

perfect sense. Vegetation required sunlight. If they found anything here, it would likely be some sort of fungus.

A sudden flash lit the night, and an explosion came from the far side of the lake. The magma spell, Crewes's trademark attack, illuminated the terrain for a moment, arcing into a creature about the size of a Krox enforcer.

The creature had a pallid white exoskeleton. Too many legs scuttled underneath it as it sought to avoid the sergeant's attack. It screeched when the magma exploded, splashing over the cluster of eyes in its hideous face. Eight eyes.

The screech wasn't pained; it was angry. A moment later, it was answered from the hillsides above—answered by many different throats.

The first creature scuttled toward Crewes, wiping magma from its face as if it were nothing but an irritation. Crewes fired again, and this time the creature dodged. It chittered a stream of what might be words in his direction, gesticulating with two of its legs. Then it charged.

Crewes charged, too. Voria judged the distance between them, then her relative distance from both. She sketched a quick *void* sigil and teleported to the opposite shore. The creature hadn't noticed her, so Voria cast a third-level void bolt.

It sailed into the creature's thorax, disintegrating a huge segment of carapace. Greenish ichor leaked out, and the creature aborted its charge.

"Yeah, you better run," Crewes taunted the retreating creature. "She's got more where that came from." He spun to face her, his confidence melting. "That thing's buddies are about to show up, and they're resistant to fire. I can feel it. My rounds ain't doing shit to them."

"You've got water magic now, as well. You must remember that, sergeant. It may save your life," Voria pointed out. "We don't know how these things react to the cold. Try ice next time, and see if you have any better luck."

Many sets of eyes appeared on the rocks above them.

31

MINI-DRAKKON

Aran tumbled into the bulkhead as the ship jerked violently, then began to spin. He caught himself, clinging to the side of the cargo hold. "We're in free fall."

Nara clung to the opposite wall. "I think the rear part of the ship just sheared off. How do you want to handle this?"

"If we leave the sergeant's armor he'll never forgive us. Can you 'port it out of here?" Aran pulled his spellblade from a void pocket, and dropped his rifle inside.

"Yeah. I'll meet you outside." She kicked off the wall and tackled the sergeant's spellarmor, then sketched a quick set of sigils with much the same skill the major would have used.

Aran blinked. Clearly he wasn't the only one who'd been training hard.

Nara warped out of existence, both her and the sergeant's spellarmor carried safely outside the ship. Aran rammed his spellblade into the wall. He used the suit's enhanced strength to cut himself a hole, then dropped the spellblade back into the void pocket.

"Let's hope we're not about to hit." He crawled through the hole and kicked off the side of the ship. It spun away from him, and Aran tumbled end over end for several seconds until he regained control of his armor. He poured a trickle of *void* into the suit, grinning like a kid when it responded instantly. He hadn't used his spellarmor since playing cat and mouse with Ree, and he'd missed it.

The rear section of the ship slammed into the valley below, detonating spectacularly. The sudden light exposed dozens of creatures that evoked a nameless dread in Aran. He knew these awful things. At some point, he'd faced one. Where or how, he didn't know.

"Arachnidrakes," he murmured into the comm.

"Is that what these things are?" Nara asked. "Let's hope they're not as hostile as they look, because there sure are a lot of them."

"We need to get to Voria before they do. Come on." Aran leaned into the turn, zipping high above the terrain as he followed the path to the cockpit crash site.

"There they are. I can see explosions." Nara pulled even with him. She carried the sergeant's armor in both hands, struggling to maintain altitude.

"Get that to Crewes. I'll lay down some suppression fire." Aran dropped fifty meters, flying fast and low just above the deck.

A creature banked above him, and Aran rolled out of the way as a spiked tail plunged through the space he'd just occupied. It had wings like a Wyrm, and its flesh was scaled, but it had eight legs, and eight eyes. "My new friend here has a seventy-meter wingspan. This thing is serious. I'm going to have to deal with him. Get to Crewes and Voria."

Aran dove, slipping into a narrow trench as the terrible drake followed. It slammed into the edge of the trench, and the collision sent a hail of rock spray down on him. He spun out of the way, dodging almost all of them. A head-sized rock pinged off his shoulder, and a light yellow warning appeared on the paper doll.

"My turn." Aran raised his spellrifle. This spell was still theoretical, but everything he'd learned from Erika suggested it was possible. He poured an equal measure of *void*, *water* and *air* into the spell.

A core of dense ice formed in the center, wrapped in a layer of void energy. Lightning crackled around it all, waiting to discharge. Aran sighted down the scope, centering the reticle over the arachnidrake's thorax. "That looks pretty important."

He stroked the trigger, and the rifle yanked still more magic from his chest. It flung the spell at the arachnidrake, who made no move to avoid it. The void energy boiled away scales and muscle, and the ice lance punctured the thorax. The lightning crackled down the ice, into the creature's flesh.

The drake shrieked, kicking off from the ledge and flapping out of sight. Aran waited several moments, but could neither see nor hear anything. He flung himself upward out of the crevasse and took evasive action the instant he reached open sky. There was no sign of the arachnidrake.

"Nara, do you copy?" Aran asked as he gained elevation.

"I've reached the rest of the Company. Crewes is getting into his armor now. The major is counterspelling their attacks so far. I'm not sure how long she can keep it up. I get the sense they're just probing our defenses." She paused for a moment and her face appeared on his screen. "I don't see how we're going to get out of this one. How the depths are we going to deal with hundreds of these things? We need shelter, but I don't see anything."

Aran glided closer, studying the creatures below. "They're communicating. If they're intelligent, then they understand self-preservation. I bet these things have never seen a Wyrm the size of Drakkon. Any chance you can create something like that?"

"I've never tried an illusion that size." She pursed her lips. "Hmm, how about a mini-Drakkon?"

She began to sketch, and a moment later light flared above them, and every octet of eyes turned up to face it. The spiders quivered, retreating slightly as they saw what Nara had created. It was Drakkon, down to the last scale. The illusion was maybe a quarter of Drakkon's actual size, but that still meant a three- or four-hundred-meter wingspan.

A group of spiders broke, scurrying for the shadows. That triggered the avalanche, and they all scattered—all but the arachnidrake Aran had tangled with. It swooped down at the illusion, which Nara guided out of its path.

"I need to focus to keep this spell under control." Nara's voice conveyed the strain; Aran was amazed she could still speak while maintaining a spell of that magnitude. "Can you stop that thing before it exposes the illusion to the little ones?"

"On it." He zipped skyward, peppering the arachnidrake with level-one void bolts. That got its attention. It winged away from the mini-Drakkon, flapping in his direction.

The drake's mouth opened and it vomited hundred of sticky white tendrils. Those tendrils each moved independently, as if alive, writhing in Aran's direction.

"Man, I hate magic sometimes. Sentient spider webs? What god thought that was a good idea?"

The tendrils snaked around Aran's legs, yanking him closer to the drake. He willed open the void pocket and snatched his spellblade, which flashed down, slicing cleanly through the webs.

The drake gave a frustrated cry as Aran rolled away from a tail slash. It reared its head back and Aran snapped his rifle to his shoulder, aimed it hastily with one arm, then squeezed off a level-three void bolt. It caught the drake's mouth an instant before it could vomit more webs. The massive creature shrieked, choking like a cat on a hairball.

Aran zipped closer and poured a large chunk of water magic into his rifle. It fired a cloud of blue motes that clung to the drake's right wing. The motes began to crystalize, and ice raced across the surface of the drake's wing. The ice thickened rapidly, and the suddenly lopsided drake fell from the sky. It slammed into the lake below, sending up a huge geyser of water.

Aran sped down to join the others. "Let's get the depths out of here before that thing gets out."

Crewes had donned his armor, and carried Pickus's unconscious body.

"Is he okay?" Aran asked.

"Hypothermia," Voria said, teeth chattering. "I think. Crewes is keeping him warm for now, but he hasn't woken back up. Let's find shelter, quickly. We need to get out of sight before those things figure out where we've gone. We can regroup, then press on to the temple."

32

DEADLY MESSENGER

"It's time," Nebiat purred. She enjoyed the way Dirk flinched when she spoke. "You know, I rather like you, little war mage. If not for your daughter, I'd keep you in my service forever. You'd certainly make a valuable asset."

"Why do you hate Voria so much?" Dirk asked quietly.

He'd done nothing to resist her, and she admired his restraint. It was the only stratagem left to him—appear weak and docile, so when the opportunity came to strike, your captor would never suspect the blow—and he'd executed it masterfully.

"You value family, do you not?" Nebiat asked sweetly, though the rage boiled inside. She leaned closer, nose to nose with Dirk. "Your daughter killed my eldest brother, and many of my younger siblings. She foiled my plans on Marid, and she even managed to salvage the Confederate lines at Starn, slaughtering our enforcers. Tell me, Dirk: what would you do to someone who did such things to your family?"

"I would kill them." Dirk shrugged. "You have Erika under your thumb, and now you have me. We're both excellent assassins, and together we could probably cut down the Tender herself. So why not just send us? Why go through all the elaborate showmanship? I'll tell you why. Because my daughter embarrassed you in front of your father, and now you have something to prove. You don't just want revenge. You need it."

Nebiat recoiled a step. Her natural impulse was to lash out, to punish him. Yet he was right. "You are very perceptive. I don't know that I've ever met someone who could read me quite so accurately."

Dirk simply stared at her.

"You thought I'd be unnerved by your outburst? Angry perhaps? You are quite right about my motives." Nebiat smiled predatorily. "That doesn't anger me. It pleases me. You are arguably the most skilled war mage in the Shayan Confederacy—perhaps even in the the sector, though there are a few on Virkon who might best you. And now, you work for me." She ran a finger along the collar of his uniform.

"You didn't answer my question. Why not kill Voria?"

"I've already tended to that particular detail." She patted him on the cheek. "She won't be returning from the Umbral Depths. No, I am after much larger game, Dirk—much larger. You're going to drop this vial into Aurelia's wine when you see her this evening. After you're certain that she's consumed it, you will tell her guards the Krox have been sighted at the second burl, and you believe they're working with Ducius. You and Erika will personally lead a team to stop them."

Dirk gritted his teeth, eyeing her defiantly. It was nice to see him beginning to crack. He wanted to appear docile, but his emotions had gotten the better of him. His daughter appeared to be the lever.

Nebiat waved dismissively, and Dirk left the chamber.

She had one more stop to make before she visited Aurelia, and it was an important one. Eros was no mere war mage. He was a true mage with decades of experience, and she needed to treat him with the respect that deserved.

Taking him down would not be easy, but if she succeeded then she guaranteed the remainder of her plan. The Tender would die, the drifters would go to war with the Shayans, and Ternus would cede from the Confederacy.

33

TOO EASY

Nara sketched the final sigil to the simplest illusion she knew. She envisioned a rock face where the cave mouth stood, and the opening vanished behind an illusionary wall of granite. "That should keep them out, I think. As long as we don't make any noise."

"Nice work," Aran said. His voice was hoarse, and she could hear the exhaustion, though she couldn't see him under the helmet. He turned to face Voria. "Sir, I didn't get a great look at the terrain. How far do you figure to the target?"

"Fifteen clicks? We could fly it in minutes, provided we can avoid detection." She tapped her lips with a finger. "I don't want to risk simple invisibility. There's too great a chance their Wyrms, if that's what those things are, can pierce it. Speaking of—Aran, you seemed to recognize that thing. Aurelia called it an arachnidrake?"

"Yeah, that's the name." Aran removed his helmet and sat on a nearby rock. He focused his gaze on the helmet cradled in his hands. "I don't know what it means, or how I know it. But I've fought one of those things before, and it scares the ever-living shit out of me."

"Out of all of us, I believe," Voria said. She looked to Nara. "You performed admirably back there. I felt your use of spells. The illusion in particular was both inventive and effective. Well done."

Nara stared at the major like she'd grown a third eye. "Thank you," she finally managed. She cleared her throat. "So, what's the plan then? How do we get from here to the temple without being overrun?"

"Those things got real pissed off when we hurt one of them," Crewes said. "If they can feel anger, all we gotta do is piss 'em off." He slammed his armored fists together. "We just need a distraction. We send a team—me—to go bust some of their heads. They all come to see what the ruckus is, and you head for the mountain so you can pray or whatever."

"That's a terrible idea," Nara countered. "If we do that, you end up dead. Aran, Voria, I know we're here unofficially, but one of you needs to pull rank." She frowned at them both.

"Do you have a better idea?" Voria asked, her voice barely above a whisper. It still felt too loud.

"Not yet, but that doesn't mean we can't come up with one." She set her helmet down, and sat next to it. "We need to recover our spells anyway. Why don't we sleep on it. If we don't have a better idea by morning, then we'll—"

A huge roar echoed off the canyon walls outside and into their sheltered cave. They all looked at each other.

Nara stated the obvious. "That wasn't an arachnidrake."

Aran put his helmet on. "Nara, why don't we go investigate? You can use an invisibility sphere. We'll go up a hundred meters or so and see if we can figure out what's going on, then come right back before anyone sees us."

"Okay, let's go." She slid her helmet into place, and her HUD sprang to life.

Crewes did the same. "Remember, kids—no petting the animals. Get up, get back. I'll wait here, but if you get into trouble I'll come running."

"We'll be fast. Nara?"

She reached into her reserves for *dream* and *air*, sketching sigils quickly and easily, more naturally than she had a few weeks ago. She needed more practice, but at least she no longer reached for her missing spellpistol whenever she cast.

The spell completed, and the invisibility sphere rippled outward around her and Aran. He zipped through the cave mouth, and she followed. She enjoyed chasing him like this, following closely as they whipped through canyons and over ridges.

Aran stopped against an outcrop at the base on a small peak, high enough to see for kilometers in all directions. She followed, pausing next to him as she surveyed the direction they'd heard the roar.

"I think it's coming from the first crash site." She floated a bit higher. "Oh, gods, its the Air Wyrm. It's tearing apart the remains of the ship."

"Yeah, I see that." Another streak of lightning split the darkness, but this one was directed at a knot of the spider creatures. "It looks like he's getting the locals' attention. If we wanted a distraction, I don't think we'll ever have a better one."

"If we head back down, I can add the rest of the company to the invisibility sphere."

"Perfect."

He shot down into a dive, and she followed. It only took a few moments to rejoin the others. Crewes carried Pickus, who'd yet to wake. At least his breathing was smooth and even.

Voria climbed onto Nara's back and wrapped her arms around her waist. "Let's make this quick. We fly low and fast, and get there as quickly as possible—hopefully before these things figure out we're there."

"All right, just get within five meters of me and I'll recast the spell," Nara instructed. She waited for the others to gather, then cast the spell again. The invisibility rippled outward and included Voria, Crewes, and Pickus. "Okay, we're good. Stick close."

They rose slowly, leaving the cave and flying toward the mountain in the distance. Aran flew a few meters ahead with his rifle cradled in both hands. Voria perched on Nara's shoulders like a toddler, and Nara wasn't sure she'd be able to cast if it came to combat. So she needed to make sure it didn't.

Their little caravan crossed two more valleys, quickly narrowing the distance to their target. The rough-hewn temple loomed in front of them, a towering mountain that rose high above the surrounding valleys.

They zoomed toward an opening on the east side. Thus far, they hadn't seen any more spider creatures. Now that they were closer, Nara had her first real look at the place. The angular slopes were too symmetrical to be natural, but so worn they appeared to be. This planet hadn't seen much weather, but unless there was some source of storms Nara hadn't yet seen, this rock was incredibly ancient.

She glanced over her shoulder, and saw another blue-white flash. Thunder boomed a moment later. The Wyrm was still tearing apart spiders. Perfect.

Aran dropped elevation and Nara followed. They came to a smooth landing just outside a yawning tunnel mouth on the pyramid's south slope. Aran turned to face her, scanning the darkness with his spellrifle. "This is way too easy."

"Why," whispered a discordant voice from the shadows in the temple, "do you assume it will be easy?" A many-legged creature scurried forward, its eyes glinting in the darkness.

34

CUSTODIAN

Voria sketched a *fire* sigil, and light flared over them, but only for half an instant. Then it was snuffed out, countered by some sort of intense magical field.

"Your spells will not work here," the sibilant voice whispered. "Come, enter quickly. The distraction that allowed your passage will not keep my more primitive brethren at bay for long."

A pair of double doors opened inward; a blinding glow washed out from the temple. Voria's hands shot to her eyes, and she grunted in pain as the sudden light blinded her. After so much darkness, it wasn't merely discomfort. It struck her like a blow.

"The discomfort will pass in a moment or two. This is the first true light your eyes have seen in some time." The soft voice's accent was strange. Clipped. The words were too short and the cadence slightly off...as if the mouth had trouble making sounds like a human mouth.

Aran's confident voice came from behind her. "You okay,

Major?" Metal clanked on stone as his armored form drew even with her.

"I just need a moment." She blinked rapidly, and shapes finally began to appear. Spots still ate at her vision, but it was beginning to pass. "You can lower your rifle, Lieutenant. If our host wanted to hurt us, I expect he wouldn't have spoken first."

She peered at the creature, which resembled the smaller ones they'd fought outside. It had no wings, and where the spiders outside had white carapaces, this thing had scales.

A more evolved form perhaps?

"I understand that my appearance must trouble you," the spider said, its chelicerae quivering. "I ask you to look beyond your instincts." The jaws were covered in thick black spines, with sharp, spear-like fangs in between.

Voria shuddered. "Please forgive my, ah, weakness. We've come a very long way to find you, and have sacrificed much. Have we found sanctuary where we can rest, and regroup?"

"Indeed." The spider clasped two of its legs before it in a sort of bow, while a third leg pointed deeper into the structure they'd entered. "You have found the Library of Neith, the greatest repository of knowledge in the omniverse."

Omniverse? That sparked a great many questions, but Voria forced them down in favor of the more pressing ones.

"Do you have a name?" Voria asked as she peered deeper into the library. She didn't trust their host—not yet, anyway. Yet they desperately needed help.

"Names are complicated things, and we do not share ours. You may call me...*custodian*. It is a term you are familiar with, and captures the essence of my purpose."

The custodian scuttled deeper into the library, and Voria eagerly followed. They passed into a vaulted room with a black marble ceiling, the backdrop for a night sky. Glowing magical runes made up the stars, mystical constellations of immense power. The vastness unnerved her, and seemed to encompass not just their galaxy, but many, many galaxies. They moved slowly, orbiting in a chaotic pattern her mind couldn't quite grasp.

She recognized that she was seeing an ocean of magical power she couldn't even begin to comprehend, but she didn't have the slightest idea what it might be used for, so she focused on the more familiar. As far as she was concerned, the library under the domed ceiling represented the real power in this room.

Row upon row of floating shelves lined the room, each holding hundreds of faintly glowing dragon scales. "Are those knowledge scales?"

"Indeed," the custodian confirmed. "Each contains a specific discipline or historical epoch. Together, they represent the sum of all remembered knowledge."

"How far back does it go?" Nara asked, removing her helmet with a hiss.

"To the beginning of all things, when Neith first drew breath," the custodian explained, as if that should have been self-evident.

"Custodian," Aran called. He removed his helmet, and bowed respectfully to the awful spider. "You were waiting at the entryway at the exact moment we arrived. That can't have been a coincidence. You were expecting us, weren't you?"

"Indeed. This day has long been foretold. We were aware of your arrival on our world, and that of the dragon Khalahk. Both events were necessary to forge this specific possibility."

Voria stopped in her tracks as the implications hit her.

"The Wyrm *had* to attack us, and *had* to follow us here. If it hadn't, there would have been no distraction to give us the opportunity to reach the temple."

The spider gave a jerky nod. "Yes, yes. Without the arrival of the Wyrm, you'd have been killed and devoured by my feral brethren. That particular dilemma took Neith many cycles to unravel. The dragon was the only way. If you will follow me, I will bring you to quarters where you may rest. In the morning, when you are ready, you will be brought to audience with Neith."

"You speak of Neith as if he—or she—is still alive," Voria ventured. "We've never met a living god. I've heard of one or two who are considered to be asleep, but no living, conscious gods."

"Neith is very much alive," the custodian explained, "one of the last surviving deities from the earliest days of the godswar." He led them through the main library and up a hallway that led off the main room.

Voria cleared her throat, drawing the spider's attention. "I don't really know how to respond to the idea of meeting a living god. If Neith is still alive, why hasn't she intervened in matters directly?"

"She has. Countless times. Your arrival marks one of the more direct interventions, but hardly the first, or even the ten-thousandth."

The spider ducked through a doorway into a jarringly ordinary chamber. Five spacious bedrooms jutted off the main dining area. A glance into the closest bedroom showed a wide, floating bed that could easily sleep three adults. The dining room itself had several comfortable couches. Crewes moved over to one and gently set Pickus down, then flopped down on another couch, which bowed alarmingly under the weight of his armor.

"We have got to take one of these back with us." He threw his arms up behind his head as he sank further into the couch and gave them a grin.

"If you wish refreshment, simply ask and the room will provide it," the custodian said, scuttling back toward the door. It was leaving, just like that.

"Custodian, our friend is injured." Voria nodded at Pickus. "Is there anything you can do?"

"There is no need for me to interfere directly. The room's ambient magical energies will heal him, and wash away your various hurts and exhaustion." The custodian gave a bow then scuttled off, leaving them in relative peace.

Voria waited until he was gone, then turned to the others. She dropped her voice to a whisper. "I may be paranoid, but I don't trust that spider. This all seems a little too convenient for my tastes."

"Seriously, sir?" Crewes asked, eyeing her like he usually did his recruits. "Ain't this the whole reason we flew out here? To meet with the locals, so they could hook us up with some Krox-slaying tools?"

"He has a point," Aran added. "If this thing wasn't on the level, and if there really is a goddess here, couldn't she snuff us out with a thought if she wanted to?"

Nara stifled a yawn. "If they want us dead, there isn't anything we can do to protect ourselves. We may as well get some sleep, and hope they're not going to eat us."

"And on that comforting note," Voria said, "I am going to bed." She walked into the first room and flung herself on the bed without even bothering to remove her boots.

Sleep overtook her in moments.

35

POWERLESS

Voria awoke groggily, raising her face from a wet spot on the pillow. "Eww."

She crawled from the mounds of pillows and blankets, rubbing sleep from her eyes as she ambled back into the sitting room. There was no sign of the others, but the rooms where they should be staying were dark. She briefly considered checking on them. It seemed dangerous to assume they were okay without verifying it.

Yet what could she do if they weren't? Nothing.

She had to accept that she was virtually powerless here; she could either wallow in it or focus on something else. Passivity galled her, in any form, and besides she was tired of waiting. Why not give in to the temptation to learn? If this really was the first library, she could learn...anything. And wasn't that what the augury had intended for her?

Voria headed out into the library. Several custodians, each indistinguishable from the one they'd met, moved among the stacks. They still unnerved her, but whatever discomfort she experienced was overridden by the knowledge they guarded.

She approached the closest one. "Excuse me."

The creature turned eight eyes on her.

"I spoke with a custodian earlier. Are you...him?"

The spider's jaws quivered. "I am not, but I can serve you just as ably. What do you require? Is something amiss in your chambers?"

"Quite the contrary. The accommodations are brilliant. I'm hoping to avail myself of the knowledge here. Is that permitted?" She didn't know if it was a gross breach of etiquette to ask, but the risk seemed worth it.

"Hmm. Certain parts of the library are available to you. You may see the past, with some stipulations—and the present, with a few more. But I cannot allow you to see any futures, especially any possibility touching your own thread." The custodian raised two bristly limbs and rubbed them together. "What do you wish to study?"

That was the real question, wasn't it? She had the chance to learn, theoretically, the beginning of all things. She could see the universe being born. Or, if this thing was correct, maybe even the instant when the last star snuffed out, billions of years from now.

"Can you track a specific person's life?" Voria asked, an idea forming. If this worked, maybe she could finally steal a metaphorical march on her enemy. Maybe she could be the hunter, instead of the hunted.

The custodian cocked its bulbous head. "Of course. Is there a thread you wish to examine?"

"Yes. I know her as Nebiat, though it may not be her true name. She is a dragon. A Void Wyrm, and child of Krox."

"What type of data do you wish regarding this individual?"

"We were attacked by Khalahk, and I know that was part of the possibility needed to get us here. But how did

Khalahk know we were going to be there at that exact instant? Why attack us?" Voria knew it was a lot of supposition, but the move had Nebiat's claw marks all over it. "Was Nebiat involved? If so, I will have followup questions."

"Come." The custodian scuttled between rows of shelves, moving unerringly through the library. Other custodians eyed their passage with great interest, though none spoke to her or her guide.

Any one could have been the creature she'd dealt with the day before. How could she know? It only made the spiders more unsettling.

They finally stopped at a shelf along the far wall. The custodian plucked a scarlet scale from the shelf. It studied it with those bulbous eyes for several long moments. The scale pulsed with magic, and a wispy image rose from it.

The light reflected off the spider's eyes. "I believe this is the information you seek."

Nebiat and Khalahk swam around each other in the infernal glow of a star. The titanic dragons conversed for some time, then departed without fighting. There was no use of magic, so whatever Nebiat had done didn't appear to have bound Khalahk. Either he'd long been her slave, or she'd somehow convinced him to attack Voria of his own accord.

Why would a dragon outside the Krox want to see her dead? She'd saved Drakkon from enslavement, and had never attacked Khalahk.

"Do you have another question?" the custodian asked. Its face might be grotesque, but the words were cultured, hinting at this creature's intelligence.

"Can you show me what she is doing at this very instant?"

"Of course." The custodian breathed across the top of the scale, and another wisp puffed up.

This one showed a small, sleek corvette. The starship had been burned into her mind over the course of decades. The *Swift Arrow*—her father's ship—currently docked at the sixth branch, at what appeared to be a resort. The wisp followed a person's perspective as they snuck aboard the ship.

Voria reached out and seized one of the spider's bristly limbs. "Is there a way we can warn my father? Please, we have to stop this!"

The custodian looked down at her hand curiously. "This is why we are loathe to show the present, or the future. Observers always seek to change, to alter. This would inflict catastrophic and often unpredictable consequences. Slow down. Think. Consider the ramifications if we were to act. What would you do? And what effect would that action have?"

Voria licked her lips, thinking frantically. What could she say to convince this creature to help her? An honest answer to its question was a good beginning. "It would require some sort of communication spell. A missive."

"And?"

"And this missive would have to travel through the Umbral Depths until it reached my father." She still didn't see where the creature was leading her.

"Spells leaves a residual signature. Missives travel in a straight line. Your own magical abilities are primitive, but even you must understand that." The custodian added no animosity to the words. It was a simple statement of fact.

"So sending such a spell would leave a trail back to this world," she realized aloud. "Warning my father could expose this place."

"More, it would expose you and your companions to immediate danger. Khalahk lurks somewhere on this world, watching. Hunting. If he were to see a spell depart this place, he would unerringly track it here."

Voria exhaled a long, slow breath. The images played above the scale as Nebiat made her way inside a spacious suite, weaving a path toward the master bedroom. The dreadlord paused just outside, peering cautiously inside. Her father was sprawled across his wide bed, naked and unarmed. Several empty wine bottles lay scattered around the nightstand.

Erika rose from the bed, and moved to stand protectively in front of Nebiat. Her father took up his weapon, but failed to cast a spell. He was quickly overwhelmed, and all Voria could do was watch as Nebiat took the man who'd raised her to near adulthood.

If Voria knew anything about Nebiat, it was that the binder left nothing to chance. Those women were plants, and the wine had almost certainly been drugged. She'd set a trap, and clearly Erika had been part of that trap.

"I know you can't risk exposing this world, but can you at least show me the future? What will she make my father do? Knowing that could influence my own actions. I could return to help, somehow."

"Your audience with Neith approaches." The spider raised a long leg and pointed at a tunnel leading off the main library. It was easily thirty meters tall, far larger than any of the others. "Go there, through those doors. They will open of their own accord when the goddess is ready for your audience."

36

NEITH

Voria arrived at a pair of titanic golden doors. Every millimeter was covered in dragon scales, each containing a vast repository of magical energy. Sigils dotted every last one, allowing the scales to be configured as the user desired.

She couldn't begin to guess what the enchantment was used for. The complexity was staggering, and she doubted even a lifetime would be enough to decipher a single door.

The doors swung silently inward, exposing a short hallway that emptied into a cavernous room. Voria steeled herself. The first step was the hardest, but after she got moving she was able to keep going, plunging into the darkness.

The doors swung silently shut behind her, a faint whoosh of air washing over her. A moment later a rush of hot, fetid wind engulfed her as something colossal moved in the darkness.

"When you gaze upon me, you will be filled with terrible wonder." The voice echoed through the room like thunder, and Voria's hands shot to her ears. "Awe. Fear. Madness. Be prepared, mortal."

A bright flame sprang into existence high above, banishing the darkness in a pool around Voria. It didn't fully expose the monstrosity in the corner, but she had the impression of giant leathery wings and long, segmented legs. An arachnidrake, like the one Aran had clashed with.

"Not *an* arachnidrake," the goddess whispered. "*The* Arachnidrake. The mother of my entire species."

Even the whisper was enough to draw blood from Voria's ears. She gritted her teeth against the pain, and forced herself to look upon the goddess. Something about the deity tore at her mind, prying open a new sense she hadn't realized she possessed.

"Yes, you begin to see. To *truly* see for the first time."

"What are you doing to me?" Voria yelled, her voice small against the darkness.

"I am awakening you, vessel. Showing you the true universe, not the static single moment most of your kind dwell within."

Voria's grip tightened over her ears as the pain increased.

"Imagine an ant walking along the forest floor, never looking up. It doesn't know the sun, or the stars. It doesn't know the mountains, or valleys, or the creatures that dwell within. Such is how your perceptions compare to mine. Look up, little ant. Look up and *see*."

Voria fell to her knees, cradling her head against the pain. Nausea roiled up, and she heaved bile onto the stone before her. She trembled violently, unable to control her body as unfamiliar magical energies washed over her.

"My work is done, vessel. This portion, at least."

"W-who are you?" Voria rasped over the shards of glassy pain in her throat.

An orb of flame sprang to life in each of the eight eyes. "I am the first witness, the seer of all things. Flame-reading is a paltry attempt to understand the universe as it truly is, but it is a rough approximation for the change I have imbued you with."

"You're the one who invented divination," Voria realized. Her head throbbed in time with her heartbeat, little flashes of light flaring in her vision with each one. She wouldn't waste this opportunity. Pain could be borne.

"Invented? No. *Discovered*, perhaps. Divination simply is, though I taught many of the first gods how they could utilize it." The spider-goddess's jaws wiggled in a most disturbing way as she scuttled closer to the light. "In the library you asked a question. What will Nebiat do next? Do you still wish the answer to that question?"

"More than anything, but if I am only allowed to ask one, I have to make it about the war with the Krox. What is my role in it?" Voria demanded—as politely as the agony made possible, anyway. "What do you expect me to do?"

"There is no need to hurry our conversation," the goddess rumbled. "I will answer all pertinent questions until I feel you are prepared for your purpose. You are meant to stop Krox from being resurrected. It remains unclear whether you will succeed in this task, though your presence here means the possibility, however remote, still exists. What do *I* expect you to do? I expect nothing. I have foreseen the possibility that you may achieve this, nothing more."

"Okay..." Voria thought furiously. What should she be asking? Damn it, she was putting herself first for once. "Can you tell me what Nebiat seeks on Shaya, and what role my father plays in it?"

"I can, but you will not enjoy seeing this possibility. Are

you certain you wish to know?" The goddess loomed closer. A musky smell suddenly pervaded the cavern—her breath, perhaps?

"Tell me. Please."

"Very well. I foresee the possibility that Nebiat will kill Tender Aurelia. Even now, the possibilities narrow. Soon, they will narrow to a fixed point." The goddess's eyes flared, and Voria saw a sorcerous battle between two women: Aurelia, and a white-haired beauty with black skin. Nebiat's human form, exposed at long last. "As for your father, see for yourself."

Possibilities danced endlessly before Voria; she could see down each, like a thousand, thousand corridors. Her father dead at the hands of Ducius. Her father standing over Ducius's corpse. Her father attacking Shaya itself.

That last possibility was stronger than the others, available on many paths. She studied it, following the corridor to see where it would lead.

Her father stood near Shaya's heart, inside the tree itself. The wood around him, one of the oldest parts of the tree, was dry and desiccated—the part nearest the wound that had felled the goddess. He guarded a robed mage, who assembled some sort of magitech device, something of Inuran construction.

The view shifted outward and looked down at Shaya from above. The second burl shattered suddenly, raining millions of tons of wood and stone on the drifter city below. An entire city rested on the burl. Both the drifters and the Shayan nobles died in a catastrophic explosion of wood and debris. Thousands upon thousands dead in an instant.

"No," she whispered, her hands falling from her ears. Each palm was sticky with blood. She looked up defiantly. "There must be a way to stop it."

"There is almost always a way. You now possess the observational tools to locate the correct possibility. When you leave this place, you will retain the ability to perceive futures. With time and study, you will possess the same advantage that already guides your opponents." The spider's eyes dulled, the flames going cold.

"May I ask more questions?"

"A few, mortal." The spider moved back into the shadows.

"Why is this world hidden here? Why don't you return to our sector, and help stop Krox directly? You're a living god. He's dead."

"Because Krox is not the only threat in the sector, or in the galaxy, or in this universe." The goddess's eyes lit again, briefly. "Once, Nefarius stalked this sector. A dark, terrible goddess of incredible strength. She subjugated the weak, and killed the strong. Before her coming, we lived in relative peace, each god ruling his or her own world. After her coming, we soon realized that if we did not band together, she would kill us all."

"The godswar," Voria breathed in awe.

"A small part of it, yes. We gathered our full might, under the leadership of Xal and his consort Marid." The eyes showed images. Memories of a terrible cosmic battle. "Over half our host died, but in the end we killed Nefarius. His heart is still in this sector, clutched within the Fist of Trakalon. Yet our victory was merely the prelude to a greater defeat.

"By the time we realized what Krox had done, it was too late. Krox had manipulated the war, arranging for those who could have opposed him to be killed. The rest were quietly subverted in a plan stretching for dozens of millennia." The spider's eyes showed a final conflict, a few dozen gods coming together to kill Krox. "Because of Marid's planning, we were able to kill Krox, scattering his magic across several sectors. His children have been slowly gathering that energy, and if not stopped they will bring the return of their dark father."

"I think I understand why you brought this world here."

"Yes. You see now. In this place we are safe. There is no possibility of our discovery. I will not allow it. The darkness in your augury? My spell, to keep enemies from finding this world. Yet adhering to this vigilance severely limits my active involvement in the war against Krox, and Nefarius." The spider's clawed feet dug furrows in the cavern floor. "I must rely on tools, vessels to carry forth my will. Vessels like you."

Voria wanted to ask more questions, but the pain had grown too acute. Each time the goddess spoke, Voria's vision doubled, and her center of gravity lurched as one of her eardrums tore with an agonizing *pop*.

She cried out, panting for several moments before she could manage words. "How can we get off this world, to return to the fight?"

"Climb the stairs on the opposite side of the cavern, and you will find your salvation."

The flame lighting the room winked out, plunging the room into sudden darkness.

37

RESHAPED

Aran awoke to the sound of a soft chiming. He flipped out of bed, yanking his spellblade from its scabbard and turning a slow circle around the room. His chest heaved, but his thundering heart began to slow when he remembered where he was.

The adrenaline dissipated quickly. He stifled a yawn, picking up his helmet from the nightstand. None of them had taken off their armor. This place seemed benign enough, but Aran wanted to be ready to bug out, just in case.

Pickus poked his head into the room. "Oh, hey, you're awake." He gave a sheepish smile, pushing some of his hair out of his eyes. "They brought us breakfast a little while ago. This green pudding stuff. It's pretty good."

The knot of tension between Aran's shoulders eased. "It's good to see you on your feet. You had us a little worried."

"Hey, I'm fine with being knocked out. I have no idea how we got from the crash site to here, and I'd just as soon not remember any of it."

He headed back out into the sitting room, and Aran

followed and dropped into a seat across from Pickus, dragging over the closest bowl and giving it a sniff. A heady cinnamon smell rose up.

Aran picked up a spoon and gave the gruel a try. "You're right. Not bad." He shoveled in food as fast as he could, a habit he'd picked up quickly after being conscripted.

"So where's the captain?" Pickus asked. He withdrew a small soldering iron from his belt, then pulled his glasses from his face. He held them up to inspect the bent frame.

"I don't know. It's odd she'd leave without a note, but if there's any single thing that might make her forget to, it would be the lure of this place. She loves knowledge almost as much as Nara does."

Nara entered the room with a stifled yawn of her own. "Almost as much as Nara what?"

"Loves books." Pickus bent over his glasses and used the soldering iron to heat the bridge. He twisted the frame, then inspected it carefully.

Aran finished his bowl and set it back on the table. "Voria's out in the library somewhere, or so we're guessing."

Nara eyed one of the bowls dubiously. "What is that?"

"Oatmeal?" Aran shrugged. "Or something very much like it. If you're hungry, have some. If not, the sooner we find Voria, the happier I'll be."

Pickus gave his glasses another twist, then applied the soldering iron again. "I'm going to stay here while you adventurous types go do your thing. I'm, uh, not a huge fan of spiders."

Nara gave the table a wide berth and moved to join Aran at the doorway into the library. "I think I'll pass on the spider goop."

They entered the library proper, and Aran started

walking toward the center. Before long, they encountered one of the arachnid creatures.

Aran approached. "Custodian?"

"Hmm?" The creature's many eyes swiveled in his direction.

"We're looking for one of our companions—Voria. Brown hair. Blue coat."

"Ah, yes. She has just completed her audience with Neith. Yours is next, I believe." The spider raised a leg covered in bristly spines and pointed it at a massive set of double doors. "Go there. Enter one at a time. Neith will make all clear."

Aran looked to Nara, who shrugged.

"Thank you." He bowed to the spider, and they moved off.

Nara walked beside him, leaning closer to speak. "These things creep me out. Do you think there's any chance they're lying?"

"There's a chance, but until we see the major, we won't know for sure." Aran frowned as he walked. "I don't like not knowing, and I don't like splitting up. Even when we're not being attacked, I feel like we're about to be. It's like I can't put it down."

"I know what you mean. I feel like we're being watched. Always." She shook her head. "At least I know you've got my back."

"Always."

They finally reached the doors, which were larger, more intricate versions of the ones he'd seen in the Tender's palace. They opened silently inward, showing cavernous darkness.

"Ladies first?"

"Yeah, no." Nara laughed. "Good luck, sir."

"Oh, now it's *sir*." He started into the darkness, settling his helmet over his head.

The doors closed silently behind him, separating him from Nara. Aran's hand shot into his void pocket, and he snapped his rifle to his shoulder.

"You'd likely have more success with the blade," something rumbled from the darkness. The words rattled his teeth, even through his suit's dampeners. "A spellblade could, theoretically at least, harm me. The rifle cannot generate a spell powerful enough to bypass my natural defenses."

Eight fires slowly warmed to life, and Aran realized they were eyes. They provided enough light to see the outlines of the creature, but most of it was still clothed in shadow. His mind filled in the arachnidrake's awful details.

Aran lowered the rifle. "You're even larger than Drakkon." He withdrew his spellblade in his free hand, but he made no threatening gestures with it. "I take it you're the goddess Neith?"

"That name is...adequate." The spider-goddess prowled closer, flapping tremendous wings as she scuttled forward. "Do you know why I have brought you here, to this place, at this precise moment?"

"Because I'm a tool," Aran answered instantly. He didn't like it, but that didn't make it any less true. "You have a specific purpose for me. Beyond that, I don't know."

"I brought you here so you could be reshaped. Your abilities, at present, are inadequate to your purpose. In exchange for accepting this purpose, I will also grant you that which you most desire." The spider-goddess leaned closer, and Aran took several hasty steps back. "I will show you your past."

"You can restore my memory?" Aran perked up instantly.

"I was told that was impossible—that the memories are gone."

"I cannot restore your memory. Or rather, doing so would require magic of sufficient strength to draw attention to this world." The spider-goddess shook her head. A single spiny hair tumbled loose, crashing to the ground not far from Aran. It was nearly as large as his armor. "However, I can show you specific moments in time—your formative memories. I can reconnect those memories to your neurological system, so you will regain full control of your martial abilities."

"So I accept my role in your plan, and you give me back some of my memories?" Aran surprised himself with a laugh. "You've orchestrated all of this, haven't you? Our arrival on this world. Me being mind-wiped. Even Nara."

"Indeed," the goddess said, her voice thrumming through Aran's armor. "Each event surrounding your arrival here has been carefully orchestrated since the atoms that comprise your body were still part of a star. Your assignment to the Wyrm Father known as Rolf was my doing. As was your involvement with the Heart of Nefarius, and later the Skull of Xal."

"I don't have any clue what you're talking about."

"You will. Very soon. But first, the reshaping."

Immense magical power radiated outward from the spider-goddess. It wasn't at all like the wave of violent energies that had burst forth from Marid, or even like the cold light of Xal. This was controlled, measured. Guided by a living god.

The power thrummed into Aran, infusing his armor, then moving within to transform him as well. Where Xal had been a fight not to be drawn into a chaos that would destroy him, Neith burned pure and steady, the cleanest of all flame.

"Your armor has more complexity than your spellrifle or spellblade," Neith rumbled. "I can infuse it with far greater strength and speed, but the ability must be fueled by fire magic. To aid this, I impart to you the magic of flame. With the mastery of this aspect, your destructive capabilities are complete. You can now be forged into the weapon you were always meant to be."

Aran noted that the spellrifle didn't change at all.

"Yes, it is limited. Marid has already touched it, and the weapon possesses no room for further enchantment. Your blade, however, does."

Aran's spellblade flared white, and waves of intense heat warped the air around the weapon.

"This magic will ensure that the weapon will pierce the scales of all but the mightiest of Wyrms. This ability, and those imparted to the armor, are chosen to address threats you will encounter in the near future. You are as well-armed as I can make you."

"Not yet, I'm not," Aran countered. He returned his rifle to the void pocket, but kept the sword out. It had changed in more than just the new ability. The blade had grown smarter. He could feel its mind, and their connection. Aran looked up at the goddess. "You said you could give me part of my memory back. You want me to be the best servant you can make? Give me back my life, and I will happily fulfill my role."

"Sit, mortal. This will not end quickly, and there may be some...discomfort."

38

ANSWERS

Aran fell backward into infinity.

The universe spun out around him, and he perceived a million billion new senses. He understood that time wasn't linear, but neither was it cyclical. It was an explosion of possibilities leading endlessly in all directions.

All secrets were clear—every scrap of knowledge generated by trillions of lives over millions of years. Neith's mind encompassed an impossible span of information, making even Xal insignificant.

Yes. Neith spoke into his mind. *You perceive as I perceive. The impression will live inside you, a constant reminder of the scope of what you battle for.*

They zoomed through space and time, tunneling through reality with a truly frightening ease. They arrived at a large, purple world orbiting a golden sun. Power pulsed rhythmically from the world, and part of Neith recognized and called out to that power.

My younger sister, Virkonna, Neith explained. *She slumbers on that world, protected by her children's children.*

"Why doesn't she wake up?" Aran asked. He couldn't feel his body, and wasn't sure how he voiced the question.

But Neith responded. *Her slumber is a manifestation of crippling grief caused by the death of our mother. It is not an easy thing for me to accept, even after all these millennia. It was much harder for Virkonna. She was closer to mother. The blow at her death was...incalculable. My sister will only awaken at the end, yet she will be present for the final battle.*

The world grew slowly larger until they were close enough to see ships lifting off from the surface. Only most of the "ships" had wings. Dozens of dragons flitted to and from the planet, spellfighters streaking in little clusters behind them.

"A world ruled by dragons?" Aran asked in wonder. Some of the ships were of Inuran design, and tiny figures in spellarmor flitted around some of the dragons. "Working with people?"

Such was once the way of things. The dragonflights protected this sector, and many others. Each Wyrm Father or Wyrm Mother ruled their own world. Some warred upon each other, but for the most part there was peace. Until Nefarious shattered that peace, and Krox dealt its deathblow many centuries later.

"Why are you showing me this?" Aran asked. They dropped through high orbit, zipping past dragons, down toward a mountainous region below.

We witness your past.

They dropped down toward a golden pyramid surrounded by several warring armies. Soldiers on all sides wore the same loose, flowing outfits, and all carried primitive melee weapons. The only thing to distinguish each side was the color of the patch sewn onto their shoulders.

The people themselves were varied, some dark-skinned,

some light. They must have come from a variety of climates and regions, all brought together here for whatever had sparked their war.

To come to be chosen, Neith explained. It unnerved Aran that she could hear his thoughts. *My sister takes a very pragmatic approach to her children. Only the most fit are elevated.*

Two of the armies—one side with black and scarlet patches, the other with gold and blue—pushed toward the top of the pyramid. Aran's perspective zipped closer, and he could make out individual skirmishes now. The style used by the combatants was familiar: aggressive, mobile. They leapt and kicked, flowing around each other in a deadly dance. Some were as old as forty or fifty, but most were young.

The perspective fell toward a boy no more than fifteen. He wore a blue-and-gold patch, and fought alongside several older soldiers.

They were surrounded by black and scarlet patches, pressed steadily backward toward the edge of that level of the pyramid. Abruptly, one of the black-and-scarlet patches was lifted into the air. A bolt of blue-white lightning shot down from the tip of the pyramid, lancing into the floating woman's chest. Power crackled around her, then a torrent of light burst from her eyes and mouth.

She landed, then straightened. Magical electricity crackled around her hands now, the same ability Aran used.

"What did I just see?" Aran asked.

Most Catalysts are simply the remains of my brethren. These fallen gods bestow power on whomever or whatever approaches, with no conscious decision on how much, or to whom. My sister sleeps, but she still lives. Her will selects those she deems worthy, and grants them air magic. That is the entire purpose of this battle, to give the victors magic so they can be elevated into the dragonflight.

The newly catalyzed air mage leapt over the blue and gold bands. She thrust out a hand as she landed, and an intense gust of wind knocked four of her opponents off the side of the pyramid, out over the abyss.

The fifteen-year-old sprinted to the edge and slammed his blade into the stone. The tip sank in, and he gripped the hilt with one hand while the other unfurled his belt. He flung the buckle to a scarlet-haired girl. She seized it, and the boy strained to redirect her momentum.

The scarlet-haired girl rolled back onto the the stone, immediately charging the air mage. The air mage's fists crackled with electricity, and she launched a quick punch. The scarlet-haired girl ducked into a slide, easily dodging the blow. Her fists came up in a flurry of blows, punching her opponent in the groin and stomach.

The boy ripped his blade from the stone, and leapt into the air. He brought it down in a wide arc, the blade humming as it picked up momentum. The tip sliced through the air mage's throat, sending a fountain of ruby droplets into the sky.

Another bolt of lightning shot from the tip of the pyramid, this time forking into both the boy, and the scarlet-haired girl.

You and your sister, gaining the favor of mine.

The siblings became a force of nature, slaughtering their way through their opponents. "Is the use of air magic instinctual? That kid is throwing lightning bolts like he's been doing it all his life."

The magic is well understood by their culture. Every child prays to Virkonna each evening. They visualize themselves having these abilities, using them. From the time they can walk

*children pretend to throw gusts of wind, or fly through the air.
They live and breathe because of the same element: air. It is their
entire culture.*

"So, if that kid is me, what happened to him now that he
was chosen?" Aran asked. The boy and his sister continued
to devastate the enemy, pushing their line further and
further back. He had a sister. Or rather, he had during this
memory. He didn't want to assume she was still alive, only to
find out she'd died years ago.

Watch.

Aran observed the passage of years, somehow able to
understand everything that was happening as it flowed by in
a blur. His younger self trained endlessly, always trying to
impress his sister. She was the gifted one, effortlessly
mastering the things he struggled with.

He had his heart broken, and a few bones. He lived and
learned alongside dragons, moving with his part of the flight
once he was old enough. His sister was assigned to the same
flight, and rose quickly through the ranks. Aran did not.

*You wonder if you possess some defect. No. This possibility
was manufactured. It was important that you be unremarkable
in all ways, your potential stifled. This made it nearly impossible
for even other gods to track the possibility of your existence. Especially after the mind-wipe eradicated all but a few possibilities
with you in them.*

"So...you sabotaged my training and advancement, then
arranged to have my memories stolen? Wow. You guys are
hard core."

Indeed. Gods do tend to be hard core. *You have viewed the
universe through my eyes; you know the stakes, and understand
the parameters of the war.*

"Yeah, and I'm not complaining. I probably would have
an hour ago, but seeing all this, I get why you do what you

do. What seems unfair to me personally ensures the survival of whole worlds." Aran hated that he was accepting this, but wasn't it the smartest path? Like it or not, he'd been picked for something greater, and he could either fight it tooth and nail or accept the fact and try to adapt.

This, too, was part of the possibility. Your mind has been shaped, all in service of this precise moment. Now witness the rest of your past.

Aran stayed an apprentice far longer than his sister, and didn't become a full Outrider until he was twenty-two. Time slowed, and focused on an Aran the same age as he currently was. He prowled with a deadly grace, the same instinctual grace he used now. This couldn't have been too long ago.

I return this to you.

Wave after wave of magical power rushed through him, each containing another memory of him fighting, or training. Blinding agony shot through his temples, then flowed down his entire nervous system in a river of awful flame. It seared him, scouring away conscious thought.

Forms and stances flowed into his mind, fleeting memories of thousands of hours of practice. He understood the movements now, remembered practicing them endlessly. Finally, the fire ceased.

He stood once again in the dimly lit cavern, staring up at Neith's bulbous eyes. Any fear he might have felt was gone now, replaced by confident reverence. He bowed low to Neith, who gave an amused laugh.

"Did you find what you sought?"

Aran looked down at himself in wonder. "I know Drakon Style."

"Yes, and just in time. Now you must use the abilities I have given you. Save them, vessel. Save them all."

"Save who?" Aran asked, blinking up at the goddess.

She retreated back into the shadows, and smothering darkness drenched the room. A pair of double doors at the top of a set of long stairs suddenly opened, showing a sliver of light.

39

SMARTER

Nara shifted from foot to foot, wishing she knew what was happening on the other side of those terrible doors. Since she had nothing but time, she started trying to trace the sigils with her mind, to understand the myriad spells the dragon scales and their sigils had constructed. It involved all eight aspects, and if she was reading it correctly, all eight greater paths.

Granted, she had only a few weeks of magical training, but Eros had been quite clear that such a combination was impossible. It shouldn't surprise her that a goddess's understanding of magic would dwarf their own.

Nara had no idea how much time had passed when the doors swung silently. She stepped hesitantly into the darkness, straining to catch any sound as she shuffled forward. "Hello?"

The doors swung silently shut, smothering the room in total darkness.

"Welcome," a voice boomed, terrible and ancient.

Nara dropped her helmet with a clatter, and her hands shot up to cover her ears. She gritted her teeth, snatching up her helmet and locking it into place as quickly as she could manage.

"A wise precaution," the voice rumbled again, thankfully muted now that she was fully encased in her armor. It still hurt, but the pressure lessened considerably.

A single flame burst to life high above. It revealed a colossal creature with eight legs, and two wings. Nara studied it. The resemblance to the arachnidrake Aran had fought was unmistakable, but Neith was far, far larger.

"Size seems to correlate to age for Wyrms," Nara ventured. "Are you the first arachnidrake?"

"Yes," the voice confirmed. Neith scuttled forward, but stopped twenty or thirty meters back.

Nara floated into the air and guided her spellarmor up to the spider's face. "I don't want to be rude, but I have so many questions."

"Sort them in order of importance, and ask," the spider suggested, watching her with eight eyes, the smallest of them dwarfing Nara's armor.

What did one ask a living god? Should she seek power? Or maybe her past? Did she even want to know what she'd been like?

No. And power by itself wasn't very appealing. Maybe it was stupid, but what she wanted most right now was answers.

The spider seemed amused, though she hadn't spoken aloud. "And this is why, of all your companions, your mind is the most similar to my own. Do you know what I am called in the oldest tales?"

"The keeper of secrets?" Nara ventured, remembering the passage from the book.

"Precisely. I sought all knowledge. I could not help the desire to know. I still cannot help it." The spider sounded both amused and exasperated. "And, given that our minds are similar, I believe I know which alterations you will most properly benefit from. Your ability to process and encode knowledge is insufficient."

"Alterations?" Nara asked, flying back several meters. "Uh, I'm not sure I want to be altered."

"The plant does not refuse the light of the star."

Sudden power flared in those dark orbs, and the energy pulsed out over her in waves. Warm, fiery motes of light swam around Nara's armor, zipping inside at random. Each time, she felt a jolt of heat—not painful, but too intense to be pleasant. She flinched with every mote, finally pulling herself into a fetal position when the barrage intensified.

The energy suffused her body, collecting in her chest and her head. She felt the power flowing through her brain, warming neural pathways.

"What are you doing to me?" she whispered, more in awe than fear now.

"I am increasing your cognitive recall, spatial reasoning, deductive capabilities, and several other ancillary abilities," Neith rumbled. "In short, I am making you more intelligent."

Nara had no idea how to describe the sudden changes in her mind. Her senses hadn't been enhanced, but her understanding of the data she absorbed had. She could analyze and come to conclusions much more quickly now. Even *that* conclusion had come in a fraction of an instant.

"How long will this last?" She already dreaded returning to her previous state.

"Last?" The spider cocked her head. "I have remade you. This is what you are now."

In just a few heartbeats, Nara considered many things. She

considered everything occurring around her, the situation with Khalahk waiting for them, and the possibility that Nebiat was up to mischief back on Shaya. She considered her role, and that of her companions. Finally, she considered what other information she might be able to secure from the god.

"You want us to succeed. You're far more intelligent than any of us, and can perceive time differently." She paused. "Can you give Aran his past back?"

"Your compassion is a variable I did not foresee." Neith's jaws quivered as she studied Nara. "Will it enhance your chance of success, or doom you, I wonder? No matter. I will complete my work."

Another cloud of motes appeared, but these clustered around Nara's staff. They shot into the silvery metal, and a scarlet sigil appeared wherever one touched. The staff grew half a meter in length, and four glowing fire rubies winked into existence around the void orb at the top. They rotated slowly, adding their power to that of the onyx.

Nara wanted to examine the staff further, but that would mean squandering her last few moments with a living goddess. She couldn't waste it. "What else do I need to know to keep my friends alive and fulfill whatever purpose you have for us? What other tools should I be given, or should I be asking for?"

"More astute questions than any of your companions, though each left with the tools they will require. You have yours as well, now." Neith gestured with a titanic leg, and a pair of doors opened at the top of wide stairs on the far side of the room. "You require nothing further in order to fulfill your role. Carry forth my will, vessel. Stop Krox."

The room plunged into darkness, showing only the sliver of light from the top of the stairs. Nara flew in that direction, her mind racing. The staff pulsed a greeting in her hand, and she turned her attention to that.

"You're alive now, aren't you?"

It vibrated again. Eros would be pleased.

Nara glided over the stairs in her power armor, making for the light.

40

AIN'T HALF BAD

C rewes slowly cracked his knuckles, then reached into the void pocket and pulled out his spellcannon. He rested the barrel on his shoulder, whistling as the gigantic golden doors opened silently before him.

He ambled between them, but a bead of sweat dripped down his temple. Damn this room was dark. Anything could be out there. They were still in the depths; he couldn't afford to forget that. The others had let down their guard. But him? Yeah, that wasn't going to happen. Guess he needed to take the initiative.

"I didn't expect my first god to be shy. Hope you don't mind if I light the place up." Crewes activated the external microphone and his voice boomed through the room. He brought the spellcannon up and lobbed a flare spell into the air. It shot up, driving away some of the shadow.

Something massive shifted at edge of the room, a living mountain, covered in scales, and smelling like the deep jungle. Crewes stared up at the thing. "Hope I didn't ruin your entrance or nothin."

"Your simplicity is refreshing." The creature lumbered forward, its many eyes glittering under the flare. It peered down at him, unblinking. "You lack the complex motivations your companions exhibited."

"You like that I'm dumb?" Crewes snorted, then shook his head at the spider thing. "I ain't Nara or nothing, but somehow I get my own diaper changed every day."

"You misunderstand me. Your intellectual capacity is not meaningfully different from that of your peers. Rather, your worldview is much more reductive. You see violence as the most employable solution to nearly every circumstance." The spider cocked its head, and a single hairy spine tumbled free. It slammed into the round with a thunderous boom.

"Well, my granddad said if you've got an axe, and you ain't got nothing else, then every problem looks like a sugar tree." Crewes engaged the thruster on his armor, rising slowly into the air. He circled the god-spider-dragon thing. "My brother's got a whole tool kit. He's got a spanner, and a screwdriver, and a hammer. Me? I just got that axe."

"Your sense of worth is predicated upon your relation to your progenitors," the spider-god rumbled. "You believe you are worth less than your brother, because he utilizes his mind, and you your body. Because your progenitors value those qualities, over your own."

It unnerved him how much that hit home. He did rate himself against his brother. He always had, and he'd always come up short. Always.

"Well, yeah. I mean, I don't hate him for it or nothing, but Mercelus is good at everything. He brought our folks from Yanthara to Shaya. He's the reason they even got a place on the sixth branch, with proper sunlight and everything. Without him my mom would be down in the dims."

Crewes shook his head. He flew a little closer, staring at the spider thing. "Listen, man, I'm sure you're real good at this shrink stuff, but I got shit to be about and you probably charge a lot for therapy. Why don't you give me the secret handshake or whatever, and point me in the direction the major took?"

"You do not fear your own death, but you do fear the deaths of your companions," the god mused, ignoring Crewes. "You seek to protect them. You see their fate as your responsibility. Fitting, then, that you possess the tools with which to do so."

"Come again?" Crewes backed his armor away a few meters. "Now don't you go and—."

A wave of brilliant multicolored light burst from Neith's eyes. The energy crackled over his armor, and his rifle. Heat burst through the armor and Crewes roared. The heat burned, at first. It didn't lessen. If anything, it increased. But the pain stopped. Crewes became one with the fire, drinking deeply of the magical power.

"What the depths are you doing to me?" He roared up at the god, a puff of flame coming from his mouth.

"I have granted you true mastery of flame, not the rudimentary control you previously possessed. It dwells inside you, a living shard of my own power. When you engage your foes, they will truly learn to fear you, even the greater Wyrms. But first, you will use the power to stop the death of the one you are most loyal to."

"Now I like the sound of that. All heroic and such. You know what, spider-guy? You ain't half bad. I mean, we ain't friends or nothin, but I appreciate you giving me the tools to help with my—what did you call it—reductive world view. Now where's the major? I got baddies to roast."

The spider thing's jaws quivered. Was it laughing? "Indeed you do, mortal. Indeed you do."

41

ALL OR NOTHING

Nebiat hurried into the library, effecting the manner of a new apprentice scurrying to her next lesson. In her experience, few people paid any attention to apprentices, and she'd used an illusion to mute her beauty. People noticed beauty, and while she'd have been the first to admit to her own personal vanity, even she was willing to set it aside occasionally.

She fingered the bracelet in the inner pocket of her robes. It was a powerful eldimagus, but since it had no direct spell effect, most defensive wards wouldn't be triggered by its presence. That loophole was how she planned to take down Eros. If she failed...she stood a real chance of dying.

Nebiat quickened her steps among the shelves, avoiding the occasional gazes of students. No one bothered her or impeded her in any way. It never ceased to amaze Nebiat how far one could get with simple social engineering. Magic was amazing, but many mages were too reliant on it. One could often effect better results with simple deception.

The steady glow of magical light came from the office

ahead, a study set into the wall along the outer ring of the library, as far from his students as Master Eros could get. Normally, she wouldn't blame him for wanting that little distance—she lacked the patience for the endless questions students inevitably had—but in this instance it also kept those students from coming to his aid.

She paused at the last shelf, sketching a morph spell. Her features became less angular, her hair longer and darker. Freckles sprouted across her face, and down her neck. When the spell had completed she examined herself in a pocket mirror. Perfect.

"Master Eros?" she called timidly from the doorway. She let her thick, dark hair cover her eyes. Hopefully she'd duplicated the freckles well enough to fool him.

"Hmm? Pirate girl?" Eros looked up from his desk. He removed a pair of magical spectacles and set them down next to the tome he'd been reading. "Aren't you supposed to be off on Voria's mad quest? You've only been gone four days."

"We returned less than an hour ago. We had magical help getting back." Nebiat waited outside the room, shifting from foot to foot. "Voria asked me to bring you an eldimagus we discovered. She says it's vital you unlock it's potential as soon as possible."

"Stop prancing out there. Come show me whatever it is Voria insisted I see." He waved at her to enter, and Nebiat stepped across the threshold.

Fire and *void* exploded furiously around her, the hellish flames boiling away her clothing, and much of her skin. Nebiat shrieked, but made it her only concession to the pain. Discovery made the next few seconds a literal matter of life and death.

Eros rose from his desk, a confident smile spreading

across his devilishly handsome face. "You really thought a simple illusion would fool me, dreadlord?" he asked contemptuously.

She flipped across the room, sketching a counterspell even as he began to cast. Her counterspell zipped into the sigils forming around his hand, and the spell shattered. She landed on his desk and delivered a kick that shattered his jaw.

He tumbled from his chair and landed on the floor with a grunt. He began sketching again, but Nebiat's hand flashed forward and snapped the bracelet around his wrist. Eros completed his spell—a disintegrate—and the magic flashed down his arm. Instead of emerging as a bolt that could have ended her life, the magic poured into the bracelet and was shunted harmlessly away in a puff of purple magic.

Nebiat seized Eros by the throat. He beat at her wrist with both hands, but she ignored the feeble blows. "You could always try another spell if you like, I'll wait."

Eros reached for the catch on the bracelet...only to find that it had been removed.

Nebiat brought his bloody face closer to her own. "That's right. Flail all you like. Your magic is worthless, so long as you wear that bracelet."

Eros went limp. He choked out several words. "W— What do you want with me?"

"You're arguably the most powerful true mage on this world." Nebiat sketched a binding at him, but the defensive wards in the room instantly countered it. "Hmm, that won't do. A moment please." She strode from his study into the un-warded hallway outside. "There we go. Much better."

She cast another binding, and this one worked as intended. The magic seeped into Eros. She added a second, slightly different binding. Then a third, more insidious than either of the other two, and therefore more difficult to detect if her enemies somehow freed Eros. She relaxed finally, after the third spell had taken effect.

Duels of this nature were always settled quickly, and it might just as easily have been her on the losing end. She could never afford to forget that, as it meant making the same prideful mistake Eros just had. The same mistake that had cost Kheftut his immortal life.

As much as she hated to admit it, she'd gotten lucky. Eros had phenomenal mystic wards, but had done little to protect himself physically. If not for that, and for the bracelet, she'd likely be dead right now.

"Oh, don't worry, Eros. I won't keep you in suspense. I have a very special task for you. You're going to kill an entire city full of drifters—and, in the process, spark a civil war."

Nebiat set Eros down.

He stood there, shoulders slumped, a prisoner in his own mind.

"Here is what you will do…"

42

THE TALON

The cavernous doors closed behind Voria, and she surveyed the room she'd arrived in. It looked a good deal like the rest of the library, complete with floating shelves. But a large area of the room had been left empty, and the sky above had no ceiling, exposing the yawning darkness.

"It's a starport," she realized aloud. She started in that direction, scanning the area for a vessel. "There has to be one. How else would we escape this world?"

A brilliant sapphire light blazed to life directly ahead of her. She shielded her eyes, approaching cautiously as the light dimmed.

A staff floated in the air—and not just any staff, but the single most advanced eldimagus she'd ever seen. Its golden haft had layer after layer of tiny sigils woven into it, and she spotted at least a dozen magical materials used in its construction.

The head of the staff was the most striking, and it more resembled a pike than a traditional quarterstaff. A pair of sharp golden prongs jutted gracefully from the top, one artfully shorter than the other. A fist-sized sapphire sat directly beneath the prongs like a single watchful eye, and a pair of golden spikes curved outward below it, almost mimicking a jawline.

An amused male voice emanated from the staff. "If you keep staring like that, I'll start to get self-conscious." The sapphire pulsed in time with the words. "Let's get the introductions out of the way. I've been standing here for...well, a really long time. I was meant for greater things, so let's go."

Voria cautiously approached the staff, scanning for any sign of a trap. There appeared to be no hidden bindings, no touch-triggered fireballs. She tapped into her new senses, examining the timeline to see what might happen if she touched the staff. Nothing bad, so far as she could see.

She settled her hand around the warm metal, and it thrummed in her grasp.

"Ah, another wielder at long last. I'm called Ikadra, by the way."

"Ikadra?" Voria asked. She cocked her head. "I think I've heard a myth about you."

"Well, I used to cruise around with some pretty legendary heroes, so I'm not surprised." The voice was smug now. If the staff could have preened, Voria was certain it would have. "If you'll head right this way, we can be off." A ball of scarlet flame shot from the staff's tip, zipping over to the only starship in the starport.

A sleek, black vessel that would have blended into any star field sat under the pool of light. She was a corvette class, designed for a dozen people or fewer, Voria guessed. Less than forty meters from bow to stern. A wicked spellcannon jutted from either wingtip, and the entire vessel reminded Voria of a swooping bird of prey with its wings outstretched.

"Before we can leave, I need to retrieve my companions. They are having audiences with Neith," Voria explained. She started back toward the double doors she'd arrived from, using Ikadra as a walking staff. "So, I'm afraid I must be rather indelicate. I'm a military commander, and I'm used to orders being followed. Are you normally this chatty?"

"No," Ikadra said forlornly. "Most of the time it's *don't speak unless spoken to*, unless I'm warning you of a threat. I have additional latitude right now since I'm supposed to instruct you about a whole bunch of boring stuff. You don't have to worry about my constant, awesome commentary after that. I mean, unless you want to remove that particular limitation?"

"No, I think I'll leave that bit in place for now." Voria stopped in front of the doors. She shook her head in wonder. "I'm still waiting for the dragon dung to drop, so to speak. We haven't been attacked in two full days, and we're actually receiving resources to fight with. I feel like someone's made an awful mistake, and they're going to correct it any moment."

The staff was blessedly silent and Voria relaxed a hair. She took long deep breaths, considering how best to proceed. She wanted a ready solution when Aran and the others arrived, so they could get out of here, get back to Shaya, and deal with Nebiat.

The doors finally swung open. Voria stepped out of their path, watching the darkness as footsteps approached. Aran emerged a moment later, encased in spellarmor and holding a naked spellblade. His armor had changed again—grown larger and sleeker. The armor's alloy had gone from a deep grey to a dark, angry crimson.

"Are the others here yet?" Aran asked in a subdued

voice. He placed his spellblade in a void pocket, then removed his helmet. The doors closed silently behind him.

"Not yet, but you arrived only moments after I did. I doubt it will be long before the others join us. Which gives us our last moment of real privacy."

"And you want to talk to me about falling into line?" Aran asked. Whatever awe he felt for Neith had been replaced by amusement.

"Quite the contrary. I want you to do more questioning," Voria countered. She stroked Ikadra's runes with her thumb. "Thalas was a blowhard, but he was a competent first officer. I don't know where we're going to end up, or even if we'll continue to be affiliated with the Confederate Marines. I hope so. But either way, I need a strong first. That might have been Davidson, but he's back on Shaya, or already shipped off to someone else."

"I'll follow your orders, but I won't do it unquestioningly." Aran spoke with a quiet confidence. "I'll try not to be an ass about it, but, especially after learning about my past, I'm not going to take anything lying down any more. The Confederacy—you—screwed me. The reasons make sense, but that doesn't change the facts. I'm not just some Marine. I'm an Outrider."

"That's exactly the tenacity we will need, I think." Voria smiled at his determination and candor—at his growth, really. The Tabula Rasa had been replaced with a strong, confident war mage. "We are both of us tools, Aran. Tools with complimentary purposes. If we work together, I don't know that anything can stop us. Not even the Krox."

Aran offered her a hand, and Voria shook it. He cleared his throat. "I blamed you for a lot initially, but I get that it isn't your fault now. I'm sorry if I was a little...assholish."

"Thalas did not set the bar very high." She laughed and

pointed to the starport. "I know you want to wait for Nara, but I think you'll approve of the transportation Neith has provided."

"I'd wondered if they were going to give us a ship." Aran's spellarmor rose from the deck and he peered into the area where the ship was parked.

The doors opened again, and Nara drifted slowly up the stairs. Her staff was clutched in her armored hand, the end now pulsing as fire rubies slowly orbited the tip. She glided to a halt next to Voria, and stowed her staff in a void pocket.

Nara slowly removed her helm, and her dark hair spilled out. "Now that was a...fascinating experience."

"Agreed." Voria brushed a few stray strands of hair from her face. "We'll have plenty of time to discuss it on the ship, but the sooner we get underway, the better."

"Ship? The *Talon* isn't the ship. She's just a shuttle, to get us to the ship," Ikadra said. Aran's blade snapped into a guard position, while Nara merely gawked at the staff. "Oh, uh, sorry. I thought Voria was going to introduce us."

Voria cleared her throat, and held up the staff for their inspection. "This is Ikadra, a guide left for us by Neith. He's yet to explain what he is a guide to."

"I was just doing that," the staff explained jubilantly. "I'm supposed to guide you to the real ship. As in the first spellship. I act as a super charismatic key."

"Where is this spellship?" Voria demanded.

"Why not store the spellship here?" Aran asked, right on the heels of her own question.

"I don't know where it's stored, but it isn't stored here, because that would bring too much risk. If this world were discovered we couldn't have both the key and the vessel fall into the hands of our enemies."

The door opened again, and Crewes strode through with

his helmet tucked under one arm. He wore the largest smile —and one of the only smiles—Voria had ever seen on the man. "That hairy, eight-legged dragon ain't half bad. So what did I miss?"

"We're about to board the vessel left for us." Voria's glee faded. "Once we take off Khalahk will almost certainly attack us. But I may have a plan." She started striding toward the ship.

"Wait!" Nara called. She pointed back at the door. "Pickus, remember? He hasn't come out yet."

"Oh, yeah," Crewes muttered. "The kid can fix things. We should keep him breathing."

The door opened a final time and Pickus came stumbling out, his mouth hanging open. He stared wide-eyed around him, then thrust a hand into the air. "Check. This. Out!"

His fist burst into flames.

"Excellent," Voria said. "Another fire mage. Nara, will you take charge of his training?"

"I'd be happy to." Nara perked up, and Voria smiled.

Being a commander, as it turned out, involved more empathy and trust than she'd have guessed.

43

VANISH

Aran turned around slowly in wonder, drinking in the interior of a vessel older than the Confederacy, or Ternus. "This thing is amazing."

The spellship didn't resemble any vessel he'd flown on. The walls were sloped, golden metal, with tall, arched hallways that easily accommodated spellarmor.

Several rooms radiated off the main entryway where they stood, and a ramp sloped up toward what Aran guessed must be the battle bridge.

"These rooms are larger on the inside." Nara's head poked out from one of the rooms. "Like a void pocket. They're incredibly spacious. They even come with a full reference library! This place is a palace."

Aran started for the room, but Voria raised a hand to block him. "Wait. I realize we are all eager to explore, but could I see you all on the bridge first?"

Aran headed that direction, and the others fell into line behind him. He didn't mind following orders, but mostly he wanted to see the *Talon*'s battle bridge.

He paused at the top of the ramp, a grin spreading across

his face as he moved immediately to the the command matrix. A black, contoured chair floated within, and would allow the pilot to touch any part of the rings without needing to stand. The pilot could be comfortable for hours, without ever needing to duck out and sit while another mage took a standing shift.

Two other matrices sat at the corners of the room, each identical to the command matrix.

"Which is offensive, and which is defensive?" he asked.

"I can't distinguish any differences between the matrices. Ikadra?" Voria looked at her staff.

It spoke in a warm pleasant voice. "The matrices are interchangeable. The practice of segregating them was introduced as a cost-saving measure, long after this vessel was constructed, but before Shaya died."

"How long is that?" Aran asked.

"Many millennia," Voria supplied impatiently. "So any mage can cast a spell from any matrix?"

"Yes, and the ship also possesses a fourth matrix: me." Ikadra's sapphire flared. "You may cast spells directly through me, and I will funnel them through the appropriate spellcannon."

"Four pilots? That's a pretty hefty tactical advantage, especially on a ship this small." Aran slid into the command matrix and sat in the floating chair. It flowed around his body, the contours adjusting to fit his posture. "We could have two dedicated offensive casters, a counterspeller, and a pilot."

"And that's going to form the foundation of our defense." Voria moved to stand before a floating scry-screen comprised of clear magical energy. She waved a hand before it, and the scry-screen flared to life. Right now it showed the sky above, empty black.

"Strategy? Does that mean you have a plan to deal with Khalahk?" Aran asked slowly. He'd been chewing on the problem himself, without a lot of success. Even a pre-godswar spellship might not be enough to deal with a Wyrm as old as Khalahk.

Nara had moved to the second matrix, and climbed cautiously into the chair. Crewes watched her do it, and only moved to the last matrix after she seemed comfortable.

"Man I hate this piloting shit. We gotta get someone better for the last spot." He climbed in, his comically large armor spilling over the sides of the chair. "At least this thing will hold me in my armor."

"Yes, I do have a plan. We're going to leave the planet, very openly," Voria said. "The dragon will, in all likelihood, attack us immediately. It has no idea what this vessel is capable of, and we don't really either—which means we don't know how we'll fare in the first confrontation." She turned from the viewscreen, touching Aran's gaze, then the others. "This fight still doesn't favor us. First, let's compile our resources. Ikadra, what's the highest level spell this ship can cast?"

"Up to ninth-level spells," Ikadra supplied happily. "Is there a specific spell you have in mind?"

"Possibly. Ikadra, can *you* cast spells?" Voria asked.

"A few. I can only cast the spells stored in me by the last owner. Would you like a list?"

"Yes."

"Icy Storm of Death, Disintegrate Shit, Impervious Bubble of Coolness—"

"You named these spells, didn't you?" Voria put a hand to her temple. "We're given the key to the most powerful ship in the galaxy, and it has the mind of an eight-year-old. Do any of the spells involve poop?" She sighed. "Continue."

"Vanish, and a ninth-level counterspell," Ikadra finished.

"What does Vanish do?" Aran asked.

"We fade from one location, and appear in another. When we reappear, it will be under the effects of a hardened invisibility."

"Which will work against the dragon?" Nara asked. "I'm not familiar with the term *hardened* as it pertains to a spell."

"Hardening increases the magical resonance, allowing it to defeat most counterspells or defensive responses," Voria said. "In this case, yes, it means the dragon will not be able to see us. We can use that spell, and escape toward Shaya."

"He'll be waiting for us when we arrive. That thing is still faster than us, even in the *Talon*," Aran pointed out. He reached out for the spelldrive, syncing with it. The ship thrummed eagerly, a living thing, just like his spellblade. "I can feel the limits. For its size, this thing is insanely fast, but Wyrms are faster than every spellship I've ever heard of."

"That's fine." Voria gave a grim smile. "It will take three days to reach our exit point. By the time we arrive, we'll have a plan."

"This assumes we can get the past the dragon in the first place. Are we ready to take off?"

"Do it," Voria ordered.

"On it." Aran smiled slowly as he tapped the initiation sequence. The corvette drew a sliver of *void* from his chest, then rose slowly into the air. "Okay, here goes."

He poured power into the ship, and she shot from the starport, into the sky. The speed was incredible, but there was no increased g-force as they accelerated toward orbit. "This thing's internal dampeners are phenomenal."

"The excess gravity is channeled into additional velocity," Ikadra explained.

They'd nearly reached orbit when a dark shape

appeared on the horizon. Wings unfurled as the dragon sped in their direction. The scry-screen tracked its progress, and the thing was growing larger at an alarming rate.

Aran's eyes narrowed, and he guided the ship into a steep climb. "It's on us in fifteen seconds."

"I want erratic flying as soon as it fires the first lightning bolt. I'll counter it." Voria moved to the scry-screen, pacing back and forth before it. "Crewes, cast a fire bolt when the dragon is within range."

The dragon closed, and finally loosed a lightning bolt. Aran jerked the ship out of its path, but the bolt adjusted to track their flight. Voria tapped a *spirit* sigil, then an *earth*. A dark brown counterspell shot from the spellcannon under the main body, slicing the lightning bolt in two. The energies were then sucked toward the counterspell, completely negated as the whole ball popped out of existence.

A moment later, a scarlet fire bolt shot from the side cannon, then a void bolt from the left cannon.

"Improvisation. I approve, Lieutenant."

Aran smiled, unsurprised that she realized he'd been the one to add the void bolt. Both spells streaked toward the dragon. It dodged the fire bolt, but the void bolt slammed into its side. The creature shrieked silently as scales on its rear leg disintegrated, exposing muscle underneath.

"I'd say that's pissed it off sufficiently. Ikadra, if you'd kindly cast your stored vanish spell, we'd be grateful." The staff began to glow around the tip, and waves of pink-and-white energy flowed through it, into the floor. All three spellcannons exuded dark, violet light, and the perspective on the scry-screen jumped suddenly.

"How far did it move us?" Aran asked, scanning the space around the ship.

"About twenty kilometers. Enough to avoid any response from the Wyrm." Ikadra sounded pleased with himself.

Aran found himself liking the staff. He bet it would get along great with Bord. He spun his matrix to face Voria. "Well, that went a heck of a lot better than the last time."

"That it did." She smiled warmly. "And we did it without revealing any of our other resources. The Wyrm isn't even aware of Nara yet. We've bought ourselves a few days, and by that time we'll know what this vessel can do. Well done, all."

"What will we do now?" Nara asked. "I mean how will we prepare?"

Aran stifled a yawn. "First, I'm going to get a good night's sleep."

"He's right," Voria said. "We can convene in the morning to discuss tactics. Why don't we enjoy some well-earned rest? I doubt the coming days will allow for much sleep."

44

FINAL PREP

Nara combed her fingers through her hair, then tugged it into a tangled ponytail.

Good enough.

She resisted the urge to bring her staff, because she knew she was only carrying it around so much as a sort of *look at me* aimed at the rest of the crew. She was proud of being a true mage, but there was no need to rub it in everyone else's faces.

She headed up into the mess—a spacious dining chamber with a quartet of tables, each large enough to seat six. Aran, Crewes, and Voria sat together chatting in wide, comfortable chairs.

"What is that amazing smell?" Nara asked, as she entered the room.

"It's whatever you want it to be. See that golden disk over there?" Aran pointed with a drumstick. "It's a food conjurer. You can make whatever you want. We might be dead in a couple days, but at least we'll die happy."

"Give me a slice of Shayan layer cake," Nara ordered.

The disk flashed, and her cake appeared. "This is incredible."

"And it breaks several laws of physics," Pickus said, entering behind Nara. "But this thing can make chicken wings, so I don't really care."

"Nara," Voria said, "would you please join us?"

Nara brought the cake to the table and sat next to Aran. "Did you finish hashing out the plan to deal with the Wyrm?"

"We have, but what I want to discuss is what happens when we reach Shaya." Voria's face went hard. The major was back. "I won't require anyone to speak about their experience with Neith, but I am willing to relate part of my own encounter. Neith gave me the ability to see possibilities the same way gods do. I've been studying this ability in my quarters. Using it, I believe I have discovered Nebiat's plan—or the shape of it, at least."

Voria planted her palms on the table. She eyed them all to make sure they were paying attention. "Nebiat is going to kill Tender Aurelia."

"How the depths is she gonna do that?" Crewes asked. "The Tender can summon her royal guard. Those guys scare me the way I scare Bord. I don't care how good that scaly bitch is, she can't deal with the Tender *and* her guards. They got spellfighters. Lots of 'em. Even dragons don't like fighters."

"What if her guards were called away by someone they trusted implicitly?" Voria countered. "Sent away to deal with a threat to Shaya, led by a talented military strategist...like my father."

"Are you saying...she's bound Dirk?" Nara asked, setting down her cake. Her appetite was ashes.

"That's brilliant and ruthless." Aran clenched a fist.

"Send us away, so we can't interfere. Arrange our buddy Khal to make sure we don't make it back. Bind Dirk, and use him to respond to a fake emergency, then assassinate the Tender. She leaves Shaya in chaos, without ever facing us directly."

"You begin to see why I'm terrified—only there's one part of her plan you are mistaken about. It's not a fake emergency my father is being dispatched to deal with." Voria's scowl deepened. "She plans to use my father to detonate one of Shaya's dead limbs. The second burl, which contains Caretaker Ducius's manor. It will look like my father murdered a full Caretaker in a fit of rage."

"And possibly start a war in the process," Nara murmured as her mind flew through the implications. "If that limb detonates, it will crush the drifter city underneath."

"Turning my father from a hero into a pariah, on the same day the Tender is assassinated. And, if her plan works, Ducius will die, too. We'd lose our entire leadership caste in an afternoon, and it would take years to recover." Voria eyed them all soberly. "Even if we did recover, we'd be without a guardian for the first time in centuries. Can you think of a better time for the Krox to invade?"

"Or to invade Ternus," Pickus pointed out. "If they know Shaya can't help, they could focus on us. We wouldn't last a year."

"Nara, knowing our capabilities, how would you choose to address this issue?" Voria asked.

Nara blinked a few times. She licked her lips, and gathered her thoughts. "Which issue is paramount, saving the Tender, or saving your father?"

"That isn't the choice." The lines around Voria's eyes tightened. "The choice is save the Tender, or save the dims.

If my father can be saved, we will do so. But not at the expense of the drifters. Tensions are high enough as it is. This could cause a civil war, as you said. We cannot allow that."

"Okay. The drifter city, or the Tender. So which is the priority?" Nara pressed. She didn't want to be callous, but they were going to have to make an unenviable choice.

"Saving the drifters. If the Tender is killed, a new guardian can be declared," Voria finally said. "The damage of losing a limb from Shaya herself will do catastrophic damage to our society."

Nara considered that. "Then I'd send you and Ikadra to help Aurelia. Ikadra has several spells that could kill or hinder Nebiat, which means you could make the difference in a duel between her and Aurelia. I'd send the rest of us to stop Dirk. We have a full team, and should be able to overcome Dirk."

"Aran?" Voria asked.

Nara glanced his way. His beard had thickened, but at some point Aran had found time to trim it. It fit him, and it matched the authoritative weight to his gaze. Something significant had changed, something to do with Neith, but Nara hadn't pressed him about it.

"I'd agree with Nara's assessment. We can't ignore the threat to the Tender, but odds are good we're going to see some serious combat if Dirk is involved. We'll need to bring our A game, and that means we can't afford to send anyone else with you to help Aurelia." Aran leaned back in his chair. "Crewes?"

"Shit, man, I don't care. Let the major decide. And yeah, I know the Confederacy thinks she's a captain. That's bullshit. She's the godsdamned major. She earned that rank." Crewes thumped the table for emphasis. He shook his head suddenly, giving a half-laugh. "This *share my feelings* crap about the mission is lame. We need to ditch it, and get back to a proper chain of command. You give orders, and we follow."

"He's not wrong," Aran added. He looked to Nara, then Voria. "In order to even reach Shaya, we've got a Wyrm to kill. Let's cover the plan one more time, then get to our stations."

45

KHALAHK

Aran buckled himself into the command chair, then took a deep breath. The matrix rings rotated slowly around him, giving up their steady *whum whum*. He grounded himself in that bit of normalcy. There was so much to take in, so many disjointed memories. Neith hadn't given him everything.

In fact, Neith hadn't given him back much at all. His combat abilities, sure. All that training, every memory, had been returned. But his childhood? His parents? His favorite food? All absent. He needed time to process, but now wasn't that time.

Aran compartmentalized his emotions. Duty first.

He nodded respectfully at the major. "I can bring the drive online any time, sir."

"True Mage Nara, please open a Fissure." Voria stood not far from the scry-screen with Ikadra cradled in one hand. The sapphire had dimmed, and the staff hadn't spoken since they'd escaped Khalahk. "Lieutenant Aran, warm up the drive. Sergeant, what is that colorful phrase

Corporal Kezia used back at Starn? The one when you killed the enforcer that nearly killed her."

"Uh, blast the shit out of 'em, sir," Crewes supplied.

"Yes, well, if the dragon appears...blast the shit out of 'em." The major gave a half-smile.

Aran allowed himself to share it. The mood couldn't have been more different than their first confrontation with the Wyrm. Then, they'd been in a crappy little frigate. Now? They had a full godswar-era spellship, one of only a few hundred in the entire sector. That ship was crewed by four talented mages, all of whom had learned to work well together.

Nara gracefully tapped sigils, and the familiar crack split the sky. Aran guided them smoothly through, into the smattering of asteroids around the edge of the ring. The Fissure snapped shut in their wake, and he flew deeper into the asteroid field.

"Steady yourselves," Voria called, tapping her staff against the deck. "The strike will come soon." Aran noted a glazed look in her eyes, and cocked his head as he studied her. She was utilizing an unfamiliar magic, something with bits of *fire* and *dream* in it. "Now!"

Aran responded instinctively, jerking the ship down into a steep dive. A blue-white lightning bolt shot through the space they'd occupied, obliterating an asteroid in a shower of rubble. His heart quickened as he twisted the ship around the largest chunk, shielding them temporarily.

Crewes grunted as waves of fire poured from his hands into the rings. He fired a third-level magma ball as the Wyrm came around the asteroid into view. Hunks of smoldering stone shot from all three cannons, peppering Khalahk's scaly face with flaming rock. The dragon roared, squinting as a rock caught it in the eye.

Aran dove, taking the ship deeper into the asteroids. It was nimble and considerably smaller than the *Hunter*. The battleship was easily five hundred meters long; this thing was only forty meters from end to end, about twice the size of the spellfighter he'd recently piloted.

Khalakh tore through rocks, following them just as Kheftut had back at Marid. This time, though, they had a lot more firepower. Aran flipped the ship, angling all three spellcannons at the dragon.

"Fire!" Voria roared.

Aran tapped *void*, then *fire*, then *void* again. He poured the energy into the ship. Crewes added more *fire*. Voria added both *fire* and *void*. Finally, Nara completed the disintegrate with a substantial chunk of both *fire* and *void*.

The bolt shot from the central cannon, dissolving an asteroid as it shot toward Khalahk. The Wyrm twisted to avoid the spell, nearly dodging it entirely. Instead, the bolt caught a leathery section of his right wing, dissolving a huge swath of scales and flesh.

It would have hindered the Wyrm in an atmosphere, but meant nothing out here in the void.

"Nara," Voria barked, "blink us."

Nara tapped a flurry of sigils, and the ship winked out of existence. They reappeared a kilometer away, in a relatively empty patch between asteroids. Aran adjusted course, drifting slowly over an asteroid as he sought a visual on Khalahk.

"There he is," Aran growled. "Major, permission to modify the plan."

"Sell me on it, and do it fast, Lieutenant." Voria kept her attention focused on the scry-screen. The Wyrm had spotted them, and had already started in their direction.

"I need Nara to make several illusions of us. I've seen her

use that spell on Crewes back aboard the *Hunter*." Aran willed the ship to drop below the asteroid, then flipped it around and dove deeper into the field. The scry-screen still showed the Wyrm in full pursuit. "We let the Wyrm catch up to us in the densest patch of asteroids, and we engage. We're unlikely to land a disintegrate, but if we use fire and void bolts, almost all of us can contribute shots."

Nara perked up in her matrix, swinging the chair around to face him. "I think I see where you're going with this. A bunch of illusions make passes at the dragon. It doesn't know which ones are real, so it can't dodge or counter them all."

"Exactly. Some of the bolts will get through, and we can wear that thing down." Aran turned to the major. "Sir?"

She nodded. "Do it."

Nara's fingers flew across the sigils again, moving with a grace and speed not even the major could match. She'd grown during her time on Shaya—but it was more than that. Aran didn't know what Neith had done, but Nara had been enhanced in some way.

Six copies of the ship appeared, each zipping out in a different direction. Khalahk came over an asteroid near one of the ships, and belched a lightning bolt. It crackled through the space the illusion occupied, shattering it into mana shards.

"Light it up," Aran roared. He took control of the central cannon, firing a flurry of level-two void bolts as he guided the ship into an attack run.

Nara fired from the second cannon, and Crewes from the third. Fire and void bolts streaked into the dragon, and the spells were mirrored five more times from the surviving illusions. The Wyrm pulled its wings up protectively, diving suddenly to avoid as many spells as it could.

Real bolts peppered its wounded wing, and a lucky void bolt carved a furrow just over the Wyrm's eye. It bellowed silently, then raised a claw and began to sketch a spell.

"My turn, you scaly bastard." Voria raised Ikadra, and a wave of power pulsed from her, followed by one from the staff. The energies sank into the deck, and the central cannon fired a counterspell far more quickly than the *Hunter* could have managed.

A bolt of pure white streaked into the sigils gathering around Khalahk's claw. Those energies shattered, spraying mana shards into space. The dragon gave a frustrated roar, but Aran had already guided them around an asteroid and out of sight.

"Excellent piloting, Lieutenant," Voria said. "Bring us around for another pass."

Aran gave a grim smile as he brought the ship around. They came up under an asteroid, streaking toward the Wyrm. This time, the creature dove directly at them, ignoring the illusions.

"We've been detected." A bolt of lightning slammed into the side of the ship, and it shuddered. "I can feel the damage. The wards blunted that, but we don't want to take another one of those if we can avoid it."

Crewes and Nara poured destructive energies into their respective cannons, and a stream of void and fire bolts drove Khalahk into cover behind a city-sized asteroid.

"Nara," Aran asked, thinking aloud, "can you ready a blink?"

"What do you have in mind?" Her finger hovered over a *void* sigil.

"I'm going to take us to the side of the asteroid where Khalahk is hiding. You blink us around it, so we're in range to fire, and we're doing it from an unexpected angle." Aran flew toward the asteroid he had in mind. "Switch to a disintegrate."

"That will utilize a significant chunk of our resources," Voria cautioned.

"Sure, but so will pass after pass of void bolts," he countered. "Let's end this, fast. If we continue the same tactic, the dragon will adjust to match. We need to keep it guessing."

"Ready," Nara called. "Just give me the word."

Aran guided the ship toward the asteroid, coming around fast. He knew Khalahk was aware of them, likely preparing to breathe at the exact area where they'd appear.

"*Now!*" Aran roared.

Nara cast the blink, and the ship's location shifted. They appeared on the exact opposite side of the asteroid, coming at the dragon from the rear instead of the front. Khalahk was already pivoting to face them, twisting in midair.

"Too late there, stain," Crewes barked, with a laugh.

Aran poured as much *void* and *fire* as he could into his matrix, and the others added their power to the choir. All three cannons fired, and the bolts converged on the dragon's chest. Scales, flesh, and bone dissolved into atoms.

The disintegrate punched out the other side, coring a hole through the dragon.

It twisted and thrashed several times, hot blood freezing into crystal droplets as they sprayed away from the Wyrm in a glittering scarlet fan.

The light left Khalahk's eyes, and the Wyrm's corpse began to drift.

Aran threw up a fist and roared a cheer. The rest of the crew took it up.

He grinned at the major. "Time to deal with Nebiat."

46

INTO THE TREE

The *Talon* broke through the asteroid field, and into Shaya's upper atmosphere. The re-entry didn't trouble the ship, and Aran couldn't even feel the friction. A single jewel glittered in the sky above the tree, the Tender's palace catching the setting sun.

"Ikadra, can you get me from here to the palace?" Voria asked. The glazed look hadn't faded from her eyes, and Aran wondered what it was exactly that she saw when she looked at reality.

"Of course. I can teleport us directly outside the palace, though the wards prevent me from entering the structure." The staff pulsed with eagerness. "Shall I?"

"Not yet. Aran, you understand what you need to do?" The major looked at him, but Aran wasn't really sure she saw him.

"Near enough. I need to find Dirk, and stop him from detonating the second burl."

"And how do you plan to do that?" Voria asked.

"I'm going to start with Erika. She knows Dirk, and

might be up to speed on his whereabouts." Aran waited for the inevitable protest, and wasn't disappointed.

"You believe she'll give you that information?" Voria cocked her head in confusion. "You remember she's been bound, yes?"

Aran tapped a *fire* sigil as he guided the ship lower into the atmosphere. "Erika doesn't know we know that. She could try misdirecting us, but if she's following Nebiat's orders I'm betting she can't risk us going to help Aurelia."

"So she'll tell us where Dirk is, then ambush us when we show up," Nara interjected.

"Theoretically," Aran offered. It wasn't the best plan, but when you were out of time, you had to improvise.

"It's as good a plan as any." Voria looked to each of them in turn, a proud smile growing. "There's a very real chance some or all of us are about to die. If that happens...I've never served with a finer crew."

"At least we'll die well." Crewes gave a whoop. "Give Nebiat hells, Major. I still owe that bitch for Marid, so please bring her my very warmest regards."

"I'll send your best, Sergeant." Voria walked to Nara's matrix, and leaned close to the rings. "I'm leaving them in your care, True Mage. Bring them home safe, if you can."

"I'll do my best," Nara offered. "That's a lot better than it was back on Marid."

"It will be enough," Aran said. "And if it isn't then we'll make them damned sure they respect us on our way out." He meant that, and it felt good. He was ready to die, if it came to it. Seeing Neith's mind had crystalized things for him. This war was bigger than all of them.

"Luck to you all. Ikadra, take me to the palace." Voria disappeared almost instantly, with an audible *pop*.

"Okay, guess that's our cue." Aran tapped a *fire* sigil, then a *dream*. He triggered a missive to Erika, waiting patiently for the spell to locate her. The edge of the scry-screen flared red, and her face appeared.

Aran didn't recognize the room behind her; beyond the fact that it was shayawood, it had no distinguishing features. It could be anywhere, which was probably by design. There was nothing about Erika to suggest she was anything other than a friendly mentor, her smile as genuine as they came.

"I'm pleased to see that you survived the Umbral Depths, but now isn't a good time, Aran. What do you want?" she asked. Her demeanor was perfect.

"I've received a tip about Dirk," he said, suddenly cautious. "I'm told he's going to destroy the second burl, along with Ducius's entire compound." He mentioned nothing about Nebiat, or binding.

"Where did you hear that?" Erika eyed him intensely.

"Does it matter?" He countered.

"I suppose not," she gave back smoothly. Too smoothly. Her first slip. "He's made his move on the burl, and I've sent Ree to stop him. Ducius has been evacuated, along with his family. Ree's got a full squadron of war mages. Dirk is good, but no one is that good. I know you're close to Voria. You can reassure the captain we'll do our utmost to spare her father's life, but also make it clear we make no promises."

"Of course. Thanks, Master Erika. I'll be in touch." Aran killed the spell, and the scry-screen returned to a view of Shaya's trunk. They'd nearly reached the second burl.

"We ready to engage, sir?" Crewes asked.

"Not yet, I have one more missive to send." Aran tapped *fire* and *dream* again, triggering another spell.

The edge of the screen turned red, and Kezia's face filled the view. "Aran! You survived the Umbral Depths. I'm so glad to see you alive." She turned from the screen, and yelled over her shoulder. "Hey, Bord. They're back! Aran's on the scry-screen."

"Kezia, I need you to listen very carefully." Aran licked his lips. "Look up, out your window. See that burl?"

"Yeah, keeps the sun off the little ones for most of the day. What of it?" Kezia asked, blinking wide blue eyes.

"Nebiat is here. She's bound Voria's father, and he's trying to detonate it."

"If that thing comes down..." She shivered. "What do you need me to do?"

"Get people out, as many as possible. We're going to try to stop Dirk, but we have no idea if we can even get there in time." Aran guided the ship to a smooth landing beside several other ships, at the edge of Ducius's compound.

"We'll do what we can. Shaya watch over you, sir." She gave a quick salute, then the connection terminated.

Aran leapt from the command matrix, sprinting down into the cargo room. The rest of the crew followed, and found Pickus already down there.

"I know I don't have a suit of your fancy armor, but I want to help. I can fire a spellrifle, at least." He held up a rifle he'd apparently taken from the armory. Aran made a mental note to catalogue the contents of that armory, at the first opportunity. He couldn't believe he'd forgotten to do that on their voyage home.

"Have you ever fired *any* type of rifle?" Crewes demanded as he hastily donned his armor.

"Uh, well, no. But how hard can it be? You point it at something, and shoot, right?" Pickus protested. He pushed his mop of hair out of his eyes. "Nara does it."

Aran winced.

"Nara does it?" Nara's eyebrows knit together and she loomed dangerously over Pickus.

"Nara is a seasoned Marine," Aran shot back. He took a breath. Pickus might not realize how he'd insulted her, though her cold stare was a big clue. "She's fought Krox enforcers, walking corpses, and full Wyrms."

Pickus deflated. "So what can I do? I don't want to just sit here and watch holos."

"Hang out near the command matrix," Aran instructed. "If we can't stop Dirk our parking space is going to detonate. If that happens, I need you to be ready to pilot. There's a manual up there that will walk you through the basics."

"A manual you say?" Pickus perked up a bit. "A thick one?"

"It's like seven hundred pages. Get to work, fire mage!" Aran thrust a finger toward the bridge, and Pickus sprinted out of sight.

"You're not really going to trust him with piloting the spellship, are you?" Nara asked. Some of the fire had left her gaze, but Aran could still feel the anger radiating off her.

"Of course not. If we get into trouble we'll 'port back up here, but I want to keep him out of trouble, and I think this will keep him busy." Aran sketched a *void* sigil and slid into his armor. "Now let's get out there and stop this."

The ramp lowered and Aran burst out into the Shayan sky. Nara followed, then Crewes. The sergeant's armor was a lot less maneuverable, but what he lacked in finesse he made up for in power.

"Halt!" Boomed a voice from the far side of the parking area.

Aran spun his armor to see two suits of golden Mark X spellarmor, both raising spellrifles in his direction. He landed and made no move to reach into his void pocket. "Calm down. We're on the same side. I know you have to recognize us. We were just at the Tender's palace the other day."

"So was Dirk, but he's gone renegade. Until we have proof you aren't bound, you're going to step out of that armor and sit very quietly." The woman called confidently.

"Yeah, that's not going to happen." Aran reached into his void pocket and yanked out his rifle. The woman in the golden armor fired, but Aran stepped nimbly out of the path of the spell. It came easily. Effortlessly. His armor moved with a grace that could only be the result of Neith's augmentation.

Aran kept the barrel of his spellrifle pointed at the ground. "I'm going to give you one chance. You're standing between us and a battle that will result in the entire second burl crushing the city below. Now we've just returned from a trip into the Umbral Depths where we met a living god. You really want to test yourselves against us?"

"Bet it'll be an interesting fight," Crewes called. He raised his spellcannon, resting the fat barrel on the shoulder of his spellarmor. "I've always wanted to kick some Shayan noble ass. Since I never really got to punch Thalas, I'm happy to punch you two stains instead. You wanna dance?"

The leader hesitated, then lowered her rifle. Aran released the breath he hadn't known he'd been holding.

"If you get past us you come up behind our strike team. If you're working with Dirk, that could guarantee we lose. So convince me. Why should we let you past? I'm willing to listen." The woman asked rigidly.

"All right. We returned with Major Voria, and she's been touched by a god. That god showed her that the Tender would be attacked by a Krox dreadlord. You've heard of Nebiat?"

"Every Shayan has," the woman breathed. "Nebiat is the

very worst the Krox can bring to bear. She slaughtered my men at Vakera."

"She's going to take a shot at the Tender. We've sent help, but I have a feeling more would be a really, really good idea." Aran started walking slowly toward the jagged hole in Shaya's trunk. "If you're not going to go help her, then at least come with us. You want to walk behind us with your weapons out? Great. You'll see which side we're on soon enough."

"The Tender is in danger?" the woman choked out. She turned to her companion. "We have to gather the Caretakers. She cannot be harmed."

"What about Shaya? What about our post?" the man in the other set of armor asked. "Even if you trust this...human, what about honor?"

"Honor be damned," she cursed. "We're going to save the Tender, or die in the attempt. 'Aran,' you said your name was? I'm going to trust you. I hope I'm not a terrible judge of character."

She turned and sprinted toward a spellfighter. After a moment her companion turned and ran for another.

"Aww." Crewes thumped his fists together. "I was looking forward to a good scrap."

"I have a feeling we're about to get one." Aran lifted off and guided his spellarmor inside the corpse of a goddess.

47

NEW FRIENDS

Nara's heart thundered as the adrenaline surged through her. She piloted her spellarmor after Aran into Shaya's musky interior, gazing around in wonder. It wasn't much different than the inside of a redwood tree, just on a massive scale. Sap ran thickly down the walls of the smooth tunnel, the tree's attempt to seal the wound.

They flew through the tunnel Dirk had bored into the goddess, through the thick bark, and into a soft, golden wood. Their path took them down at an angle so steep anyone without a suit of spellarmor wouldn't have been able to make the climb.

Spells flashed ahead, dozens of them.

"Nara, can you get us under cover?" Aran asked confidently. He'd definitely settled back into the officer role, especially after whatever Neith had done to him. The lingering doubts he always seemed to carry were simply...gone. Like he'd been made whole somehow.

Nara sketched a *dream* sigil, then an *air*. She added another, and another, humming softly as she completed the illusion. Not so long ago she'd needed a potion to cast a sphere of invisibility.

The illusion rippled outward, enveloping Aran and Crewes. The instant the spell completed, Aran dropped slowly down the tunnel. Nara followed closely to ensure he didn't get out of range. Having him suddenly appear in the middle of a firefight because he left the spell's radius would probably ruin their whole day.

The tunnel leveled out, and they finally got a look at the combat. Several war mages had been pinned down behind thick chunks of wood. They were trying to make it deeper into the tree, but several Krox enforcers were firing spirit bolts at any war mage who left cover.

"I recognize their leader," Aran called. He pointed at a suit of silver Mark IX armor. "That's Reekala, one of the war mage instructors from Erika's kamiza."

"Can you reason with her?" Nara asked dubiously. Her mistrust of Shayan nobles only grew over time. They'd yet to meet one who wasn't a total ass. Even the major came with a healthy dose of insufferability.

"Probably not," Aran admitted. "Not quickly anyway. I doubt the Krox have access to pierce invisibility though. The best way to get Ree to trust us is to start dropping Krox."

"Well we do want to make friends." Nara started counting opponents, and considering possible spells. "If we save her ass I'm going to have to rub it in her face. Just warning her up front."

"She'd deserve it after the way she treated you. Let's give it a shot. We'll fly over them and Crewes and I will exit the sphere and begin our assault. Nara, get into cover and see if you can drop a couple of these guys without exposing yourself." Aran didn't wait for confirmation, instead zooming from the invisibility sphere as they neared the Krox.

He fell on the enforcers like a comet, demonstrating a ferocity the made Nara glad he was on their side. He led with a level-three void bolt, which caught the first enforcer in the eye, killing it instantly. Then his blade was in his hand, larger and longer than the last time she'd seen him wield it.

The blade flared white as heat shimmered out from it. Then Aran's familiar void lightning crackled down the blade, adding to the destructive power. Aran leaped on the back of the next Krox, and buried the blade deep through its shoulder and into its chest. The creature's body went rigid, and smoke rose from its eyes as the magic cooked it from the inside.

Nara blinked. She remembered the first time they'd engaged enforcers. Not so long ago, they'd had Thalas, too, and the four of them had still struggled to overcome a pair of enforcers. Aran had just dropped that many in his opening attack. The way he flowed from attack to attack was beautiful and terrifying, and his speed was incredible now.

Crewes hit the other flank, shoving his cannon into an enforcer's face. "Hey there. How about some surprise magma?" Molten rock burst into the creature's face, and it shrieked as it tried to claw the burning magma from its face. Crewes shot it again, this time in the groin. The enforcer collapsed, not dead, but definitely incapacitated.

Another Krox had become aware of Crewes, and leapt at him, wings extended. Crewes fired his thruster, ramming his helmet into the Krox's face. Bone and scale met enchanted metal, and both lost. Crewes's helmet shattered, but so did the Krox's face.

"Want to see what a god gave me?" Crewes roared. "You're gonna love it. Trust me." He sucked in a deep breath, and exhaled a river of boiling white flame. It flowed into the

Krox's mouth, into its gullet. The creature shrieked, flapping weakly away as it released the sergeant. "That's what I thought, stain."

The last few enforcers leapt away, quickly retreating around a bend in the tunnel.

"Pursue?" Nara called.

"Not yet. Let's link up with Ree," Aran yelled back.

"Mongrel?" called a clear female voice. The set of Mark IX armor trotted forward, stopping near Aran's armor. "What in the depths are you doing here?"

"I've got bad news and worse news." Aran landed next to her, and raised his faceplate.

Something clenched in Nara when the woman glided up. Maybe it was the way she said his name, or the way he responded to it. There was something there, between them. It wasn't like she had any sort of claim to Aran, but the idea of him being with someone as arrogant and condescending as Ree twisted her guts into a knot.

The woman's faceplate came up, and sure enough, she possessed the same ethereal beauty the major did. Thick scarlet hair framed a perfect face, the kind that inspired statues. How did a normal woman compete with that?

"Tell me." Ree's mouth firmed, and her eyes tightened angrily.

Aran's eyes hardened. "The Tender is under attack by a Krox dreadlord. That's the bad news. The worse news? Erika has been bound."

A bolt of crackling energy, a mix of *air*, *void*, and *fire*, zipped over Aran's shoulder. It caught Ree directly in the chest, blasting a hole in her armor and hurling her into the wall behind her.

"Ree," Aran roared, then spun to face whoever had attacked them, his blade raised.

Nara didn't recognize the woman who'd attacked. Her hair was the same color as Voria's, but she looked older. Her late forties, though Nara had the impression the woman was both far older and far more powerful than she appeared.

"It's a pity you decided to show up, Aran. I truly regret having to kill you." The woman held a naked spellblade, but didn't wear spellarmor. Who was she, that she thought she could stand up to their entire company?

Aran's faceplate snapped shut. A moment later a video missive appeared in the corner of Nara's screen. "We're going to have a hard time taking her. Erika is a lot more powerful than she appears. Crewes, I want you to distract her while I get behind her. When she turns to face me, I'm hoping Ree and her friends will give us a hand. If not, I don't like our chances."

"Take your time," Erika called, boldly. "We can get started whenever you're ready."

48

IMPROVISATION

Aran jetted forward, the tip of his blade crackling with power as it flashed out at his mentor. He knew he'd never connect, but he also knew Erika would have no choice but to respond. If she were dealing with him, she couldn't attack Crewes or Nara.

The master hopped backward and flung a hand in his direction. A tendril of air wrapped around his leg, yanking the suit down.

He reached out with his gravity magic, struggling to maintain his altitude. Erika's magic pulled him lower, and in a few more seconds he'd be within her reach.

"You're outmatched," she taunted.

"Good thing I didn't come alone, huh?"

Crewes's shoulder impacted against Erika's back, launching her across the tunnel into the far wall. She slammed into it with a sharp crack, slumping to the ground. "This is the fancy bitch you been talking so much about? I am *not* impressed."

Erika flipped back to her feet, blood flowing freely from a gash in her forehead. She touched it with two fingers, then frowned and sprinted up the side of the wall, dodging a hail of life bolts from Ree and her war mages. She rolled from the wall into a slide, pulling a dagger from her boot sheath as she passed under Crewes. She slammed the slender weapon into the side of Crewes's knee, and green lightning played around the wound.

The sergeant gave a pained roar. "Still not impressed, bitch."

Crewes fired a napalm round into the ground ahead of Erika. It detonated spectacularly into a blanket of liquid flame and Erika slid through it. The fire clung to her like a living thing, but the flames did little more than singe her clothing. Her eyes narrowed, smoke rising in little plumes.

"You think you understand magic, tech mage?" Erika sketched a sigil and the dagger in Crewes's leg exploded. He was flung spinning into the wall, and when his body stopped moving Aran realized everything below the thigh was...gone. The spellarmor ended at a jagged, blackened stump.

Aran charged, leading with a quick flurry of strikes. He adopted Drakon stance, but this time...he understood it. Erika parried the first several blows, and Aran studied her movements, the same way she studied his.

"Interesting. You're showing improvisation. That shouldn't be possible, unless your mental block was somehow removed." Erika suddenly took the offensive, coming at him in Mantid stance. She launched a high strike, which he did nothing to defend himself against.

Her blade slid between the seam where his helmet met the chest. The weapon punched through his armor, continuing out his back. Only adrenaline kept the pain at bay long enough to respond.

Aran punched Erika in her unarmored gut. The suit

already enhanced his strength, but whatever Neith had done dramatically increased it, and he fueled it further with a burst of fire magic. His gauntlet cracked ribs and lifted Erika a meter into the air. He lunged forward with his face-plate, smashing it into the bridge of her nose. The helmet cracked, but Erika's nose shattered as she was flung backward.

Right into Ree. Ree launched a roundhouse that caught Erika in the back of the head, flinging her back in Aran's direction. He raised his blade, bringing it up in a powerful slash. Somehow Erika's foot landed on the blade, and she flipped away from them.

She landed in the midst of the war mages, her students. They eyed her uncertainly, either unwilling or unable to strike their master. Erika took full advantage of that. She snapped a tall woman's neck, snatching up her discarded spellblade. Erika carved through the rest of the war mages, dropping them with ruthless efficiency.

"No!" Ree screamed. She sprinted in Erika's direction, but the master didn't wait.

Erika leapt again, her air magic carrying her further up the corridor, and she sprinted off into the darkness, after the enforcers.

"Come on," Ree yelled over her shoulder, holding her side with one hand. Waves of warm energy flowed from her palm, into the wound, and Ree straightened with a relieved sigh. "We need to go after her. She's hurt, but if we give her time she'll use her life magic to repair the damage. We need to keep up the pressure."

"Sure thing, just let me pull the sword out of my frigging chest." Aran seized the hilt, yanking the weapon loose with a groan. He dropped it to the ground, staggering into the wall.

"I've got you." Nara was there suddenly. "Hang in there. You're losing blood."

Aran relaxed into her, thankful for the support. The adrenaline was quickly fading, bringing a tide of pain in its wake. Maybe letting Erika run him through hadn't been the smartest decision.

"Do you have any potions?" Ree asked. Her voice sounded muffled. He shook his head weakly.

"Of course we don't. We're the Confederate Marines. Beneath your people's notice." Nara snapped. "Can you help him? You healed yourself."

"Of course I can," Ree snapped back. Love at first sight, right there. Ree pressed a hand against his armor, over the wound. "Hold still, you fool. She sliced an artery, I think."

Aran held very still. The familiar warm energy took the pain, and the exhaustion. A bead of sweat trickled down Ree's cheek, and he noted the dark circles under her eyes. She was running close to the edge, which shouldn't surprise him. He had no idea how many spells she'd used against the Krox before they showed up.

"Thanks, Ree. Much better." Aran floated off the ground. "Sergeant, how you holding up?"

"Just peachy, sir." Crewes's teeth were gritted. "I think the explosion cauterized the wound. At least I ain't gonna be bleeding out." He climbed slowly back to one foot, and put the butt of his cannon under his arm like a crutch. "I ain't too fast, but I can still kill shit. Let's go. And don't wait for me. I'll be along."

Aran glanced at the blackened stump. Everything from the knee down had been obliterated by whatever spell Erika had cast. The skin was cracked and charred, masking the hideous damage underneath.

Theoretically it could be regrown, if they could afford a

mage powerful enough to do it. If they survived the next few minutes.

"Copy that." Aran took point, pouring on the speed as he zoomed down the tight corridor. It wound downward for several hundred meters, then finally spilled out into a sort of cavern. The edges of the wood here were black, and rotted.

"What is this place?"

"This is where Shaya took the spear that killed her." Nara bent to touch the rotting wood. "They must have chosen it intentionally, because the wood here is weaker."

Chanting came from further in the cavern.

"Do not let them finish that spell, people." Aran leapt back into the air, and shot toward the sound of the chanting.

49

THAT'S IT?

A ran slowed as the tunnel leveled off, widening into a large cavity of rotted wood. Dirk stood protectively in the far corner of the cavern, his spellblade clutched loosely in one hand. At least he wasn't wearing spellarmor. Eros stood behind Dirk in the center of a ritual circle a few meters back. There was no sign of Erika.

"How are we playing this?" Nara called, zooming up beside him as they neared their opponents.

Ree sprinted below them, vaulting chunks of wood as she approached the combat.

"I'm going to engage Dirk. Erika will almost certainly jump me. When she does, I want Nara to take her out. Stay hidden until then, no matter what." Aran dropped low, yanking his spellrifle from his void pocket. He snapped the butt to his shoulder, drawing a bead as he closed.

"Be careful, Aran," Nara whispered over the comm.

"Aren't I always?" Aran fired a level-three void bolt.

"No."

Dirk casually sketched a counter, shattering the spell,

then folded his arms. "Come on kid, you can do better than that."

Aran landed and took his time lining up another shot. He heard Ree sprinting up behind him. She'd be here in moments.

His feet suddenly left the ground, and Aran found himself tumbling end over end across the ground. His spell-rifle clattered away, leaving him weaponless for the moment. He flipped to his feet, then shot into the air.

Erika landed on his back, her legs encircling his waist. "Better, Outrider. Still not good enough." Her hands settled around his head and began to twist.

"Maybe you should wait till you've seen the whole show," Nara taunted from a meter away.

Pink magic slammed into Erika from the side, and her body went rigid. She tumbled limply from Aran's back, dropping toward the ground below. Nara caught her paralyzed body before she hit the ground, dumping her in a heap on the side of the room.

Aran turned back to Dirk, but it was far too late. He'd made the mistake of taking his eyes off what might be the most lethal war mage in the sector. One did not survive mistakes like that.

Dirk's rifle fired a ball of crackling black energy, which burst as it reached Aran. Void energy splattered his armor, and wherever it touched the paper doll instantly went yellow. A few moments later areas of his right torso and arm flared red.

"I'd suggest removing the armor, if you don't want to lose a limb or two," Dirk suggested. His tone was the same jovial friendliness he'd shown when he met Aran at the Tender's palace. "Nebiat insisted I keep you alive, but didn't specify how much of your body remains. I'd prefer to keep you intact, but if I have to maim you to subdue you, I will."

Aran willed the armor down to the ground, and sketched the *void* sigil needed to eject. He tumbled out the back of the armor, rolling away as the void energy continued to devour the armor. Everything below the right elbow had already been consumed by the hungry spell.

He grabbed his spellblade from the void pocket and trotted away from the armor as he waited for Dirk to engage.

"Ahh, there we go," Dirk called as Ree pulled up panting beside Aran. "Why don't the two of you figure out how you're going to assault me? You only get one shot. Make it count, for all our sakes."

On the far side of the room Nara sketched a *dream* sigil, and started to add an *air*. Dirk's hand twitched, and he flung a counterspell in Nara's direction. Her illusion spell ruptured, flinging mana shards in all directions.

"Nara," Aran called, interposing himself between Dirk and Nara. "Let us handle this. Stop the ritual. We'll deal with Dirk."

"Sending away your true mage isn't very smart. Now she's a threat." Dirk sprinted low and fast toward Nara.

Aran kicked off the ground, hurling himself forward on a cushion of air. He reinforced his blow with gravity magic, flaring the blade white as he brought it down in a wide slash. As expected, Dirk broke away from Nara to engage him. He easily parried Aran's blow, returning a wicked slash from a stance Aran didn't recognize.

Dirk might have finished Aran then, but Ree leapt at him from behind. Her spellarmor was damaged, but it still possessed all of its strength. She wrapped her arms around his chest, pinning them to his side.

"Finish it, Aran."

Before he could strike, Dirk's elbow shot back into the fist-sized hole Erika had made in Ree's spellarmor. Ree screamed as green lightning poured from Dirk's elbow, into the wound. She released him, staggering away several meters where she collapsed into a heap. Smoke poured from the wound, and the stench of burnt meat billowed out around them.

"Now what's your plan?" Dirk asked mildly. He gave his blade an experimental swing as if unlimbering himself. "Your true mage is trying to deal with her master. A fight she is doomed to lose, I might add. Your one ally can't stand up, and if she somehow does, I'll just knock her down again. This comes down to you and me—which means it comes down to me."

Aran walked slowly to a debris-free area of the floor. He watched Dirk closely. The man moved like Erika, but better. Who knew how many Catalysts he'd been to, or what abilities he might possess? He'd been training before Aran's parents were old enough to go on a date.

"How long ago did Nebiat bind you?" Aran asked. Maybe he could buy time for Ree to get up, though he wasn't sure how much that might help.

"Not long." Dirk started walking in a slow circle around the perimeter of their little circle, like it was a dueling ring. "She took me when you were in the Umbral Depths. I got careless, and she took advantage."

"And now you're going to help her kill tens of thousands of drifters, while she kills a woman you're in love with?" Aran considered launching the first strike, but sensed that would be a fatal mistake.

"Yes." Dirk's mouth went sour. "I can't fight it, kid. Do you think I want to tear down everything I've spent my life building?" He advanced slowly toward Aran, and stood only a few meters away now. Close enough to begin a strike.

Aran settled into Drakon stance. Dirk would expect it, of course, but there wasn't any other real option. Aran didn't know another style well enough to use it. Maybe he could do something similar to the fight with Erika, where he took a blow but landed one in return.

Dirk blurred forward, his blade crackling with purple lightning. Aran launched a parry, which knocked him back a step. Dirk flung a dagger from his sleeve, and the blade sliced across Aran's forearm. The wound immediately began to burn.

"Poison." Aran launched a counter attack, which Dirk easily parried.

He shook his head sadly, sighing at Aran. "Of course. You can't be surprised. A lesson for another life, kid. Use every weapon at your disposal, whatever it takes to kill your opponent. If you'd done that here, then maybe you could have beaten me and stopped this tragedy. So, in a way, this is as much your fault as it is mine."

Dirk circled slowly. Time was on his side now. Fire burned through Aran's arm, working its way toward his shoulder. How long until it reached his heart? Aran caught movement out of the corner of his eye, but studiously ignored it. He couldn't allow Dirk to realize what he saw.

"Ree, if you're going to help now is the time." Aran didn't break eye contact with Dirk, watching to see what effect his words would have. Dirk's gaze flicked to Ree's fallen form, and in that moment Aran struck.

He launched a high slash, and when Dirk knocked the blade away Aran channeled the momentum into a round-house kick. It caught Dirk in the side, flinging him backward. He stumbled, but regained his footing before Aran could follow up.

"Yes, you're definitely better than Erika described you," Dirk mused. He cocked his head. "What happened to you out there? I'd hoped whatever it was would be enough to stop Nebiat from killing Aurelia, but if this is the best you've got, then she's going to die badly."

"You're right," Aran admitted. He prowled closer, but stayed out of attack range. Not yet. "I know you're better than I am, but I can promise you this, Dirk. My sword is going to end up buried in your throat."

Aran leapt into the air, and aimed a fan of flame at Dirk. Dirk hopped backward, and Aran came down atop him. Dirk's leg scythed up and caught Aran in the chest. The move knocked the wind from Aran, flinging him twenty meters. He landed in a pile, something cracking painfully in his chest.

"That was your big finale?" Dirk shook his head and chuckled.

"No," Crewes roared, "this is."

Dirk turned to face the big man just as Crewes's spell-cannon bucked. A magma shell hit Dirk in the chest from three meters away, detonating into hundreds of shards. He was flung from his feet, and rolled across the ground.

Crewes fired again. "Did you think I was just gonna let you kill the LT? I spent months breaking in this kid. Do you know what a pain in the ass it is to train a new officer? Nah, you're out of bounds, war mage. Sit the fuck down."

Crewes sucked in a deep breath and breathed a river of flame at Dirk. Somehow Dirk rolled to his feet and away from the flame. He raised a hand and the flames parted to either side, flowing harmlessly around him.

Dirk sprinted toward Crewes, dodging to the right as

Crewes fired another spell. He leapt into the air, twisting as he somersaulted over the sergeant. Crewes tried to adjust but his missing leg made that impossible. Dirk landed behind him, and his sword punched through the sergeant's back.

"No!" Aran roared. He thrust his hand forward and seized Dirk around both legs with tendrils of air. Aran yanked, pulling the war mage from his feet.

Dirk recovered instantly, rolling away from Crewes and adopting a defensive stance. He glanced once at Crewes, who lay in a pile clutching the wound in his back. "Now that was a much more impressive finale, kid. You almost had me."

Aran's shoulder throbbed, and he could feel the poison working its way closer to his heart. Ree wasn't getting up. The sergeant was down. He was alone.

"I'm sorry," Aran said, advancing slowly toward Dirk, his blade raised high.

"For failing?" Dirk asked. He gave a heavy sigh. "Me too kid, me too."

"No." Aran raised his blade into a guard position. "For this."

His blade burst into eager brilliance, heat and light pouring out in all directions. The fire flowed up Aran's arm, into the wound. It flowed through his veins, purging the poison as it swept through his body. The magic infused every part of his body, bringing strength, and speed.

Aran sprinted three steps, then leapt into the air. He drew equal parts *fire*, *water*, *void*, and *air*. The collective energies swirled around the blade in a chaotic maelstrom, a maelstrom made brighter as the blade flared white with its own internal heat.

Dirk raised his blade to parry, and enchanted steel met

enchanted steel. A sound like a tremendous gong echoed from the impact, and Dirk's sword shattered.

Aran reversed the blow, gripping the hilt in both hands and ramming it through Dirk's spine, to the left of the heart. The weapon punched through his body, discharging the spell at point blank range. Dirk's body thrashed wildly, seizing from the lightning.

Aran yanked the blade free, whipping it around in a tight slash that sliced cleanly through Dirk's throat. Dirk's head tumbled from his body, and both collapsed into a heap.

"That was damned impressive, sir," Crewes rumbled. He hopped over, and sat on a large hunk of wood. "I hope Ree wakes up. I got no idea how bad the wound in my back is."

"We'll deal with that in a minute." Aran pulled himself to his feet. "We have to help Nara."

"Might be a bit late for that, sir." Crewes pointed.

Aran's heart sank.

Nebiat's invisible form rippled through the sky, banking on an updraft. She winged her way up over the great tree, toward the Tender's palace. It glittered high above, a jewel in the sunlight. She found it fitting that the Tender would die during their most holy time, the time they believed themselves to be strongest and most connected to their goddess.

She rose above the shayawood structure, gliding to a graceful halt on an empty landing pad. There was no sign of the Tender's honor guard. Dirk had done his work well.

Nebiat dropped her invisibility spell, and shifted back into human form. She had some gloating to do before the combat began, and wanted Aurelia to see her coming. She wanted to savor this victory. It had been a long time coming.

She pushed open a door and headed downstairs, into an opulent sitting room. Aurelia waited on the balcony. Nebiat's heels clicked across the hardwood floor as she approached, and the Tender turned in her direction. She straightened, still managing to look resplendent in her golden armor. But the image was marred now. Tainted.

"Aurelia, you don't look at all well. You're sweating," Nebiat teased. She stopped several meters away and rested her back against the railing. "I thought that was impossible. Isn't your health directly tied to Shaya herself?" Nebiat did her best impression of innocence. Admittedly, it wasn't very good.

"I finally understand," Aurelia panted. "How long have you been on my world?"

"No more than a few weeks. You'd probably have detected me, but all flame reading was blocked by the augury you are so obsessed with. I've been quite industrious during that time." She shot Aurelia a conspiratorial smile. "Between you and me I expect the fight to capture Eros was harder than killing you will be."

Aurelia hunched over suddenly, coughing violently. She spat blood onto the floor, then straightened. "I don't know what poison you used. I don't know what preparations you think you have made. If you wish a duel with the Guardian of Shaya, then you have it, dreadlord. Come. Let us put an end to this."

"Kay." Nebiat grinned.

She raised a hand and sketched a disintegrate. Nebiat raised her other hand and sketched a small Fissure. She fired the disintegrate into the Fissure, then opened a second Fissure right behind Aurelia. The disintegrate shot down at the Tender from above.

Aurelia flowed around it, rolling backward as the spell punched through her balcony, disintegrating a wide swath of the priceless shayawood. The Tender thrust out a hand and a meter thick beam of pure white lanced out at Nebiat.

She flung herself to the ground, but the light seared her back and drew a pained grunt. She sketched a blink, appearing above Aurelia. Nebiat sucked in a deep breath, and breathed. Many mortals didn't understand that a Wyrm could still breathe when in human form. Then again, most mortals didn't survive such occurrences, and thus couldn't speak of it.

A cloud of white-grey mist billowed out around Aurelia, the spirits keening as they hungrily sought her soul. Aurelia merely stood there, staring up at Nebiat. The mist faded with no apparent effect, but Nebiat wasn't daunted.

This was merely the opening gambit, and time was very much on her side. In a few minutes, Aurelia would be dead and this world at war with itself.

51

PIRATE GIRL

Turning away from Aran and abandoning him to fight Dirk was the single hardest decision Nara had ever faced. Fighting side by side was all she really knew, and her partner needed her. But so did Kezia, Bord, and the thousands of other drifters down there. She had a responsibility to those people, and that meant filling the role Voria would normally fill. She had to be the true mage.

Nara clutched her staff tightly in her right hand and flew closer to Eros and his ritual circle. She studied that circle, and the ring of wards inscribed outside of it. They were complex and powerful, but her new abilities allowed her to grasp them far more quickly than she could have managed only a week ago. She could probably understand them in minutes instead of days. Unfortunately, she didn't have minutes.

"Your wards will keep me out," she said, landing outside of the circle. "But they will also keep you and your magic in."

"An astute observation," Eros muttered. He continued to

sketch sigils, adding complexity to the ritual. "You're running out of time, so you need to make the logical leaps. I cannot tell you how to do this. She won't let me."

That got Nara's attention. "You're bound, but not completely."

"Clever, pirate girl." Eros didn't look at her, only kept sketching furiously. "The rest is up to you."

Nara slowly walked the edge of the wards, studying them and considering the problem. The quickest way to disrupt a ward was to attack it magically. Unfortunately, that was also the most destructive. Overloading a ward often caused a magical detonation powerful enough to kill the mage foolish enough to try.

She stopped.

"The wards are bidirectional," she mused quietly.

"And?" Eros called. His eyes glinted feverishly in the light of the sigils.

"Meaning that if there were an explosion, it would move in all directions, instead of outward from the blast point." Nara realized the implications. "If I can disrupt the wards, the explosion will hit us both..."

"But?" Eros pressed, still sketching.

"I don't know how much force the explosion will have. It could kill us, and Aran, or it might not be enough to hurt you." Nara bent closer to the runes, eyeing them frantically. She had no idea how to calculate the destructive force of an exploding rune. She'd only been training for a few weeks; while Neith had given her increased intelligence, that didn't automatically impart knowledge.

There was only one way she could find out what would happen, and the longer she waited the closer Eros came to completing his spell. "Screw it."

She raised her staff, and brought it down on the *life*

sigil with all her suit's strength. The tip bit into the wood, scratching a wide line through the sigil. The sigil flickered, then winked out. The entire circle flared brilliantly, and a wave of magic energy burst outward in all directions. The blast flung her backward, and she tumbled drunkenly end over end as she struggled to get control of her spellarmor. She finally came to rest against the far side of the chamber.

Nara rose slowly. The paper doll on her HUD had gone almost completely red, but the spellarmor was still moving, at least. She raised her head, scanning for Eros. He lay crumpled in a heap at the edge of the circle. His robes were tattered and burned, and most of his pristine hair had been burned away. Even his eyebrows were nothing more than singed stubble.

But the important thing was the rise and fall of his chest. He lived, and didn't seem too severely wounded, which meant he could be up and fighting in a matter of moments.

Nara sketched a paralyze and flung the spell at Eros; he went rigid. Now she could turn her attention to the spell he'd been constructing.

The ritual still appeared to be active, an immense amount of magic gathered into a sea of interlocking sigils. It was like a jigsaw puzzle with pieces missing, only she didn't know what the final picture was supposed to look like. Voria's vision suggested a magical explosion, which meant the spell must generate an immense amount of force.

How did it do that? She floated a few meters closer, gaining a little altitude to study the spell. There was a great deal of *fire*, but also a surprising amount of *void* and *earth*. Those last two were often combined into the Greater Path of summoning. So what were they summoning that would require fire magic to sustain it?

"Oh, my gods," she murmured. "You were going to summon a piece of a star. The ultimate bomb."

Eros mumbled through his paralyzed jaw. "And what do you think will happen to the spell now?"

Nara considered. Back on Marid she'd completed the spell because Nebiat had left it unattended. She'd done it because if she hadn't Nebiat would have simply returned and completed the spell.

But this was different. Eros couldn't complete the spell. Could she leave it here, unfinished? What would happen if she did?

"It's a pity I didn't have time to teach you about spell erosion. Such a funny little effect. It begins with the sigils on the fringes of the spell," Eros mused through gritted teeth.

Nara bent to inspect the tiny sigils around the outer edge of the circle. They were slowly fusing together. What did that mean? The final step before a spell solidified involved the sigils merging. Was that what she was seeing? If so, the spell was already completing.

"Spell erosion," she mused aloud. "I'm guessing a ritual can only be sustained for so long before whatever magic it currently contains fuses together and auto-casts."

"That's an interesting theory. Another interesting question, do you think Nebiat intended for me to survive? Or am I a discarded tool?" Eros asked with apparent disinterest.

Nara thought furiously. What did Nebiat want? And how could she determine the answer? For Eros to survive this, he'd have to somehow live through the spell. The only place he'd be able to do that, theoretically, was inside the ritual circle. If the spell were constructed the right way, the spell itself could be unidirectional, only blasting outward.

Could she study the spell and find out?

She looked to the edges and noted that the erosion had

begun to accelerate. She didn't know how much time she had, but it couldn't be long.

"I think she wants you to live." Nara darted from the circle and dragged Eros inside.

"And if she doesn't?" he slurred.

"If she doesn't, then we die." Nara examined the part of the spell Eros had been working on when she disrupted him. This was the last piece, and finishing it would complete the spell. "I just need to make a couple minor alterations, then we'll find out."

"What are you changing?"

Nara's hands flew across sigils, erasing some and adding others. "I'm converting all this fire into light. It won't do anything about the radioactive mass, but hopefully that will soften the explosion."

"Well done, pirate girl," Eros slurred, affectionately.

Nara took a deep breath. She placed her staff carefully in her void pocket, then glanced at the fight behind her. Aran's fight with Dirk did not appear to be going well at all. He was outclassed, and likely going to die.

She smiled grimly. He wouldn't die alone.

52

HELLS YEAH

"Ohhhh, shhhiitttttttt," Crewes's voice boomed in slow motion.

A wave of fire and light burst from the ritual circle where Eros and Nara stood. It rolled toward them in a wave of death, one that would crash over them in an instant. Aran was aware of Crewes's bulk moving to shield him. "Hold your breath, sir!"

Aran sucked in a deep breath. A moment later a wall of white flame blasted over them. As it arrived, a second wave pulsed outward, this one from Crewes's armor. A wave of ice. It engulfed Aran, covering him in thick frost until he was imprisoned in the large block of ice.

The magical explosion flowed in swirls and eddies around a perfect sphere of deep blue ice Crewes had erected. The magical force warped the outer edge, flaking it away as it worked closer to the center of their shelter. Crewes's arms shook as he poured more and more ice into the spell.

The flame passed, but black spots clouded Aran's vision from the lack of oxygen. The ice exploded outwards, and

Aran gratefully sucked in a breath. Then they were surrounded by sudden sunlight, spinning wildly as they entered free fall. Crewes's thruster fired, keeping them aloft.

Aran struggled to focus, shielding his eyes with both hands. "Oh, my gods."

Perhaps a quarter of the second burl had broken loose from the tree, and fell slowly toward the drifter city below.

"We're about five kilometers up. That thing will hit in less than a minute. Sergeant, can you see the spellship anywhere?" Aran scanned the sky, still blinking away spots.

"Yes, sir. Down there. Four o'clock from your right foot. Well my only foot now, I guess."

Aran glanced down, his heart sinking. The ship tumbled end over end, alongside manor houses, other ships, statues, and everything else contained in Ducius's villa. All of it fell directly toward the dims, right onto the unsuspecting drifters.

"You can release me," Aran roared over the mounting wind.

"Yes, sir," Crewes roared back, releasing Aran.

Aran tightened his profile, pressing his arms to his sides as he angled his body toward the ship. He reached for his air magic, using it to accelerate his flight. Crewes blasted up beside him, joining his dive toward the spellship.

"We'll never make it, sir. She's falling almost as fast as we are," Crewes shouted over the wind. "We need to get clear of the impact explosion, sir. Mission's blown."

Suddenly, the spellship's spin corrected. The thrusters flared and she began climbing unsteadily in their direction.

"Gods damn. You think that moppy-headed punk figured it out?" Crewes poured on the speed, pulling ahead of Aran as they raced toward the ship.

"It has to be Pickus. I don't know how, but he must have

read enough of the manual to operate the matrix." Aran laughed, pouring on more speed.

The ship raced up to meet them, slowing awkwardly as they neared it. The hatch on the aft side opened and Aran executed a sharp turn inside. He flew straight to the bridge, dropping nimbly into the command matrix.

Pickus sat in the starboard wing matrix, his fingers flying across the silver and gold rings. "You sure do know how to make an entrance."

"I cannot believe you learned to pilot in twenty minutes. You realize you just saved our collective asses, right? Maybe everyone's asses." Aran tapped the initiation sequence, wresting control of the ship from Pickus. She sang to him as he connected, ready to fly.

"I've been watching ever since the *Texas*, so I wasn't completely unprepared." Pickus pointed at the scry-screen. "So, uh, what are going to do about that giant hunk of wood?"

Aran guided the ship into a parallel dive, studying the falling burl. Shayawood was highly prized for how light and strong it was. There was no way to inflict enough damage to destroy that thing. Even a full disintegrate would only vaporize a small segment, and the surviving debris would still kill everyone below.

"Sir, you got a plan?" Crewes hopped his way onto the bridge, then used his cannon as a crutch to hobble into the last matrix.

"Yeah, I've got a plan, but it's pretty bad." Aran flipped the ship forty-five degrees, pouring *void* and *fire* into the ship to increase velocity. "I want the two of you to pour everything you have into the spelldrive. Maximum velocity. We need to fire this ship like a bullet shot from the largest gauss rifle in the sector. Can you do that?"

"Can do, sir." Crewes tapped a *fire* sigil. "Pickus, I know you ain't been trained, but you can push buttons right? When the LT says, push the red sigil a bunch of times. Normally I'd insult your moppy-headed ass, but since you're technically a civvie I'll be nice. Don't fuck this up, mage. Or we're gonna die."

"What are you going to do?" Pickus asked, eyes widening.

"I'm increasing our mass with gravity magic. Making us heavier." Aran tapped *air*, then *void*. He repeated the sigils on the silver ring, then the gold.

"What's the *air* for, sir?" Crewes asked.

"Watch." Aran pulled up suddenly, just above the drifter city. They were close enough that he could make out individual faces. Children pointed up at them, laughing in wonder.

The ship shot back into the air, aimed at the falling burl. They were tiny compared to it, but he had a plan to fix that. He dumped *air* into the spell, adding as much as he could safely channel. He manifested the *air* from all three cannons, into a wide disk that extended for a hundred meters in every direction.

The ship accelerated, the gravity magic increasing its mass with every meter it traveled. The burl grew larger, blotting out the sun as they approached. "Brace yourselves!"

The ship punched into the burl and the bridge lurched. Aran slammed against the chair's restraints, his neck snapping back painfully. A titanic rumble sounded outside and they burst into sudden sunlight.

Aran seized control of the ship, flipping it around to face the ground. His stomach rolled as the ship finally righted itself.

Below them one chunk of wood had become six, and all

six chunks were now falling at an angle, away from the drifter city. Aran guessed they'd impact less than five hundred meters from the outer edges.

"Hells, yeah!" Crewes roared, slapping his fists together. "That's how Confederate Mages do it."

The six chunks of shayawood slammed into the ground in the fields outside the city, broken into kindling by the impacts. Wood was flung in all directions, pelting the drifter city with debris. An enormous cloud of dust rolled over the dims, masking the extent of the damage.

They waited tensely for the dust to clear.

When it did, the drifter city stood, unharmed. "Hells, yeah, Sergeant. Hells, yeah!"

53

ICY STORM OF DEATH

Voria let out a breath she hadn't realized she'd been holding when she landed atop the Tender's palace. Her hand was wrapped around Ikadra so tightly it stung, and she forced herself to relax her grip. Flying was one thing. Flying as fast as Ikadra flew was something else entirely. That was going to take some getting used to. No matter. They'd arrived.

"Could my father have really convinced them all to leave their posts?" she asked aloud, realizing the deck was completely empty, save for her. There were no bodies, and no sign of a struggle.

Then she felt the energies roiling beneath her. "By the goddess."

She couldn't see the spells through the walls, but the power being flung about down there dwarfed the conflict at Marid. Two demigods were fighting. She steeled herself.

"I have to go down there." She started toward the doors.

"Not necessarily. I mean, you could retreat. Not that I'm recommending doing that." Ikadra's sapphire pulsed.

"I thought you weren't supposed to talk," Voria growled.

She kicked open the door and stalked down the stairs. Multicolored lights splashed off the walls, reflections of the duel taking place further down the level.

"My parameters are relaxed during life-threatening situations," Ikadra supplied.

"So you can distract me during battle, but not when it doesn't matter?" Voria ignored the staff, creeping to a corner and peering around it. She froze.

Nebiat stood there in human form, sketching a counterspell. Voria couldn't see far enough into the room to make out Aurelia, but the smug smile on Nebiat's face filled her with dread. The counterspell zipped deeper into the room, painting the walls multicolored as mana shards dissipated.

"You are weakening," Nebiat taunted cruelly. She took a step deeper into the room.

Voria took the opportunity to creep closer. She planted her back against a pillar. One of the blue hover-couches floated over, bumping her thigh. "Go away," she hissed.

She peered around the pillar to see Nebiat completing the final sigil in a complex spell. The air beside her split, opening a Fissure into the Umbral Depths. Clawed hands burst from the Fissure, and a demonic cyclops pulled its way into reality. Its shoulders brushed the ceiling, and the shaggy-headed thing bellowed a challenge.

"Destroy the Tender," Nebiat commanded, pointing deeper into the room.

Voria moved closer, finally able to see Aurelia. The Tender was paler than usual, with dark circles under her normally perfect eyes. Such things were no cause for alarm on a mortal, but on a demigod? Something was seriously wrong with her.

Aurelia sketched several more quick sigils and flung the nullification spell at the cyclops. There was no visible effect, but the cyclops's eye widened. Then it blinked several times. When it focused again, Aurelia pointed toward the dreadlord. "Destroy Nebiat."

The cyclops spun and glared hatefully down at Nebiat. It roared, trembling with rage. A bright, violet glow built in its eye, and a bolt of brilliant energy lanced down at Nebiat. The energy refracted off an invisible wall of slowly rotating sigils, exposing the ward briefly before it faded back to invisibility.

Nebiat raised a hand and the cyclops was sucked through the Fissure. It snapped shut with a *pop*.

"How many more spells can you manage, I wonder? A dozen? Less?" Nebiat gave a musical laugh. "No one is coming to save you. Your allies have all been stripped away."

"Not all of them." Voria stepped from cover and leveled Ikadra at Nebiat. She lowered her voice. "Okay, Ikadra. Time to earn your keep. Lead with something flashy. Use the ice storm spell."

"It's ice storm *of death*," Ikadra muttered. His tip flared to life and a cone of ice and sleet spilled out to quickly blanket the room. The sheer volume of ice and snow was impressive, hurled at Nebiat by gale force winds.

The spell caught the dreadlord off guard, sending her sprawling across the suddenly slippery floor. Icy shards rained down on her, shredding her dress and exposing bloody cuts underneath.

Aurelia flung a potent earth spell at Nebiat, and eight surrounding pillars ripped free and slammed into her, one after the other. They battered her across the floor, and the ice prevented her from standing.

Nebiat rolled from the mess. She glared hatefully at them, with one hand wrapped around her injured side. "I stand corrected. All but your least impressive ally have been stripped away. I'm going to kill you both, and I'll do it with relish, I assure you." Nebiat began to sketch a spell, a trickle of blood leaking from the corner of her mouth.

"Can you tell me what she's casting?" Voria whispered desperately. She only had one counterspell stored, and while it sounded like it could counter any single spell, she needed to make sure she chose the right spell to counter.

"It's awful. A curtain of disintegration," Ikadra warned.

"Counter it!" Voria shrieked.

A wall of nothingness swept out from Nebiat's outstretched hands. It enveloped everything before it, dissolving pillars, hover-couches, and everything else in its path as it shot toward Voria.

Wait, what if it couldn't be countered, like a disintegrate?

The staff hummed, and discharged a beam of pure, brilliant gold. The spell sung, the air vibrating musically as it lanced into the wall of disintegration. The entire wall trembled for a moment. Voria froze, praying it would shatter. It didn't.

But it did reverse course, flung suddenly back at Nebiat.

The dreadlord screamed in rage, sketching a quick blink spell. Nebiat's bloody form teleported out of the path, and the curtain of disintegration evaporated the wall, the balcony, and part of the level above. It continued outward, disintegrating the wards around the flying palace.

A tremendous wind rushed in through the gap in the wards, drowning out sound, and forcing Voria a hasty step backward. Ikadra pulsed and a bubble of calm appeared around them. Voria looked immediately to Aurelia. The Tender stared defiantly up at Nebiat, her golden armor glowing with power. She held no weapon, but she didn't need one.

Aurelia leapt into the air and seized Nebiat. They fell

together, and Aurelia slammed Nebiat's face into the ground, ramming her elbow into the back of it. She seized Nebiat by her long, white hair, and slammed her face into the ground again. "You come into my palace." Another slam. "You poison my goddess." Another slam. "But worst of all you corrupt my people." Aurelia slammed Nebiat's face into the ground again.

"Spare me your heroic nonsense." Nebiat burst up from the ground, flinging Aurelia away from her. The dreadlord's dark skin was slashed and bruised, and one eye was swollen shut. "At least they will say you fought before I killed you."

She wiped blood from the corner of her mouth, then she attacked.

Voria dropped to one knee, pressing her body against the side of a pillar. She minimized her profile, and made no obvious moves. Ever so slowly, Voria raised the tip of Ikadra and aimed the staff at Nebiat.

Thankfully, the dreadlord's full fury was fixed on Aurelia.

Nebiat leapt into the air, then blinked fifty meters higher, out into the sky above the palace. Her body shifted, neck elongating as her limbs grew thicker and longer. The last of the dress was shredded as Nebiat assumed her Wyrm form.

She reared a long neck, sucking in a quick breath, then exhaled a cloud of white death at the Tender. Aurelia's hand shot up, and she sketched a counterspell. It divided the breath in two, shunting it safely around the Tender. Voria shuddered as she heard the all-too-familiar keen of the spirits trapped in that breath weapon.

"Not yet," Voria whispered, still aiming the staff. She only had one shot at this.

Nebiat dove, streaking toward Aurelia. The Tender leapt backward, but Nebiat's wings came up and she adjusted course. Her tail shot out, encircling Aurelia's waist. It looped around her several times, and began to squeeze.

The armor cracked, and Aurelia gave a choked cry.

"This is the end," Nebiat taunted. The tail tightened again, and the armor over the chest crumpled inward. Aurelia went limp.

Voria aimed the staff carefully, so carefully. "Ikadra, fire the disintegrate."

The dark bolt shot from the tip of the staff and cleanly severed Nebiat's tail, just below where it met the back. Aurelia tumbled from the Wyrm's grasp as Nebiat shrieked in agony. The Wyrm spun to face Voria.

She snarled, her draconic face made even more bestial by the rage. "No! Not this time. You will not survive this encounter to bedevil me again. Your possibility ends here, little mortal."

Nebiat raised a claw and began to sketch sigils.

"I don't suppose you can amplify my spells?" Voria asked.

"Of course I can." Ikadra sounded hurt.

"Then amplify this." Voria used the tip of the staff to sketch the most powerful counterspell she knew, a third-level. The sigils were infused with power form Ikadra, strengthening the counterspell.

She hurled it at Nebiat's spell, and gave a delighted laugh when the tiny counterspell disrupted the sigils at the heart of the dreadlord's spell. It burst into mana shards, and Nebiat shrieked in rage.

Voria pulled back behind a pillar and yelled over her shoulder. "I guess you're not quite as powerful as you make yourself out to be."

Nebiat's reply was drowned out as several golden spell-fighters screamed by overhead. Their cannons fired a volley of golden spells, the life bolts slamming into Nebiat. She shrieked, twisting to avoid the last several.

"My work here is already done. Your Tender lies dying. You live, Voria, but will your father? One by one, I will take away everyone you love." Nebiat dropped into a sudden dive, streaking toward one of Shaya's lower limbs.

Voria ran to the edge of the balcony, watching as the fighters streaked after her. Nebiat's titanic form rippled, then was gone. She could have transformed into a small creature, like a native bird, or she could have gone invisible. Either way, the fighters broke off and began to circle, searching fruitlessly for the canny binder. There was no way they'd catch her.

An enormous crack echoed from below. Voria scanned for the source, her heart sinking when she saw an enormous chunk of wood break loose from the second burl. It wasn't the entire thing—more like a quarter—though that would be slim consolation to the people about to die in the impact.

She clutched Ikadra to her chest, mouth going dry as the wood fell. Spells flashed beneath the burl, then something black streaked into it from below. The burl exploded into many chunks, and their momentum was somehow redirected, flinging them to the ground outside the city.

Somehow, Aran had done it.

"V-voria," Aurelia called weakly.

Voria gave an agonized look at the path Nebiat had taken. She'd never have a better chance to pursue the dread-lord, and with Ikadra she might be able to end her once and for all.

She glanced back at Aurelia, and sighed. Voria ran to the

fallen Tender, dropping to cradle her head on her lap. "I'm here, Mother."

Voria cradled Aurelia's head. A clump of the Tender's lustrous hair, now a dull scarlet, came away as Voria stroked it.

"I—I'm dying," Aurelia managed.

"How is that even possible?" Voria tried to sound confident. "We're surrounded by life mages, some of the most powerful ones in the sector. I've seen a man come back from the dead. They will not let you go this easily, Aurelia."

"Normally, that might be true," Aurelia croaked. Her eyes were dull and cloudy, every breath shallow, probably from the ribs Nebiat had crushed. "N-nebiat poisoned me, and in the process poisoned Shaya. I do not know what she used, but it has rendered all life magic ineffective. I cannot heal, and I strongly doubt the magics that call a soul back to the body will be effective against this kind of magic."

She paused, struggling for breath.

Voria tried to think of what to say. How did one comfort a dying demigod? Was there something she could or should do? "Ikadra, is there any way we can help?"

"I suspect not," the staff said. "The poison used could be any number of varieties designed to kill life gods and their progeny. Many weapons were conceived during the godswar, and those spells still exist in forgotten corners of the galaxy. This is one such."

"I can't accept this." Voria's voice cracked.

"Y-you do not have a choice." Aurelia gave a weak laugh that turned into a bloody cough. "I am sorry, Voria. For involving you. For your father."

"He died in that explosion, didn't he?" Voria said numbly.

"He did. I felt it. I'm sorry."

Voria closed her eyes, holding back the tears. "It's just one more debt I owe Nebiat. A debt I will find a way to pay back."

"I believe you will," Aurelia whispered.

"Stay with me, Tender." Voria squeezed her hand.

"I must...cast." The Tender raised a trembling hand and sketched a *fire* sigil, then a *dream*. She added several more of each, and the missive activated. It displayed the royal archives, at the library. "Head archivist Abal, I ask you to stand witness."

"Of course, Tender." The dark-skinned man bowed. "How may I be of service?"

"I am dying. I have two matters that will need to be attended to, which have not already been addressed in my will." She paused for long moments, her breathing labored. "First, the new Tender. Bring Eros to the chamber of choosing, and let him be judged. If he cannot be found, or if he is unworthy then Ducius may be judged." She closed her eyes, her skin going a shade paler. "Finally, I urge you to contact Confederate Command, and Ternus directly. Ask them to read the major's report about my death, and to reinstate Voria to her rightful rank. She is our only hope of victory against the Krox. C-can you do this, archivist?"

"It will be done, Tender," he whispered. A tear slid from the archivist's eye.

"Thank you." Aurelia closed her eyes, and died.

55

FOOLED YOU

Nebiat's rage consumed her, to the point where she very nearly sacrificed her own life to destroy Voria's tiny, fragile body. She flapped her wings once, considering.

No. She would not throw away an endless future for momentary satisfaction. She winged away from the fighters, sketching a blink spell to gain maneuvering room.

The golden fighters streaked above, quickly narrowing the gap. They were nearly as fast as she, and their pilots were fresh. Her confrontation had burned much of her magic, enough that she didn't want to expend more unless she absolutely needed to. And, much as she hated to admit it, she'd never been this badly wounded. Her tail could be regrown, but only if she survived.

Nebiat dove suddenly, willing her body to transform. By the time she reached the sixth branch she'd become a completely unremarkable raven. She winged toward a flock, losing herself amongst many similar birds.

The spellfighters opened up with their cannons, firing light bolts into the flock. Ravens scattered in all directions, those lucky enough to escape the destruction. The fighters circled above, trying to determine if they'd killed her.

Nebiat zipped into a fern and morphed into a squirrel. Many mages lost cognitive ability while morphed, but Nebiat had long since mastered the improved version of the spell. She hopped up a redwood, skittering up the trunk and into the canopy.

Two of the fighters landed and their war mages stalked into the forest below her. She watched them search, chittering insultingly at them as they scanned the undergrowth with their spellrifles. One even looked up and saw her, then casually dismissed her as a regular squirrel. She shook her head. These mages had *just watched* as she'd morphed. The idea that she could do it again should have occurred to them.

Amateurs. She scampered down the tree, morphing into human form when she'd reached the ground. This time she used the appearance of one of Erika's students, an unremarkable girl with nothing about her that might draw attention.

Nebiat walked casually to the closest spellfighter. She trotted up the translucent blue stairs and leapt into the cockpit. It took only moments to close the canopy and bring the ship online. She seized control of the ship, pouring void magic into the spelldrive. The ship zipped up into the sky, winging away from the sixth branch.

Perfect cover. Who would expect her to flee Shaya in one of their own spellfighters?

She glanced at the scry-screen, an amused smile improving her mood. The former pilot of her new ship wore a panicked expression, unsure what to do as she flew away in his vessel. His companion sprinted to her own fighter, but there was no way she'd be able to catch Nebiat in time.

Nebiat summoned a simulacrum, one of her last fifth-level spells. She stepped from the matrix, and the phantom version of her continued to pilot the vessel. She raised a delicate finger and sketched an invisibility spell.

Then Nebiat blinked out of the vessel, suddenly in the naked sky. The spellfighter shot away, roaring into the upper atmosphere. It sped toward the planet's Umbral Shadow, clearly fleeing into the Umbral Depths. Unsurprisingly, several more spellfighters began to purse.

Nebiat grinned wickedly. Then shifted into her Wyrm form again. She cast a reduce spell, making her no larger than a falcon. She flew toward the House of Enlightenment. There was one more stop to make, one more seed to plant. Then she could be rid of this world, until she returned to destroy it.

56

BIG DAMNED HEROES

N ara was awakened by the vertigo. Her eyes snapped open, and she watched in confusion as the world spun drunkenly around her. She was draped over someone's shoulder, peering between a pair of armored legs at the ground a kilometer or two below them.

She blinked again, examining the HUD in her armor. Everything had turned red, with some parts of the chest and legs having been greyed out entirely. She doubted the armor would ever fly again.

The person carrying her also wore spellarmor, though hers was a golden set of Mark IX. "Ree, is that you?"

The wind tugged away the words as the golden armor dove again. The pilot used their free hand to snatch another figure from the rain of flaming debris. It was Master Eros. He dangled unconsciously in her grip.

"Are you all right?" Ree's voice boomed over the speakers.

Nara triggered her own speakers, but they fizzled once then died. Nara gave Ree a thumbs up.

"I'm taking us down to the surface, outside the impact

site." Ree dropped lower, circling around the flaming branches. "You're lucky I was there."

Nara privately agreed. She didn't know who Ree was, not outside of a couple bad experiences, but Nara owed her, like it or not.

They finally reached the ground, and Ree deposited Nara gently. Nara sketched the *void* sigil and the armor reluctantly went translucent. She slipped out, dropping onto her hands and knees, panting.

"Now, that," Bord said from behind her, "is the nicest view I've seen in weeks."

"You had better not be staring at my ass," Nara said wearily. She rose to her feet, and offered a hand to Ree. The other woman raised her faceplate, showing the too-beautiful face she'd seen briefly back up in Shaya. "Thank you, Ree. You saved me, and Eros. I won't forget that."

Ree stared silently at her for several moments. She was on the verge of saying something, but then seemed to think better of it.

"You and Aran may be mongrels, but we couldn't have won today without you," Ree admitted. She still eyed Nara strangely, and Nara wasn't sure what to make of it. "Is Master Eros magically bound? Does he need to be contained?"

"I paralyzed him, but he'll be a threat once the spell wears off. Which could be any minute."

"I'll keep him under guard." Ree withdrew her spellrifle for a shoulder harness, and trained the barrel on Eros. She laid Eros down on his stomach, then took a big step back, the rifle never leaving a position where it could fire.

"Who's your friend, Nara?" Bord asked as he sauntered up. He thrust out a hand toward Ree. "I'm Bord. I'm a good friend of Nara's, and you said you knew Aran right? I've saved his life, like six times. Why just last week alone we—"

Ree's faceplate snapped down and her rifle swung around to Bord. He grinned up at her, delivering the least smooth wink anyone had ever attempted. "You're flirting with me, aren't you? I hear you noble types are into the rough stuff."

Ree took a threatening step toward Bord and he retreated backward. "Okay, okay. Not interested right now. Maybe some other time. I'll keep my schedule open." He dropped his voice to a conspiratorial whisper. "Think I've got a chance?"

"No. Where's Kezia?" Nara asked, scanning the chaos for her. Looking around now she realized it wasn't as catastrophic as she'd feared. Those weren't screams of pain or anguish. They were cheers, and whoops of joy. "And why are they cheering?" Maybe they were celebrating still being alive.

"Are you serious?" Bord gave a whoop of his own. "Nara, you guys made everyone here rich. You just rained a fortune in shayawood all around the community. Every last drifter is out there right now, carting off as much as they can. By the time the Tender gets her people down here, all the best stuff will be gone. These people will never have to worry about where their next meal is coming from, not ever again."

"The Tender! Where's Aran?" Nara spun around looking for the spellship. She breathed easier when she saw it slowing to a smooth landing about a hundred meters out.

The ramp extended, and Aran came limping out first. His clothing was burnt and tattered, and she had no idea what had happened to his armor. If it had been left behind, he must have lost it in the explosion. Behind him came Crewes, who used a piece of shayawood as a makeshift crutch to compensate for his missing leg. Pickus emerged in their wake, shielding his eyes from the sun as he scanned the crowd.

"Aran!" She darted in his direction and he ran toward her. They met in a fierce hug. "We did it."

"I can't believe we pulled it off." Aran picked her up and spun her, then finally set her down.

"Have you heard anything from the major?" Nara darted a self-conscious look at Ree, who appeared to be studiously ignoring them.

"No." Aran tensed. He looked so tired, and soot caked his face. He shaded his eyes and looked up at the Tender's palace. "That thing looks like it's been through a war." Smoke poured from a giant hole in the side.

Something glittered in the sky, resolving into a glowing ball that approached rapidly. It zoomed down in their direction and came to an instant halt several meters away. The shimmering bubble winked out of existence, revealing the major holding Ikadra. Her eyes were red and swollen, and she didn't speak.

"The Tender?" Aran asked.

Voria shook her head, a tear leaving the corner of her eye. Nara looked away in embarrassment. It wasn't like the major to display this kind of emotion.

"Report," she ordered, with a ghost of her usual primness.

"Nara blunted the explosion so it only took a piece of the burl, instead of the whole thing," Aran explained. He wiped his forehead, smearing the soot. "Master Erika, Master Eros, and Dirk had all been bound. We were able to save Erika and Eros, but, Dirk…"

"I already know. You did what you could." Voria's face was a mask of cold anger, concealing whatever grief might lurk underneath. Nara suspected the major would pay a price for it later. "What else?"

"We successfully saved the dims, and apparently Aran is now some sort of local hero." Nara pointed at the drifters frantically gathering shayawood.

Voria followed Nara's finger. She smiled, then began to laugh. She laughed until tears streamed from her eyes.

"What do you find so funny?" Ree asked frostily, finally approaching their little group. "These little pikeys are going to be running around on every branch now, causing chaos."

"That," Voria wheezed, "is why I'm laughing." She finally brought the laughter under control. "The nobility have tried so hard to keep them out, and the only way they've been able to do that is by keeping them at the edge of poverty. Now the drifters have money. Instead of *causing* a class war, Nebiat has ensured there won't be one."

"Major, I don't want to interrupt, but Eros is still bound. I don't know how to remove the spell." Nara nodded at his unconscious body. "Is there anything you can do?"

"This, at least, I can fix." The major moved to Eros and knelt at his side. She inspected him carefully, then looked up at Nara. "Watch closely, Nara. You'll want to learn this. Nullification is difficult, but worth knowing."

Voria began to sketch, and Nara studied the sigils, memorizing each one. The major blended *void*, *earth*, and *spirit* together. She applied the collected energies to a lattice-work of dark energy covering Eros's chest and head. The energy dissolved, clumps falling away like ash from burnt wood.

"There, that's the last of it. He wasn't too far gone. I doubt Nebiat had much time to sink her hooks in." She rose to her feet and dusted off her hands. "I'm no life mage though. I don't know when he'll wake."

"I can wake him," Ree offered dubiously. "I've only been waiting because he was a threat. He has a mild concussion, but that's easily repaired." Ree knelt and placed her hands on Eros's head. A warm white glow passed from her hands into his scalp, and the master's eyes fluttered open.

"We're...alive?" He sat up, blinking up at the sun. Eros shot to his feet. "Where is Nebiat?"

"Long gone." Voria ground her teeth. "I wounded her, but she accomplished what she set out to do. Aurelia is dead."

"By the goddess." Eros stared at the ground, his shoulders slumped. He looked back up a moment later. "You were with her. Who did she name as successor? Please not Ducius."

"She named you." Voria folded her arms. "The head archivist witnessed the missive."

"You're going to be the Tender?" Nara blinked at Eros.

"You think that's amusing?" Eros narrowed his eyes at her.

"Of course not." Nara's eyes dropped to the muddy ground.

Eros arched an eyebrow. "You are still an apprentice, and I am in a position to make your life hells. And now that you're back from your little jaunt into the Umbral Depths, that's precisely what I intend to do." He rose to his feet, futilely dusting off his burnt robe.

"As long as you're teaching me more about magic." Nara wrapped an arm around Aran's waist. "And as long as you allow me a little time to visit friends."

"Speaking of, what happens now, Major?" Aran asked. He stared up at the smoking burl, high above them.

"Well, we hope Confederate command listens to the Tender's dying wish, and reinstates me," Voria said. "Aurelia asked them to do that, and I expect they'll honor it. If they do, they'll refit the *Hunter*. That's going to take months though."

"Good," Ree snapped. She stabbed Aran hard in the chest. "Because Mongrel here will need every bit of that time. He has a great deal of training to do."

"So does this one." Eros nodded in her direction.

Voria licked her lips. "We all do. Make good use of the time. Nebiat is still out there, and she won here today. We lost the Tender, at a time when we most need our unity. We are without a Guardian."

Aran's face hardened, and he shifted his attention to Voria. "The Krox assault is coming. If we're going to resist them the *Hunter* isn't going to cut it. We need to go after the spellship Ikadra told you about. We all know the hammer is going to fall, and we're not strong enough to stop them. The gods left us a weapon. We need to find it. We just need to know where to look."

"Ikadra has already informed me." Voria met Aran's gaze, and something significant passed between them. "The ship is located somewhere on Virkon."

EPILOGUE

Frit rushed into her room, but her excited words died as she exhaled a wispy puff of smoke. She looked from Nara to the stuffed pack on the bed. "You're leaving."

Nara looked up, blinking. Exhaustion painted dark circles under her eyes, but she smiled affectionately as she sat on the bed next to the pack. "I know, I know, I just got back. But Eros has asked me to move into the Tender's Palace now that he's, you know, Tender."

"Are you...sleeping with him?" Frit ventured. She hadn't come into the room yet, not fully. Somehow she knew if she entered, it was over. Her one brief friendship would be taken away, and she'd once again be alone, and ignored.

"What?" Nara cringed. "Gods, no. There's no way I'd ever sleep with that self-important blowhard. But he can teach me destruction magic, and I'm going to need that. This war is just beginning."

Frit entered the room. She walked slowly to her bed, and sank down onto it, across from Nara. Just like on the first day they'd really become friends. She took a deep breath, burning the oxygen and exhaling smoke.

"I understand." She finally managed. It hurt, but Nara was her friend, and she should want what's best for her. "And you have to leave right now?"

"I'm afraid so." Nara bit her lip. She rose from the bed and opened her arms toward Frit. "Give me a hug at least."

"But your clothes..." Frit rose, but didn't cross the space between them.

"Will be fine. Neith was a *fire* Catalyst. I'm resistant now." Nara walked forward and embraced Frit. Frit tensed, then relaxed into the hug. It was the first time anyone had ever hugged her and it felt...amazing.

Hot, flaming tears sizzled down her cheeks. "I'm going to miss you, Nara. But I know you have to do this. If you can, maybe convince Eros to let me come along, too?"

Nara disengaged and took a big step back. She smiled broadly, and Frit realized she was crying too. "I will pester him relentlessly. You have my word. I doubt it will take much. He likes you more than you realize. This time tomorrow, I bet he orders you up to the palace."

"I'll hold you to that. You'd better get moving." Frit sat back on the bed and smiled. This time she didn't have to force it.

Nara picked up her pack. She hesitated a moment, then took a deep breath and headed for the door. She gave Frit a brief little wave, and Frit shot one back. She hoped Nara was able to convince Eros to bring her up to the palace. Then, maybe she'd have her friend back.

She moved to the window, gazing up at the twinkling structure high above. Once again, she'd been forgotten by the people who'd enslaved her. Frit blinked when a tiny dragon landed on the ledge just outside the window. It couldn't be more than half a meter long, from snout to tail.

The creature's midnight scales glittered in the sun, and it gazed up at her with ancient eyes. Frit moved to the window, and sketched a rune before it. The window dissolved, allowing a gust of fresh air into the room. Frit's skin smoldered, drinking in the oxygen.

"Who, or what, are you?" She asked, peering at the little creature. She'd never seen a Wyrm this small. It wasn't an illusion, she was certain of that.

The little Wyrm preened its scales, just outside the line of glowing wards along the window sill. If the creature mistakenly touched them, it would be incinerated instantly. Perhaps that was what had happened to its missing tail.

"Before I divulge that," the creature whispered, craning its long neck in her direction, "I will tell you why I've come. Tell me, little Frit, do you know who and what your people really are?"

"I know we come from the Blazing Heart," she ventured. "I also know I shouldn't be talking to you. This could get me in a great deal of trouble."

"Yes, it certainly could. Your masters are indeed harsh," the little dragon said. It shook its head sadly. "You have my sympathy, cousin. The collar you wear is one of many injustices perpetrated by the Confederacy."

Frit's hand rose to her neck, touching the glowing sigils. Direct contact hurt, but she ignored the pain. For a moment at least. Then she lowered her hand. "You called me cousin. Why?"

"Because it is an accurate term. You come from the Blazing Heart, but your people have been kept ignorant." The little dragon sat on its haunches, and folded its forelegs before it, like a cat. "The Catalyst's true name is the Blazing Heart *of Krox*."

Frit took a step backward. "You're a dreadlord, aren't you? I'm going to get help."

"Help? I am not the one who snatched you from the bliss of basking in the light of Krox. I did not force you into a pattern inducer, and make you into a beautiful toy, to be broken and discarded at will." The dragon eyed her soberly. "The Confederacy has enslaved you. And they have kept a secret from you, from all your people. You, like me, are children of Krox. And very soon you will need to ask yourself an unavoidable question. Which side of this war has enslaved you and uses your kind as fodder? Which one seeks to return you to the Catalyst that birthed you, so you can be reunited with your god?"

"I won't betray...the Confederacy." She'd been about to say she wouldn't betray Nara, but she had a feeling that giving the name of her only friend to a dreadlord was a quick way to remove that friend forever.

"I'm not asking you to. I'm not asking you to do anything. I merely came to offer my sympathy. We are family, Frit. Consider that. And consider your future. What is best for you and your people? Slavery? Or Freedom?" The little dragon leapt suddenly into the air, winging away from the window and up into the sky.

Frit sat on the bed. She had a great deal to consider.

CHARACTER SHEETS

The Magitech Chronicles grew out of years of pen & paper roleplaying sessions, tossing dice around a table. As such, I've made character sheets for each of the major characters.

These list things like spells known and abilities for various magic items they possess. I've included them here for those people who are as geeky as me. =D

If you'd like to see more lore, stories, artwork, and even videos please join us at magitechchronicles.com!

-Chris

Aran
Class: War Mage

Equipment

Mark V Inuran Spellrifle
Max Catalizations: 1
Abilities:
Frost Boost- Once per day the caster may enhance a spell with additional frost damage. This ability may be manually recharged by expending a single spell point.

Feathersteel Spellblade
Max Catalizations: 3
Abilities:
Pierce Ward- The blade has been void-enhanced to unravel magic, and ignores the first 5 points of spell resistance when discharging a spell.

Mark XI Inuran Spellarmor
Max Catalizations: 3
Bonuses: +4 Strength, +4 Constitution, +4 Dexterity
Abilities:
Ice Block- Once per day the user may cover the armor in a thick sheet of ice. This supernaturally hard ice is impenetrable to most attacks, and offers some resistance against

magic. The block may be dispelled or destroyed, and the subject cannot move or cast so long as they are encased in ice.

Spells Known

1st Level
Crackling Touch (Air)
Ice Shield (Water)

2nd Level
Void Lightning (Air/Void)
Air Tendrils (Air)

Voria
Class: True Mage

Equipment

Unknown

Spells Known

1st Level
Void Bolt (Void)
Fire Bolt (Fire)
Acid Bolt (Earth)
Ice Bolt (Water)
Dream Bolt (Dream)
Lesser Counterspell (Spirit)

2nd Level
Lesser Scrying (Fire + Dream)
Counterspell (Spirit + Aspect)

3rd Level
Fissure (Void)
Gravity Sphere (Void + Earth)
Greater Counterspell (Spirit + Void + Aspect)
Scry-Portal (Fire + Dream)

Nara
Class: True Mage

Equipment

Mark VI Inuran Spellpistol
Max Catalizations: 1
Abilities:
Frost Boost- Once per day the caster may enhance a spell with additional frost damage. This ability may be manually recharged by expending a single spell point.

Mark V Inuran Spellarmor
Max Catalizations: 1
Abilities:
Ice Block- Once per day the user may cover the armor in a thick sheet of ice. This supernaturally hard ice is impenetrable to most attacks, and offers some resistance against magic. The block may be dispelled or destroyed, and the subject cannot move or cast so long as they are encased in ice.

Spells Known

1st Level
Shift (Void)

Icy Armor (Water)
Sleep (Dream)
Void Bolt (Void)
Sleep (Dream)
Lesser Counterspell (Spirit)

2nd Level
Instant Growth (Earth)
Paralyze (Spirit)
Invisibility (Air + Dream)
Counterspell (Spirit + Aspect)

Sergeant Crewes
Class: Tech Mage

Equipment

Mark VI Inuran Spellcannon
Max Catalizations: 2
Abilities:
Flame Boost- Once per day the caster may enhance a spell with additional fire damage. This ability may be manually recharged by expending a single spell point
Enhanced Accuracy- Spells fired from this weapon are more likely to hit, and more difficult to counterspell.

Mark VI Inuran Spellarmor
Max Catalizations: 2
Bonuses: +2 Strength, +2 Constitution, +2 Dexterity
Abilities:

Spells Known

1st Level
Fire Bolt (Fire)
Water Bolt (Water)

2nd Level
Magma Ball (Fire)

Corporal Kezia
Class: Tech Mage

Equipment

Mark V Inuran Spellhammer
Max Catalizations: 1
Abilities:
Enhanced Strength- The hammer increased the wielder's strength by 2. This stacks with any bonuses from spellarmor.

Mark V Inuran Spellarmor
Max Catalizations: 1
Bonuses: +2 Strength, +2 Constitution, +2 Dexterity
Abilities:
Passive Healing- The user regenerates one hit point each round, to a maximum of 20 points in a day. This ability may be recharged by expending a 2 spell points. Only life points may be spent.

Spells Known

1st Level
Life bolt (Life)

Specialist Bord
Class: Tech Mage

Equipment

Mark V Inuran Spellgauntlet
Max Catalizations: 1
Abilities:
Enhanced Life Magic- All life spells channeled through these gauntlets are considered one level higher than normal.

Mark V Inuran Spellarmor
Max Catalizations: 1
Bonuses: +2 Strength, +2 Constitution, +2 Dexterity
Abilities:
Endless Healing- The suit provides a pool of ten spell points that may be spent on life spells. This pool recharges each day.

Spells Known

1st Level
Treat Wound (Life)
Ease Pain (Life)
Erect Spell Ward (Life)

Want to know when **Spellship: Magitech Chronicles Book 3** goes live?

Sign up to the mailing list!

Check out MagitechChronicles.com for book releases, lore, artwork, and more!

Made in the USA
Middletown, DE
26 August 2020